FUTURE CITY

FUTURE CITY

edited by

ROGER ELWOOD

 TRIDENT PRESS • NEW YORK

First printing
SBN 671-27103-2
Library of Congress Catalog Card Number: 72-96814
Designed by Eve Metz
Manufactured in the United States of America

CONTENTS

Preface
ROGER ELWOOD

Ideally, an anthology should not be a loose compendium of stories that bear little or no relation to one another. In the days of innocence, books that were anthologies could get away with sort of a potpourri design because readers were fascinated by the format itself and the multiplicity of authors represented therein.

But such times are gone; science fiction readers are becoming more and more astute; much more than simply "format" is demanded—there must be quality as well as a *raison d'être* for the book itself.

Future City meets both these demands, I believe. Its quality will become apparent as you sample the contents. Its reason for being is commentary on the future of that overwhelming entity, the city. The city in its massiveness, its intricate problems, its concentration of power and resources is indeed overwhelming, and seldom in an awe-inspiring sense, either. It *overwhelms* the eyes and the nose with noise pollution, air pollution and God knows what else; it fosters deep-seated anxieties of every description; and it harbors such an assortment of crimes and acts of violence as to make the mind recoil in outrage and fear.

Some sociologists have compared cities to dinosaurs, certain to be edged out of existence by the forces of evolutionary change; cities have far outlived their usefulness, therefore they are doomed to extinction.

Be that as it may, there are no concrete answers as to *what*

7

exactly will happen. If the cities on this planet *are* doomed, then *how* will they expire? And what will eventually escalate the process of decay, disruption and dissolution?

The authors of the stories and poems herein have tried to provide possible answers to questions about the future of the city. But it should be stressed that, like chapters in a novel, it may be impossible to read one or more out of context. This is one anthology that must be taken quite as a whole.

For example: The tone of "In Praise of New York" by Tom Disch seems deceptively light and optimistic. But read on to "The Sightseers" by Ben Bova, then "Meanwhile, We Eliminate" by Andrew J. Offutt, then "Thine Alabaster Cities Gleam" by Laurence M. Janifer and you will see a gradual process of disintegration; therefore, Disch's poem—if read with care and insight—is not really optimistic at all, for it begins that process, that inevitable progression along to such stories as "Death of a City" by Frank Herbert, "Assassins of Air" by George Zebrowski and "The Most Primitive" by Ray Russell, until you come to "5,000,000 A.D." by Miriam Allen deFord which—but then that is up to you to find out.

In my opinion, there are a number of stories herein that qualify as award winners or, at the very least, trend setters. I doubt that science fiction has often had a story as outspoken as Barry N. Malzberg's "Culture Lock," a condemnatory treatment of homosexuality; or that Robert Silverberg has ever done really better than his "Getting Across" novelette; or that Thomas N. Scortia will soon top "The Weariest River," a tour-de-force treatment of sadomasochism, gorgonism and other not-for-Sunday-school-picnic matters.

"In Dark Places" by Joe L. Hensley hardly pulls any punches in its depiction of black/white relationships; and Harlan Ellison shows a soft, tender side of his talent with "Hindsight: 480 Seconds"; and I have not found it easy to forget "The World As Will and Wallpaper" by R. A. Lafferty, "Violation" by William F. Nolan, "Apartment Hunting" by Harvey and Audrey Bilker, "The Undercity" by Dean R. Koontz, "Revolution" by Robin

Schaeffer, "City Lights, City Nights" by K. M. O'Donnell and "Chicago" by Thomas F. Monteleone.

Then, of course, there are two examples of *nonfiction* writing by two science *fiction* pros—Clifford D. Simak's Introduction and Frederik Pohl's Afterword, both intelligent, perceptive and invaluable to this anthology. Add to these the poems by D. M. Price and Virginia Kidd entitled, respectively, "As a Drop" and "Abendlandes," and you have, I feel, a diverse and stimulating anthology.

All the material contained in *Future City* is original and was written especially for this book. All the stories have been chosen with care and put in more or less chronological order.

But it is not a happy book. And it may be too strong for some readers. Yet it is a book that makes—through the collected talents of more than twenty authors—a powerful over-all statement on the terrible inadequacies and corruptive atmosphere of a great many cities. (Some authors would say *all* cities.)

All of us hope you find the contents of this book worthwhile and meaningful. We have tried, as best we can, to give you an anthology that is *created* rather than *packaged*.

ROGER ELWOOD

Margate
New Jersey

Foreword
CLIFFORD D. SIMAK

The city at one time served a purpose. It developed out of the evolution of our civilization and for many centuries served mankind well. It first was conceived in the Neolithic Revolution when men found it was to their advantage to forgo their nomadic wanderings and settle in one place. The formation of the communities that were the prototypes of cities and some of which later became what we think of as a city made possible the division of labor and the development of specialization in certain crafts and professions, attracted trade, made government feasible and gave religion an operating base. A city gave the people who dwelled within it a sense of unity stronger than the tribal unity they previously had known, providing a real sense of home. Once it was fortified, it became a place of comparative safety, which was not easily come by in those days. The fortifications were a necessity, for once a city had grown rich, it became a prize for raiding outland bands and added to war a new dimension—profit. There was a time when the city was more important than the state, when it often was the state. The people who lived within its walls were citizens of the city rather than the state. The first patriotism displayed by men belonged to a city rather than a state.

Today there has to be some reasonable doubt that a city any longer serves a worthwhile function. So long as travel was slow and communications were not only slow but unreliable, the city had a function to perform. There was a day when a man to transact business with another man had to go down the street to see him or send off a messenger with a letter. Today business can be transacted with almost anyone in the world by simply lifting a phone or employing any other of the means of almost instantaneous communication available to us.

Commerce today is on a national or an international basis, no longer merely between one city and another. Business transactions no longer call for togetherness. Travel and transportation no longer are local matters. There is no longer any need of the protection that was once furnished by the city. The danger to human life and property now lies within the city, not outside of it. And, unlike the days of the city-state, a city no longer is needed for the function of a government.

The city today lives on as an anachronism propped up by tradition. At great cost we rebuild the central core of a city and when we are finished with it we find that we have a glittering business district surrounded by rings of ghettos. We jam our highways each morning and again each evening with automobiles carrying workers who long since have fled the city because it has become an intolerable place in which to live.

All the cities in existence have grown by accidents of history. They have developed without plan, simply responding to the uncontrolled demands made upon them, bending to the stresses of the moment. Heroic efforts have been made to keep them alive and habitable, but these efforts have been of a patchwork nature as expedience demanded. They resemble, in their organic structure, nothing quite so much as a cancerous growth. Urban decay has eaten into them and what was in one generation a street of proud homes becomes a ghetto in the next. The city today is strangling and suffocating and there does not seem that much can be done with it.

Experimental cities, new cities designed for living, have been talked about. Ideally, such a city would be self-sufficient, with all matter recycled again and again. There would be no slums, for there would be employment and equal opportunity for everyone; pollution would be controlled, partially by the recycling process; there would be no urban decay, for the city would be designed for only so many people and so much production and when either of these exceeded the limit a new city would be started. Such a city, say its advocates, would not be designed as an organism, but as a machine. For such a city to work there would have to be controls—upon its population and production—more stringent controls than anyone in our nation knows today. There would be no room for industrial or business expansion and perhaps little for personal initiative, for the city would be a closed system.

But why save the city at all? If it has outlived its usefulness, if it no longer serves the functions for which it was designed, why spend money on it?

The day may come, sooner than we think, when business and industry, as well as people, will have fled the city. The way has been pointed by the drift to suburban communities in the last forty years. And, indeed, the abandonment of the city by a number of business firms and industries already has taken place. Many small business firms have shifted from their city locations, either to suburban shopping centers or to new locations. The larger retail establishments that still maintain their stores downtown have branches in the shopping centers. Hospitals are built outside the city; more and more office buildings are appearing beyond the city limits.

Today a man sitting in his home, in an office equipped with all the communication facilities within our capability, could transact his duties as well as and perhaps more efficiently than he could from an office in the city. It would seem to make little sense for thousands of people to travel miles through heavy traffic to sit down at desks in an office and there carry out the duties that they might do as well staying at home. If we ever have the sense to realize this, we'll be doing a number of things—making large office space in the central city no longer necessary, taking a great deal of the pressure off our highway systems and more than likely cutting down the incidence of heart attack.

CLIFFORD D. SIMAK

Science fiction writers, through the years, have been fascinated by the problems that a city poses. They have dreamed many kinds of cities—some idealized, some portraying by logical extrapolation the stifling horror that can exist within them. I am certain that in reading the stories selected for this anthology you'll find some rather startling concepts of the future city—if there is to be a future city.

In Praise of New York
TOM DISCH

As we rise above it row after row
Of lights reveal the incredible size
Of our loss. An ideal commonwealth
Would be not otherwise,
For we can no more legislate
Against the causes of unhappiness,
Such as death or impotence or times
When no one notices,
Than we can abolish the second law
Of thermodynamics, which states
That all energy, without exception, is wasted.
Still, under certain conditions
It is possible to move
To a slightly nicer
Neighborhood. Or if not,
Then at least there is usually someone
To talk to, or a library
That stays open till nine.
And any night you can see Times Square
Tremulous with its busloads
Of tourists who are seeing all of this
For the first and last time
Before they are flown
Back to the republic of Azerbaidzhan
On the shore of the Caspian,
Where for weeks they will dream of our faces
Drenched with an unbelievable light.

The Sightseers
BEN BOVA

My heart almost went into fibrillation when I saw the brown cloud off on the horizon that marked New York City. Dad smiled his wiser-than-thou smile as I pressed my nose against the plane's window in an effort to see more. By the time we got out of the stack over LaGuardia Airport and actually landed, my neck hurt.

The city's fantastic! People were crowding all over, selling things, buying, hurrying across the streets, gawking. And the noise, the smells, all those old gasoline-burning taxis rattling around and blasting horns. Not like Sylvan Dell, Michigan!

"It's vacation time," Dad told me as we shouldered our way through the crowds along Broadway. "It's always crowded during vacation time."

And the girls! They looked back at you, right straight at you, and smiled. They knew what it was all about, and they liked it! You could tell, just the way they looked back at you. I guess they really weren't any prettier than the girls at home, but they dressed . . . wow!

"Dad, what's a bedicab?"

He thought it over for a minute as one of them, long and low, with the back windows curtained, edged through traffic right in front of the curb where we were standing.

"You can probably figure it out for yourself," he said uncomfortably. "They're not very sanitary."

Okay, I'm just a kid from the north woods. It took me a couple of minutes. In fact, it wasn't until we crossed the street in front of one—stopped for a red light—and I saw the girl's picture set up on the windshield, that I realized what it was all about. Sure enough, there was a meter beside the driver.

But that's just one of the things about the city. There were old movie houses where we saw real murder films. Blood and beatings and low-cut blondes. I think Dad watched me more than the screen. He claims he thinks I'm old enough to be treated like a man, but he acts awfully scared about it.

We had dinner in some really crummy place, down in a cellar under an old hotel. With live people taking our orders and bringing the food!

"It's sanitary," Dad said, laughing when I hesitated about digging into it. "It's all been inspected and approved. They didn't put their feet in it."

Well, it didn't hurt me. It was pretty good, I guess . . . too spicy, though.

We stayed three days altogether. I managed to meet a couple of girls from Maryland at the hotel where we stayed. They were okay, properly dressed and giggly and always whispering to each other. The New York girls were just out of my league, I guess. Dad was pretty careful about keeping me away from them . . . or them away from me. He made sure I was in the hotel room every night, right after dinner. There were plenty of really horrible old movies to watch on the closed-circuit TV; I stayed up past midnight each night. Once I was just drifting off to sleep when Dad came in and flopped on his bed with all his clothes on. By the time I woke up in the morning, though, he was in his pajamas and sound asleep.

Finally we had to go. We rented a sanitary car and decontaminated ourselves on the way out to the airport. I didn't like the lung-cleansing machine. You had to work a tube down one of your nostrils.

"It's just as important as brushing your teeth," Dad said firmly.

If I didn't do it for myself, he was going to do it for me.

"You wouldn't want to bring billions of bacteria and viruses back home, would you?" he asked.

Our plane took off an hour and a half late. The holiday traffic was heavy.

"Dad, is New York open every year . . . just like it is now?"

He nodded. "Yes, all during the vacation months. A lot of the public health doctors think it's very risky to keep a city open for more than two weeks out of the year, but the tourist industry has fought to keep New York going all summer. They shut it down right after Labor Day."

As the plane circled the brown cloud that humped over the city, I made up my mind that I'd come back again next summer. Alone, maybe. That'd be great!

My last glimpse of the city was the big sign painted across what used to be the Bronx:

NEW YORK IS A SUMMER FESTIVAL OF FUN!

Meanwhile, We Eliminate
ANDREW J. OFFUTT

"Yes, there are indeed too many men in the world. In earlier days it wasn't so noticeable. But now that everyone wants air to breathe, and a car to drive as well, one does notice it. Of course, what we are doing isn't rational. It's childishness, just as war is childishness on a gigantic scale. In time, mankind will learn to keep its numbers in check by rational means. Meanwhile . . . we eliminate."

—Hermann Hesse, *Steppenwolf*

Fred Lapidus stared in shock as the big car passed him easily on the left. Everyone else was watching too, he saw, by the position of their heads. It was hard to tell where people were looking when everyone wore one-way glasses, but you learned to gauge by the way their heads were turned, or by their eyebrows when they weren't wearing the newer Supr-PrivT goggles-type affairs that covered brows and most of the nose as well.

The car that passed him was an ancient automobile, a gasoline-engine dinosaur, right here in the city! Noisy, roaring and growling (although he couldn't hear it) and capable of speeds of up to a hundred miles an hour or so. Maybe more. A road car. A country car! Moving unconcernedly along among the almost silent miniks and maxis. As if its owner owned the damned street, as if he had a right to put out all that poison!

Fred Lapidus checked the pollution gauge on the instrument panel before him. He was amazed that its needle did not jump all the way across the gauge. It did move. It moved constantly, of course, but he was sure the needle's little quiver up the scale was caused by the monster.

The son of a bitch!

Why didn't he drive on, get away from here, stop trying to kill poor Fred Lapidus in the electric minik, all the other Fred Lapiduses in *their* towncars, all the people crowded together in the big double-decker electric maxibuses? Certainly he had the horsepower. The son of a bitch! Where the hell were the police?

The minik in front of Fred swung off the freeway, angling down the ramp onto the approach to Market and the West End. The minik in front of that one swung into the center lane, and Fred increased his speed almost to maximum. Racing along at thirty miles an hour, he watched the back end of the maxi ahead rush toward him.

Then he had to jam on his brakes. Cursing. Eyes bulging. The gasoline dinosaur whipped into his line, directly in front of him. God, the speed and pickup of that thing! But how the devil was the driver able to handle it? It was so *huge.* Five or six passengers, Fred remembered, and right up to a hundred miles an hour on the Interstates. His father had had one. Fred had even ridden in it, but he couldn't remember, not really. His father had moved into Louisville when Fred was seven, looking for better work than the farm dominated by the weather, for better housing than the ramshackle farmhouse on a hundred and sixty-eight acres, for better living conditions than direct exposure to countless insects and all the other horrors of farm life.

Fred shivered, glancing about for a way to get out from behind the old automobile. He couldn't. Behind him and on either side of him were solid lines of miniks and maxis, moving thousands and thousands of persons home from work or to work from home; to this place or that. Mingled among them were the blue and white of city police vehicles, armed and armored, and the silvery-brown-and-green vehicles, tanklike affairs with windshields that could be closed just like a house's windows: Feps. And here was he, Fred Lapidus, $16,000 a year and in the 53 per cent tax bracket, by God, and damned proud of it—stuck behind a poison-breathing dragon from the past!

It was from out of town, of course. Such monsters were illegal in cities. They were poison. He knew his ecohistory. Sometime in the sixties—he wasn't sure about the year—fourteen thousand tons of guck had been added to the air above megatherian Los Angeles every day. It wasn't enough that the city was a cesspool, but even its air had become a garbage dump. And over 87 per cent of that guck came from just such a monster as the one bellowing along so unconcernedly right in front of Fred Lapidus. Right here in the *city*!

One of Fred's childhood memories was the arrival of the family in Louisville. How strange that dark sky had looked; how he had stared and wondered. (You didn't study "photochemical smog" in the first grade.)

"Daddy," he'd asked, "What's that? Why's the air so dark?"

"That's civilization, son," his father told him, not without pride. "That's Ahmurrica. That comes from the factories where Daddy's going to work and make good money and have a nice house with neighbors and ice-cream men and everything."

"That's what killed the crops," Mom said.

But it hadn't been factories. The factories were doing their part in poisoning the air of course, but their specialty was rivers. The broad old river that flowed down past Louisville, coming from up north, past Cincinnati, where there were signs in public rest rooms: PLEASE FLUSH. LOUISVILLE NEEDS THE WATER. It had been the automobiles, cars just like the one they were riding in. But they hadn't known it then. And then out of the midday darkness had loomed the buildings! Their feet vanished into their closely crowded neighbors and their spearing summits vanished into the darkness above. But— buildings! A City.

And little Fred Lapidus had forgotten all about darkness at noon, and the thought didn't occur to him in those terms until he was twenty years old and had to read Arthur Koestler for a course, just before they closed the colleges.

Helplessly following the old automobile, a relic from the days of the triumphant domination of the country by what Lewis Mumford had called Detroit's infantile fantasies, Fred tried to remember. Let's see, that thing was spewing out lead, and who hadn't heard of lead poisoning? And an assortment of organic compounds and nitrogen oxides, which were the prime sources—with sunlit oxygen—of the smog of the old days. Then there was carbon monoxide, and everyone knew that was poison, and if you got to the point where you really couldn't take it all anymore you could always go into the garage and let your automobile carry you off to eternity—without even moving.

Let's see, was that all—Oh, God, no! There were sulfur oxides, and they were really nice, here on the river. They combined with water vapor to form a lovely compound known fancily as H_2SO_4. Sulfuric acid. What that did to nylon stockings and the like was nothing compared with what it had done to Fred Lapidus' mother.

He began to sweat.

The car ahead did have an afterburner. But after all, what had that ever solved? There had been one on the next car his father had bought, seven years after arriving here in the land of milk and honey. (That was the year they were able to move out of the West End. Luckily; the next year it was proclaimed sovereign and separatist, right after the bloodbath. A part of the Black Nation of Aframerika.) His father had been very proud of that new car. Its afterburner eliminated the stuff that everyone could pronounce by then: the horrible hydrocarbons, worst menace since Communism, Koestler's *Darkness at Noon*. But, born in California like so many other pernicious plagues with attractive exterior wrappings, the afterburners didn't last long.

The car ahead of Fred Lapidus had an afterburner, so it wasn't filling the air with hydrocarbons, which killed slowly, building and building toward doomsday. No. It was squirting out pound after pound of nitrogen oxides instead. They had always reacted with hydrocarbons, and now they were liberated, and it didn't take long to learn that they were worse. (Or better; it was a matter of personal preference: Would you rather die quickly or slowly?) The nitroxides weren't as patient as the h-carbons.

They killed swiftly. Fred could well remember his constantly bleeding nose, and the thousands and millions of other almost permanently bloody noses, as mucous membranes reacted in helpless agony to the nitroxides emitted by afterburner-safe automobiles.

Sweating, biting his lower lip, he tried frantically to get into the left lane. Nothing doing. He saw the other driver's mouth moving in vituperation (justified) before he opaqued the window on that side of his car.

Fred sweated. He was two miles from his exit. Why wasn't someone *doing* something? Tentatively he raised a finger to his nose. Pushed carefully. Looked at the finger. Sighed. No blood. He tried holding his breath, wishing he'd had his minik's oxyrator checked last Saturday. Maybe he was safe so long as he remained in his minik with the oxyrator on. He reached over to switch it on Full, listening to its whine with a little frown.

Why were the local police and the Feps letting that guy just drive along here this way, right in town, killing them all?

He glanced around. Where had they gone? There wasn't a police vehicle in sight. Funny, there had been several just a minute ago. He must have been thinking about something else and failed to notice when they gunned off. Probably over to the West Side again. So somebody was getting ripped or raped or somebody had gotten pissed off and was sniping or torching a building or two. Serve them right, the scum. So what the hell, this creature up ahead was poisoning *thousands*; he was complacently killing *Fred Lapidus*, him and his stinking steel dinosaur with its Indiana plates.

Might know the bastard wasn't even a Kentuckian!

Somebody did something. The electric towncars were not long on speed or pickup, but they were supremely parkable and maneuverable. Which was all they needed; what need of mutlihorsepower in cities, when every vehicle was jammed together and couldn't get anywhere anyhow?

But the man in front of and to the left of the gasoline monster swung his eminently maneuverable minik over in front of the automobile. The Indiana driver responded with the usual reaction time, twenty or so seconds to get his foot from accelerator to brake, and Fred jerked his foot off the accelerator as he realized that the machine ahead had jolted to a stop. Instantly his minik responded to the decreased pedal pressure. Instantly it braked. Fred gasped and clapped a hand over his pounding heart as he came to a stop a few feet from the back of the monster. He could read the strip of old, broken chrome now: PONT AC.

He sat shaking. The door of the old car swung open and a man swung out. A big man whose clothes didn't look right; they looked like *clothes*, perm stuff, rather than the city dweller's usual uniform of disposables. He saw the man's broad shoulders and small butt move forward, around his machine to the one that had pulled in front of him. Then Fred saw the other driver, also out on the pavement. Lord, he was a garink! His suit showed that clearly; it was one of the disposables the government handed out once monthly to everyone on the guaranteed income rolls. The guy was a $7,500-a-year man, for God's sake!

Fred cut off his engine. Well, he had status; his own paid-for jacsuit would show that. He'd go stick up for the guy, a fellow Louisvillian, and while he was at it he'd raise hell with that out-of-state hick in his poison-breathing monstrosity of an illegal vehicle! He used left thumb and right hand to unlock the door, then pushed it open.

And yanked it shut, wincing. The noise! He'd forgotten, sealed up in the fortress keep of his car and in his frightened fury. Quickly he poked in his earplugs, but he decided against the respirator. He got out of the car. Already others were stopping, too. Getting out.

"—right out in front of me that way!" the auto driver was saying loudly, and even his accent was wrong.

"I gotta be in this lane, dammit! I turn off in two blocks. If you'd been driving a decent car you'd have stopped automatically. Now just look what you did to my minik!"

"I wish my foot'd slipped off the brake and ground you into

mincemeat, you damned smartass! Drive that car like some kind of a kid, no regard for anyone else whatever."

Bowling-alley thunder interrupted; a jet went over.

"I really think," Fred Lapidus said, stepping up to them in his black-and-silver vylon suit, "that you shouldn't be talking about regard for others."

Both men looked at him. So did two or three others who'd gotten out to see what was the matter, and to give the out-of-stater a good piece of mind.

Fred pointed disdainfully at the aged Pontiac. "You come into the city in that thing, just driving along poisoning us all and our kids—"

"Yeah," said a fat man in a shapeless charbrown jacsuit. "Our *kids*!" He glanced about at the five or six others who'd stopped their cars to join him. "Our kids. Look at that thing he's driving! A regular old poison factory. Don't you know the law about city cars, buddy?"

The big man from Indiana looked around, frowning. "I was just—"

"Scaring the life out of all of us," Fred said, "not to *mention* polluting our air and endangering the lives of our kids!"

There was a dissonant chorus of agreement from the eight or ten others gathered about. The Indianan looked around at the faces, eyeless because of their opaque glasses. He wasn't even wearing any; didn't he care about privacy?

"Look, I'm on my way home. I had to come in to get a part for this thing," the out-of-stater said quietly. "I'm not crazy about it myself. It's all I can afford. I didn't have the *money* to rent a minik at the bridge."

"Shit," said the man he'd hit from behind. "All you had to do was show 'em your card, Jack. You wouldna had to pay."

"Ought to close that damned bridge," someone else muttered, "and seal us off from these clowns from the other side of the Ohio."

The big man seemed to grow taller. "Card!" He spat out the word. "I don't have any card. I raise food, mister, and sell it to feed you city people so you don't starve. I made over four thousand last year with my own hands. But I be damned if I'll accept anything from the government. That ain't right!"

God, Fred thought, *doesn't the Mongoloid idiot know he's talking to a garink?* There were several others, too, among the twelve or thirteen men gathered around the scene of the accident.

Silence. Wide-eyed, staring silence. Naturally; how long had it been since they'd heard anything like that, since anyone had *dared* indicate there was something wrong with accepting enough money from your neighbors, via the federal government, to bring your income up to a livable seventy-five hundred?

A big jet went over and smashed the silence. Only the hick looked up.

"Well you, you better have *insurance!*" the fat man said.

"*It wasn't my fault!* He pulled right in front of me! I couldn't—"

"Hasn't got *insurance!*"

"Poisoning our *kids!*"

"Everybody in Louisville may be sick tomorrow just because of this son of a bitch—and he isn't even from *Kentucky!*"

CRASH.

No one knew who threw the brick or where he'd found it. Probably carried it in his car; sensible!

No one ever knew who started things. It just came flying out of the air, whizzed past the out-of-stater's face and smashed into the door of his old pale-blue Pontiac.

He bellowed, stared at the ugly dent. Turned horrified, enraged eyes on the clot of angry Louisvillians. Then he bent for the brick.

"Watch out!" the fat man yelled. "He's gonna throw that brick at us!"

CRASH.

Another brick. This one slammed into the Pontiac's window,

near the roof, and bounced off and hit the driver's back. He grunted. The shatterproof window became a cobwebbery of radiating cracks. The brick dropped to the ground. With the first brick in his left hand. the driver reached for the second.

The fat man stepped forward and jammed his booted foot down on the sun-browned hand.

A jet screamed over.

The man behind the fat man bent quickly and snatched up the brick.

The Hoosier hit the fat man's calf and ankle with the brick he'd picked up. The fat man screamed. The man beside him swung his brick and threw it, missing the Hoosier and clanging his car again, and a rock came arching in from behind him, from an invisible hand again, and the driver of the minik hit by the Pontiac snarled and bent to pick up the rock after it bounced off the Hoosier's upper arm and Fred felt a surge of anger and desire to punish this man who had endangered their lives and insulted them all and the Hoosier vanished beneath a wave of cursing, stamping, pummeling Louisvillians. Some used fists, others feet, others briefcases or whatever they had in their cars for defense: macesticks and wrenches and the like.

Fred Lapidus took a wrench across his wristwatch and staggered back, his wrist dangling. He moaned. The fat man fell out of the mass of twisting, swinging, writhing bodies with blood all over his face. Someone screamed. The Indianan seemed to make no noise at all, just flailing and grabbing and taking blow after blow. The noise of the overflying jet didn't even drown out their noise.

"Put 'im back in his stinking car and get the sonuvabitch off *our* freeway!" someone yelled.

They put him back in his stinking car, limp and bleeding and helpless, and slammed the door. Then they put their backs to it and got the sonuvabitch off their freeway.

By the time the F.P.F. chopper—a terrible polluter, but what are you going to do?—swung down overhead, twenty or thirty men were straining and the old Pontiac was poised with both left tires off the pavement by a foot or more.

"THIS IS THE FEDERAL POLICE FORCE. STOP WHAT YOU'RE DOING AND MOVE ON AT ONCE!" the big voice bellowed down from the Fep chopper.

One last good strain and the old Pontiac and its driver went off the freeway. It dropped ten feet, struck a support with a terrible clang and a shrieking grate of metal on metal and was catapulted outward. It dropped another thirty feet and sheared off a This Is My Country flagpole just before smashing at an angle across the roof of Borstelmann's Delly. The roof and front wall of Borstelmann's Delly resisted momentarily, then collapsed together with the Pontiac onto the sidewalk and street. Mrs. Benson R. Carrithers and her daughter Evie were killed instantly. Miraculously, little Teddy, whizzing down the sidewalk in the pram his mother had been pushing, was totally unhurt. Sam Borstelmann rushed out of his delicatessen, looked upward at the faces staring down at him from the freeway and rushed back inside. A jet rocked the hovering chopper.

"EMERGENCY IS DECLARED," a Fep overhead warned with his microphone, and the man whose minik had been struck in the rear by the Hoosier jumped into his machine and drove off as fast as he could.

"LAST WARNING!" a Fep in the chopper said.

Bleeding profusely from the face, the fat man got to one knee and then to his feet. He started lurching toward his car.

"Here! This one's getting away," a man shouted. He had just pulled up and stopped, and he reached back into his car and grabbed a defenser. He swung it. The needly little beam of light cut the fat man half in two, cauterizing the wound nicely.

Fred Lapidus, moaning and clutching his broken wrist close to his chest, tried to push his way to his car.

"Where the hell you think you're going, buddy?" a man snarled, and Fred had an instant's view of a garink suit sleeve before the fist protruding from it slammed into his left eye.

"Look at the suit the bastard's wearing," the man said, kicking Fred as he collapsed. "Rich son of a bitch!"

Below, Sam Borstelmann emerged from his delly. Almost without aiming, he let go with both barrels of his old shotgun.

Seven or eight men screamed when pellets struck their faces and necks and hands, and other pellets tink-tinked off the hovering chopper.

The door-mounted laser sent a pencil-thin beam down to widow Mrs. Sam Borstelmann. The man behind the gunner tossed three gas grenades out to burst on the freeway. Stupid, but even Feps have been known to do the wrong thing. Extraordinary powers aren't conducive to making a man stop and think carefully.

Six men jumped from the freeway to their deaths in an attempt to escape the vomit gas. Three others fell or were knocked off the freeway. Within seven minutes thirty-one miniks and three maxibuses were piled up in the swirling mist of yellow-pink gas.

They dragged Fred Lapidus from under one of the maxis three hours later, but by that time he had bled to death. Besides, everyone was very, very busy with the riot in the street below. The torched automobile and ensuing riot eventually burned out 3.2 blocks, or so the official reports said. Fortunately, only nineteen persons were killed and only seventy-three were hospitalized, twenty-one in critical condition.

But a French-made SST crashed just inside the Chinese border that day, and the Chinese attacked the Indians on the border, and Peking and New Delhi started screaming at each other, and the incident in Louisville made only the back page of the first section of most papers.

Mrs. Lapidus waited supper till ten-thirty. Then came the phone call from the Federal Police Force, and she fainted.

Thine Alabaster Cities Gleam
LAURENCE M. JANIFER

The lights of the city below went right on shining, just as if nothing had gone wrong with the Seawell Building. After a while the sight of the normal city had begun to irritate Hanlon, but of course he didn't let that show: a display of petty emotion would be worse than useless, it would be demeaning. Instead, he continued to signal with his pencil flashlight, three long and three short and three long again. The tiny flash, a present from his six-year-old son which he was sentimental enough to carry, didn't seem to throw much light; he could feel himself slowly losing touch with hope. Kitty wasn't making any sound that he could hear, but when he managed to turn away from the window and the lights below, he could see her, still at her post six or seven feet away, scratching at the unbreakable glass with her ring.

Hanlon felt the need of contact between them, the need of some communication. Maybe it would ease things a bit. After a few seconds he said, "How's it going?" at random, and his voice sounded surprisingly loud in the small room.

Kitty stopped scratching as if she too had realized that the time had come for a break of some sort. You can't overwork your assistants, Hanlon thought. The human factor. "It's all right," Kitty said flatly. "I guess it's lucky I have this ring here."

"Diamond ought to cut through glass," Hanlon said, just to keep the conversation going. Disaster made everybody equal, after all. "Even unbreakable glass."

"It's making scratches, anyhow," Kitty said. She squinted hopefully at the transparent wall and then, as she relaxed,

29

seemed to notice for the first time the lights beyond it. "I wonder when they'll miss us," she said.

"Any time now," Hanlon said, as cheerfully as he could. That was the executive's job: to maintain hope for his workers —even when there was only one worker—for as long a time as possible. But it wasn't working, not really: Kitty only nodded cynically.

"Sure," she said. "Sure. On Saturday night, two people working alone, the cleaning staff gone, nobody expects either of us home—isn't that right?"

There was no point in deluding the child, Hanlon told himself. Not anymore. "That's right," he said. "I said I'd stay in town. Some hotel or other." He thought fleetingly of the suburbs, where there were no unbreakable-glass buildings, locked, unbreachable, serviced by air conditioning—natural targets for a blowout. If the blowout had been city-wide or even district-wide . . .

Such thoughts were useless. Hanlon put despondency away and tried to look strong and confident. It seemed the least he could do.

"Likewise," Kitty said. "I mean—anyhow, working so late, anyhow, who's going to miss us?"

Hanlon turned back to the glass wall and pushed the button of his flashlight again. Three long and three short and three long. Maybe, he thought suddenly, he had it wrong.

"What is SOS, anyhow?"

"Long, short, long," Kitty said. "Three of each."

"Not the other way around?"

"What other way?"

"Short and long and short," Hanlon said. Either version sounded equally probable when he thought about it. And it didn't matter, not really: nobody was going to see the light. Not from the fiftieth story of a dark glass building at ten-fifteen at night. Nobody would be looking. All the other buildings were okay.

Useless. Hopeless. But he began again with the tiny flash, this time trying it the other way around, for variety.

"Just so it's a signal," Kitty said. "Just so people know."

The poor girl needed hope. A good secretary, but not executive material: no moral fiber, not when it counted. Hanlon tried to sound calm and sure of himself. "There have been power failures before," he said. "They get everything running just as soon as possible."

"Sure," Kitty said again. "Only maybe this time it won't be fast enough. I mean, you have to face facts."

Perhaps, he thought, she had a rudimentary strength after all. He was pleased that he had made a good choice, taking her out of the secretarial pool.

"This is just an office building, a new one. On a Saturday night, they figure everybody's gone. They won't be in too much of a hurry; everything out there is still okay." She gestured at the world beyond the glass.

Hanlon shook his head. "You think they'd realize," he said slowly. "No lights, no electricity—"

"And no air," Kitty said violently. "You might as well say it. When the power went off, the air conditioning sealed itself and went off, and there aren't any windows. Just sheets of glass, and there's no way to open a sheet of glass. Modern."

"Except with a diamond," Hanlon said, trying to gentle the girl a bit.

Kitty shrugged. "It makes scratches," she said. "That's all it does."

As brightly as he could, Hanlon put in, "Anyhow, the air's still pretty good."

"It's beginning to get stale," Kitty said evenly. "Pardon me for mentioning it."

Hanlon nodded, defeated. "Maybe we'd better stop talking for a while."

"I guess so."

But without conversation his thoughts went spinning into hopeless memory. The telephones hadn't worked, either, though you wouldn't think phones would be so hard to manage. But without a switchboard operator it was impossible to discover the right connections. One of the little buttons had been labeled with a small paper that said *079* and neither Hanlon nor Kitty knew what it meant. Another one was labeled *Cancel*, and the rest didn't seem to have any definable function at all.

He left off signaling briefly—he had been using both patterns interchangeably—and went wearily over to the water cooler. The water was getting warm, almost brackish. Just the slightest bit brackish. As he drank, he thought for the tenth or the hundredth time about making a dash for the roof or for the ground. Surely there had to be some way of getting out of the building from the ground floor, even if the unbreakable doors only worked on an electric-eye linkage. And if there was some sort of door to the roof there would be air. They could leave that door open and come back to the office for water and be perfectly okay until help arrived on Monday.

But he knew he was only indulging himself with fantasy. With the air going bad, he couldn't make the thirty-story trip to the roof and neither could Kitty. In fact, it hadn't really been possible from the first. Kitty had tried and managed eleven stories, and Hanlon had already been though one heart attack. The fifty-story trip to the ground was just as impossible.

The automatic elevators had stopped working, of course.

You'd think the air in a big box like the Seawell Building would last for weeks, but it wouldn't. The air conditioning hadn't been working at absolute peak even before the blowout, and two people used up more air per hour than Hanlon would have imagined.

Scientific facts. Slowly, he went back to his signaling, but after a few seconds he realized that there was still something left to say.

"I'm sorry I kept you late."

Kitty looked up from her own work. "Me? Doesn't matter," she said.

But it did, of course. "If I hadn't needed a secretary to get this last-minute stuff into shape—"

"Glad to do it," Kitty said. "Maybe the overtime check will

pay extra funeral expenses, after company insurance, I mean."

The words hurt. "No," he said. "No, really. If I'd thought—"

She didn't want to cause him pain, he saw by her face; she was quite a good girl for a secretary. Quite a good girl. "Oh, sure; but how could you?" she said. "It's just . . . one of those things, that's it. I didn't mean to sound nasty or anything. I really didn't."

Basically a kind girl, and efficient, too, Hanlon thought. Not that the efficiency mattered anymore. "Of course you didn't," he said as warmly as he could.

"It's just— I'm irritable," she said. "The air getting worse, I guess. Notice it?"

"I suppose so."

She stopped scratching. There were a few marks on the window, nothing more. "I guess this is it, then," she said.

Hanlon shook his head. "Fresh air goes to the bottom." There was always hope, if you could find it. "If we lie down, we'll have a long time yet. Plenty of time." There was always hope. Lying down might add an hour to their time; when that was up, maybe he would think of something else.

There was always hope.

"Okay," Kitty said. "Why not?" Of course she waited until Hanlon had settled himself, near the water cooler, before she lay down herself, some distance away. That was only right. "Be Sunday soon," she said as she lowered herself to the neat, expensive carpet.

"Yes, it will," Hanlon said. "We'll hear the church bells."

There was a little silence. Then Kitty said, "So long."

"So long." Hanlon thought of home, but the suburbs hardly existed for him anymore and what images he could recover only made him sad. Becoming emotional didn't do any good, no good at all. Briefly, he wondered what Kitty was thinking, but somehow that didn't seem important. Nothing did, not really. After a few minutes he realized that he was lying on his back and he rolled carefully onto his side to save the crease in his pants.

Culture Lock
BARRY N. MALZBERG

I

Friday is make-it. George and Fred and Karl and Miller and Kenny and me in George's apartment on the thirty-sixth floor of the project. Kenny is the complication; since we have taken up together, last Wednesday, a week ago, I have been thinking about make-it night with a mixture of fear and doubt. Should we stay away? Should we pass up the session? I know without asking him that Kenny does not want to go, that what he feels building between us etc. is important enough to take us out of the circle. Nevertheless, the forms must hold. If we do not come, there will be questions raised about the absence and the tenuous solidarity of the group itself may be menaced. What will happen between Kenny and myself will happen; exclusive of make-its. I explain this to him. Quietly, sullenly, he nods. We go into the elevator and to George's apartment, the two of us by our entrance already showing them everything they need to know.

Leers, winks, shouts of greeting as we blend into the circle. It is understood in that first moment what is going on between Kenny and me. Shouted remarks from Miller, brusque mutterings from George, who, as the host this night, must spread all of his favors equally. Fred winks. Only Karl stays away, showing his comprehension in the one bleak look we exchange. Not too many months ago, it might have been the same between Karl and me. He is bitter. Perhaps not. Perhaps I am merely projecting my own embarrassment upon him. It does not matter. I remind myself of this, clutching Kenny's hands before the lights go out; nothing matters.

Darkening. Music rises from the center; the make-it has begun. "Remember," George says ritually as we huddle together, "remember the principles." Since he is the host this week it is necessary that he make the statements; his resentment and boredom, however, come through, even under the first haze of the hit. "The principle of blending," George says, "the principle of accommodation. The principle of sharing and that of connection. Brothers all, one to one and then together for the greater good." His breath is already ragged, uneven. Our clothes come off. "For the city," George says, "for the city and thus for the country. All together. All blending."

This is one of the problems of the make-it, the posturing and formality with which, I think, none of us agree. Nevertheless, we must go through it. A tradition handed down to us by forebears. Who are we to reason why and so on? In the darkness, I feel Karl's hand on my knee and the drugs lift, they vault. He says something foul into my ear.

"No," I say, moving from him, "no, no," trying to dive into Kenny's body but in the darkness the shapes have become rearranged and I cannot find him. I feel pressure, the first tugs of entrance and then the oozing, familiar slide of Karl's entrance as he buries himself in me, the first time in many months. "No," I say again, but in a whimpering way. He has made me the woman. Karl has always made women of his partners; this is why it never could have been worked out.

"It's make-it," Karl says, moving on top of me, "it's make-it and you cannot deny. You'll have your slut later," and I feel his moments of accession then, submit to him slowly, small bits and pieces of myself yielding to Karl, and then the old fire, however unwillingly, rises. "You tramp," Karl says, slamming himself into me, and under the drugs, in the darkness, I feel my whimpers turn toward submission and at last, however reluctantly, to lust as he overtakes me.

At his peak I reach blindly, hoping that I will touch Kenny, but my fingers squirrel emptily against the surfaces of George's rug and it is only lint and dust that my palms gather as Karl works his will.

II

In the morning, in my apartment, the drugs still dissipating from my system, he turns to me in the bed, his face open and pained, and hurtles himself against me, not for connection but for comfort. I gather him against me, which is all that I can do, feel his moans against my shoulder, accept his need, which is all that I can do. He is trembling, dependent; he will always be a woman, which is, possibly, his primal attraction for me, although already, in just the eighth day of our serious relationship, he is already becoming burdensome. "Why?" he is saying to me, "Why must this be? I don't understand it. Why can't we just be together? Why can't people just live? Why do we have to go to the make-its and trade off like that? It's evil, I tell you. It isn't the way that it should be," And twenty-three years old, he begins to sob.

I pat his neck absently. "No choice," I say, and "This is the way it must be" and "We still have each other, don't we?" The aimless platitudes that, for Kenny, are as close as he can come to knowledge, and at last he quiets. Without lust I hold him, shroud him with my body.

At length he sleeps, unbonded from the drug-panic at last, and I ease from the bed, relieve myself, and then walk to the window where I look out upon the city for a long time, willing my mind toward blankness and acceptance as it is stated in the principles. Dust sifts upward, light down, light shimmers and glimmers through the one hundred stories of the project, grouped upon one another like bodies grappling at a make-it. At a far distance I think that I can see the limits and beyond that still, a hint of fire, but this must be only fatigue and I block out the illusion, going back then to the bed.

Kenny lies there openmouthed, his face a child's face, his chest moving easily, helpless against my gaze. I could mount him like a stallion and have my way; I could strangle him in his sleep and no one would know the difference; I could stagger with him toward the window and throw him down forty-seven stories of project to let him burst upon the pavement and no one could stop me. He is completely at my will; I could do anything to him that I wanted and this, then, must be part of the excitement. Standing by the bed, looking upon him, I find that my fists are clenching and unclenching in the old rhythm of masturbation, but I do not do it.

Instead I crawl beside him on the bed, carefully so as not to wreck his sleep, and roll against him, and then for a while I myself sleep, the sounds and odors of the city combating dreams for a while for attention and then disappearing at last in an oily and satisfying enclosure which I must know as rest.

III

In the morning again, but later, Kenny and I arise and leave my room quietly, journey down the forty-seven flights of the project and take a long walk around the winding paths, ending at last at the gates beyond which lies the river. Hand in hand we look at the river for a long time, talking quietly of arrangements, plans, possibilities. By some unphrased understanding, we have agreed not to mention the make-it again, not this day, maybe not for several days. We decide that the time has come in our relationship where Kenny will vacate his apartment on the fifty-sixth and move in with me, at least on a temporary basis. After that, who knows? We will see where the relationship goes. His fingers against my palm begin to excite me; I rub the small of his back, feeling the slow beat of him radiating. "Will it work?" Kenny says. "Will it work between us?" He has already told me that at the beginning of his relationships he is sentimental, hoping for permanence, hoping that this one at last will grant him stability. *It's only later that I become a bitch,* he has warned me, *when I realize that I will never find that stability and then you will hate me.* But that is a good way off, weeks at least or perhaps months until my relationship with Kenny becomes sour and embittered, and even though I can see the patterns coalescing faintly, like the shapes of dead animals in the river, they do not concern me now.

"Yes," I say, "yes, it will work between us." Looking at the river, thinking of the city, all of the city seeming to overtake me now on this late and strange morning, my body still aching from Karl's penetration but yearning toward this new lover by my side. "It's got to work," I say. "I promise that it will work." Thinking of the city and how we have come to survive in it and how wrong, how wrong all of the sociologists and analysts of forty years ago were because the patterns that they detected as the sickness of the city were, indeed, only those of health; it was the accommodation that they saw, but locked into their culture as we are not, they did not understand the cure for the illness but, instead, gave it a different name.

"I know it will work," I say quietly, testing the firmness of his rectum with a delicate finger, feeling the gentle pulsations from that flower as all unconscious it wraps itself around me, and then he slumps against me and I gather him in, my lover, my friend.

"I don't think," he says then, "I don't think that I could stand it if it went wrong again, I've been hurt so much. Last night at the make-it, when George came into me I thought—"

"Quiet," I say, putting a hand against his lips, "Quiet. We agreed we wouldn't talk about the make-it. That's a long way off. We don't even have to think about it for six days." And he laughs, gently at first, then harder, the bursts of his laughter carrying him into my arms, my arms taking him in, little whiffs and smells of the river compounding my excitement, and right there, against the gates, with all of the project looking down —and who could care if they were? who could care?—we have at each other, the clothes falling away, our bodies joining, the lifting and the joining together, and "Oh!" he cries at the climax. "Oh, Bert, I never thought it could be this way!" He is twenty-three years old, I am twenty-eight, but it is not a matter of ages. There are things I understand all too well that will never touch him, and it is this, his frailty, his accessibility to pain, that more than anything else must thrust me over and I dissolve into him, groaning and beating against the gate, against the river, the project revolving slowly above us as we thrash together on the ground.

At length we separate, but hands interlocked we walk back toward the project to make the transfer of quarters in perfect silence and understanding. The make-it is far behind us. And it will be six days more until we must test our partnership again.

IV

At the beginning with Karl, in the second week or the third it must have been, we too came down to the river; oh, this must have been months ago, six or seven at least, Karl now being as dead to me and distant as the spaces of the countryside I forsook to return to the city, but at that time what was building with Karl seemed significant or then again maybe it was not, maybe nothing was significant, and we stood against the gates looking upon the river, just as I had with Kenny this day, and he turned to me then, dropping his hand, and looking at me, he said, "Bert, we're sick. We're sick and we're totally insane. Bert, do you see what's become of us just so that we could survive? Is it worth it? Is it worth it?" And there was nothing to say to him, there was never anything to say to Karl in any of these moods, and so I let it pass, I the submissive one then, leaning against the gate, letting my posture go slack, and at this impression of vulnerability (how he always made me the woman!) Karl came upon me then and gathered me in. "I didn't mean to hurt you," he said. "I didn't want to hurt you. Forget I said it. Forget everything. Just let me hold you." And so on and so forth. "We aren't sick," he said. "It's just a dream, a dream of the city, and so it will pass." And against the gate then we did the necessary, but it was never as good as the way it was going to be later with Kenny (I believe this, I must believe this), and as I rolled under him, eyes fixed way above the project on the damp and obtrusive sky, eyes rolling in the spasms of the approaching orgasm, I told myself even then that it was temporary with Karl, a way station, and that at the very next make-it I would have to keep my eyes open for someone else, someone who would reconstitute me at the level of health I deserved, and this is how I met Kenny, Kenny, who had not been mine in other than a casual way as part of the group for three full years, and I knew then, looking at the sky, just as I know now, embracing my lover yet again in an ecstasy of connection, that the city is good and the city is merciful because it has given us, in its justice and wisdom, the opportunity to do without penalty exactly all of those things that we must in order to bear it.

The World As Will and Wallpaper

R.A. LAFFERTY

I

A template, a stencil, a pattern, a plan.
Corniest, orneriest damsel and man,
Orderly, emptily passion and pity,
All-the-World, All-the-World, All-the-World City.

13th Street Ballad

There is an old dictionary-encyclopedia that defines a City as ". . . a concentration of persons that is not economically self-contained." The dictionary-encyclopedia being an old one, however (and there is no other kind), is mistaken. The World City *is* economically self-contained.

It was William Morris who read this definition in the old book. William was a bookie, or readie, and he had read parts of several books. But now he had a thought: If all the books are old, then things may no longer be as the books indicate. I will go out and see what things are like today in the City. I will traverse as much of the City as my life allows me. I may even come to the *Wood Beyond the World* that my name-game ancestor described.

William went to the Permit Office of the City. Since there was only one City, there might be only one Permit Office, though it was not large.

"I want a permit to traverse as much of the City as my life allows me," William told the permit man. "I even want a permit to go to the *Wood Beyond the World*. Is that possible?"

The permit man did a skittish little dance around William,

41

"like a one-eyed gander around a rattlesnake." The metaphor was an old and honored one, one of the fifty-four common metaphors. They both understood it: it didn't have to be voiced. William was the first customer the permit man had had in many days, though, so the visit startled him.

"Since everything is permitted, you will need no permit," the permit man said. "Go, man, go."

"Why are you here then?" William asked him. "If there are no permits, why is there a Permit Office?"

"This is my niche and my notch," the permit man said. "Do away with me and my office and you begin to do away with the City itself. It is the custom to take a companion when you traverse the City."

Outside, William found a companion named Kandy Kalosh and they began to traverse the City that was the World. They began (it was no more than coincidence) at a marker set in stone that bore the words "Beginning of Stencil 35,352." The City tipped and tilted a bit, and they were on their way. Now this is what the City was like:

It was named Will of the World City, for it had been construct-ed by a great and world-wide surge of creative will. Afterward, something had happened to that surge, but it did not matter; the City was already created then.

The City was varied, it was joyful, it was free and it covered the entire world. The mountains and heights had all been re-moved, and the City, with its various strips of earth and sweet water and salt water, floated on the ocean on its interlocking floaters. As to money values, everything was free; and every-thing was free as to personal movement and personal choice. It was not really crowded except in the places where the people wanted it crowded, for people do love to congregate. It was sufficient as to foodstuff and shelter and entertainment. These things have always been free, really; it was their packaging and traffic that cost, and now the packaging and traffic were virtually eliminated.

"Work is joy" flashed the subliminal signs. Of course it is.

It is a joy to stop and turn into an area and work for an hour, even an hour and a half, at some occupation never or seldom attempted before. William and Kandy entered an area where persons made cloth out of clamshells, softening them in one solution, then drawing them out to filaments on a machine, then forming (not weaving) them into cloth on still another machine. The cloth was not needed for clothing or for curtains, though sometimes it was used for one or the other. It was for ornamentation. Temperature did not require cloth (the temperature was everywhere equitable) and modesty did not require it, but there was something that still required a little cloth as ornament.

William and Kandy worked for nearly an hour with other happy people on the project. It is true that their own production was all stamped "Rejected" when they were finished, but that did not mean that it went all the way back to the clamshells, only back to the filament stage.

"Honest labor is never lost," William said as solemnly as a one-horned owl with the pip.

"I knew you were a readie, but I didn't know you were a talkie," Kandy said. People didn't talk much then. Happy people have no need to talk. And of course honest labor is never lost, and small bits of it are pleasurable.

This portion of the City (perhaps all portions of the City) floated on old ocean itself. It had, therefore, a slight heave to it all the time. "The City is a tidy place" was an old and honored saying. It referred to the fact that the City moved a little with the tides. It was a sort of joke.

The two young persons came ten blocks; they came a dozen. For much of this traverse the City had been familiar to William but not to Kandy. They had been going west, and William had always been a westering lad. Kandy, however, had always wandered east from her homes, and she was the farthest west that she had ever been when she met William.

They came to the 14th Street Water Ballet and watched the swimmers. These swimmers were very good, and great numbers of curiously shaped fish frolicked with them in the green salt-fresh pools. Anyone who wished to could, of course, swim in the Water Ballet, but most of the swimmers seemed to be regulars. They were part of the landscape, of the waterscape.

William and Kandy stopped to eat at an algae-and-plankton quick-lunch place on 15th Street. Indeed, Kandy worked there for half an hour, pressing the plankton and adding squirts of special protean as the people ordered it. Kandy had worked in quick-lunch places before.

The two of them stopped at the Will of the World Exhibit Hall on 16th Street. They wrote their names with a stylus in wax when they went in, or rather William wrote the names of both of them for Kandy could not write. And because he bore the mystic name of William, he received a card out of the slot with a genuine Will of the World verse on it:

This City of the World is wills
Of Willful folk, and nothing daunts it.
With daring hearts we hewed the hills
To make the World as Willy wants it.

Really, had it taken such great will and heart to build the City of the World? It must have or there would not have been a Will of the World Exhibit Hall to commend it. There were some folks, however, who said that the building of the World City had been an automatic response.

Kandy, being illiterate (as the slot knew), received a picture card.

They stopped at the Cliff-Dweller Complex on 17th Street. This part of the City was new to William as well as to Kandy.

The cliffs and caves were fabricated and not natural cliff dwellings, but they looked very much as old cliff dwellings must have looked. There were little ladders going up from one level to the next. There were people sitting on the little terraces with the small-windowed apartments behind them. Due to the circular arrangement of the cliff dwellings, very many of the

people were always visible to one another. The central court-
yard was like an amphitheater. Young people played stickball
and Indian ball in this area. They made music on drums and
whistles. There were artificial rattlesnakes in coils, artificial rib-
skinny dogs, artificial coyotes, artificial women in the act of
grinding corn with hand querns. And also, in little shelters
or pavilions, there were real people grinding simulacrum corn
on apparatus.

Kandy Kalosh went into one of the pavilions and ground
corn for fifteen minutes. She had a healthy love for work. William Morris made corn-dogs out of simulacrum corn and sea-
weeds. It was pleasant there. Sometimes the people sang
simulacrum Indian songs. There were patterned blankets,
brightly colored, and woven out of bindweed. There were buf-
foons in masks and buffoon suits who enacted in-jokes and
in-situations that were understood by the cliff-dwelling people
only, but they could be enjoyed by everyone.

"All different, all different, every block different," William
murmured in rapture. It had come on evening, but evening
is a vague thing. It was never very bright in the daytime or
very dark at night. The World City hadn't a clear sky but it
had always a sort of diffused light. William and Kandy traveled
still farther west.

"It is wonderful to be a world traveler and to go on forever,"
William exulted. "The City is so huge that we cannot see it
all in our whole lives and every bit of it is different."

"A talkie you are," Kandy said. "However did I get a talkie?
If I were a talkie too I could tell you something about that
every-part-of-it-is-different bit."

"This is the greatest thing about the whole World City,"
William sang, "to travel the City itself for all our lives, and
the climax of it will be to see the *Wood Beyond the World*.
But what happens then, Kandy? The City goes on forever, covering the whole sphere. It cannot be bounded. What is beyond
the *Wood Beyond the World?*"

"If I were a talkie I could tell you," Kandy said.

But the urge to talk was on William Morris. He saw an older and somehow more erect man who wore an arm band with the lettering "Monitor" on it. Of course only a readie, or bookie, like William would have been able to read the word.

"My name-game ancestor had to do with the naming as well as the designing of the *Wood Beyond the World*," William told the erect and smiling man, "for I also am a William Morris. I am avid to see this ultimate wood. It is as though I have lived for the moment."

"If you will it strongly enough, then you may see it, Willy," the man said.

"But I am puzzled," William worried out the words, and his brow was furrowed. "What is beyond the *Wood Beyond the World?*"

"A riddle, but an easy one." The man smiled. "How is it that you are a readie and do not know such simple things?"

"Cannot you give me a clue to the easy riddle?" William begged.

"Yes," the man said. "Your name-game ancestor had to do with the designing of one other particular thing besides the *Wood Beyond the World.*"

"Come along, readie, come along," Kandy said.

They went to the West Side Show Square on 18th Street. Neither of them had ever been to such a place, but they had heard rumors of it for there is nothing at all like the West Side Show Square on 18th Street.

There were the great amplifiers with plug-ins everywhere. Not only were the instruments plugged in, but most of the people were themselves plugged in. And ah! The wonderful setting was like the backside of old tenements all together in a rough circuit. There were period fire escapes that may even have been accurate. They looked as though persons might actually climb up and down on them. Indeed, light persons had actually done this in the past, but it was forbidden now as some of the folks had fallen to death or maiming. But the atmosphere was valid.

Listen, there was period washing on period clotheslines! It was flapped by little wind machines just as though there were a real wind blowing. No wonder they called this the show square. It was a glum-slum, a jetto-ghetto, authentic past time.

The performing people (and all the people on that part of 18th Street seemed to be performing people) were dressed in tight jeans and scalloped or ragged shirts, and even in broken shoes full of holes. It must have been very hot for them, but art is worth it. It was memento of the time when the weather was not everywhere equitable.

There were in-dramas and in-jokes and in-situations acted out. The essence of the little dramas was very intense hatred for a group or class not clearly defined. There were many of those old-period enemy groups in the various drama locations of the City.

The lights were without pattern but they were bright. The music was without tune or melody or song or chord but it was very loud and very passionate. The shouting that took the place of singing was absolutely livid. Some of the performers fell to the ground and writhed there and foamed at their mouths.

It was a thing to be seen and heard—once. William and Kandy finally took their leave with bleeding ears and matter-encrusted eyes. They went along to 19th Street where there was a Mingle-Mangle.

It was now as dark as it ever got in the City but the Mangle was well lighted. Certain persons at the Mangle laughingly took hold of William and Kandy and married them to each other. They had bride and groom crowns made of paper and they put them on their heads.

Then they wined and dined them, an old phrase. Really, they were given fine cognac made of fish serum and braised meat made of algae but also mixed with the real chopped flesh of ancients.

Then William and Kandy padded down in the great Pad Palace that was next to the Mangle. Every night there were great numbers of people along that part of 19th Street, at the Mingle-Mangle and at the Pad Palace, and most of these folks were friendly, with their glazed eyes and their dampish grins.

II

Pleasant most special to folks of the Club!
Pleasant for manifold minions and hinds of it!
Stuff them with plankton and choppings and chub!
Simple the City and simple the minds of it.

20th Street Ballad

The world's resources are consumed disproportionally by the intelligent classes. Therefore we will keep our own numbers drastically reduced. The wan-wits have not strong reproductive or consuming urge so long as they are kept in reasonable comfort and sustenance. They are happy, they are entertained; and when they are convinced that there is no more for them to see, they become the ancients and go willingly to the choppers. But the 2 per cent or so of us superior ones are necessary to run the world.

Why then do we keep the others, the simple-minded billions? We keep them for the same reason that our ancestors kept blooms or lands or animals or great houses or trees or artifacts. We keep them because we want to, and because there is no effort involved.

But a great effort was made once. There was an incredible surge of will. Mountains were moved and leveled. The sky itself was pulled down, as it were. The Will of the World was made manifest. It was a new act of creation. And what is the step following creation when it is discovered that the Commonalty is not worthy of the City created? When it is discovered also that they are the logical cattle to fill such great pens? The next step is hierarchies. The Angels themselves have hierarchies, *and we are not less.*

It is those who are intelligent but not quite intelligent enough to join the Club who are imperiled and destroyed as a necessity to the operation of the City. At the summit is always the Club. It is the Club in the sense of a bludgeon and also of an organization.

Will of The World Annals—Classified Abstract

In the morning, Kandy Kalosh wanted to return to her home even though it was nearly twenty blocks to the eastward. William watched her go without sorrow. He would get a westering girl to go with him on the lifelong exploration of the endlessly varied City. He might get a girl who was a talkie or even a readie, or bookie.

And he did. She was named Fairhair Farquhar, though she was actually dark of hair and of surface patina. But they started out in the early morning to attain (whether in a day or a lifetime) the *Wood Beyond the World.*

"But it is not far at all," Fairhair said (she was a talkie). "We can reach it this very evening. We can sleep in the *Wood* in the very night shadow of the famous Muggers. Oh, is the morning not wonderful! A blue patch was seen only last week, a real hole in the sky. Maybe we can see another."

They did not see another. It is very seldom that a blue (or even a starry) hole can be seen in the greenhouse glass-gray color that is the sky. The Will of the World had provided sustenance for everyone, but it was a muggy and sticky World City that provided, almost equally warm from pole to pole, cloyingly fertile in both the land strips and the water strips, and now just a little bit queasy.

"Run, William, run in the morning!" Fairhair cried, and she ran while he shuffled after her. Fairhair did not suffer morning sickness but most of the world did: it had not yet been bred out of the races. After all, it was a very tidy world.

There was a great membrane or firmament built somewhere below, and old ocean was prisoned between this firmament and the fundamental rock of Gehenna-earth. But the ocean-monster tossed and pitched and was not entirely tamed: he was still old Leviathan.

Along and behind all the streets of the World City were the narrow (their width not five times the length of a man) strips, strips of very nervous and incredibly fertile land, of salt water jumping with fish and eels and dark with tortoise and so thick with blue-green plankton that one could almost walk on it, of fresh water teeming with other fish and loggy with snapping turtles and snakes, of other fresh water almost solid with nourishing algae, of mixed water filled with purged shrimp and all old estuary life; land strips again, and strips of rich chemical water where people voided themselves and their used things and from which so many valuable essences could be extracted; other strips, and then the houses and buildings of another block, for the blocks were not long. Kaleidoscope of nervous water and land, everywhere basic and everywhere different, boated with boats on the strange overpass canals, crossed by an infinity of bridges.

"And no two alike!" William sang, his morning sickness having left him. "Every one different, everything different in a world that cannot be traversed in a lifetime. We'll not run out of wonders!"

"William, William, there is something I have been meaning to tell you," Fairhair tried to interpose.

"Tell me, Fairhair, what is beyond the *Wood Beyond the World*, since the world is a globe without bounds?"

"The World Beyond the Wood is beyond the *Wood Beyond the World*," Fairhair said simply. "If you want the *Wood*, you will come to it, but do not be cast down if it falls short for you."

"How could it fall short for me? I am a William Morris. My name-game ancestor had to do with the naming as well as the designing of the *Wood*."

"Your name-game ancestor had to do with the designing of another thing also," Fairhair said. Why, that was almost the same thing as the monitor man had said the day before! What did they mean by it?

William and Fairhair came to the great Chopper House at

20th Street. The two of them went in and worked for an hour in the Chopper House.

"You do not quite understand this, do you, little William?" Fairhair asked.

"Oh, I understand enough for me. I understand that it is everywhere different."

"Yes, I suppose you understand enough for you," Fairhair said with a touch of near sadness. (What they chopped up in the Chopper House was the ancients.)

They went on and on along the strips and streets of the ever-changing city. They came to 21st Street and 22nd and 23rd. Even a writie could not write down all marvels that were to be found at every street. It is sheer wonder to be a world traveler.

There was a carnival at 23rd Street. There were barkies, sharkies, sparkies, darkies, parkies, and markies; the visitors were the markies, but it was not really bad for them. There was the very loud music even though it was supposed to be period tingle-tangle or rinky-dink. There was a steam calliope with real live steam. There were the hamburger stands with the wonderful smell of a touch of garlic in the open air, no matter that it was ancient chopper meat and crinoid-root bun from which the burgers were made. There were games of chance, smooch houses and cooch houses, whirly rides and turning wheels, wino and steino bars and bordellos, and Monster and Misbegotten displays in clamshell-cloth tents.

Really, is anyone too old to enjoy a carnival? Then let that one declare himself an ancient and turn himself in to a Chopper House.

But on and on; one does not tarry when there is the whole World City to see and it not to be covered in one lifetime. On 24th (or was it 25th?) Street were the Flesh Pots, and a little beyond them was the Cat Center. One ate and drank beyond reason in the Flesh Pots region and also became enmeshed in the Flesh Mesh booths. And one catted beyond reason in the honeycomblike cubicles of the Cat Center.

Fairhair went and worked for an hour at the Cat Center; she seemed to be known and popular there.

But on and on! Everywhere it is different and everywhere it is better.

Along about 27th and 28th Streets were the Top of the Town and Night-Life Knoll, those great cabaret concentrations. It was gin-dizzy here; it was yesterday and tomorrow entangled with its great expectations and its overpowering nostalgia; it was as loud as the West Side Show Square; it was as direct as the Mingle-Mangle or the Pad Palace. It was as fleshy as the Flesh Pots and more catty than the Cat Center. Oh, it was the jumpingest bunch of places that William had yet seen in the City.

Something a little sad there, though; something of passion and pity that was too empty and too pat. It was as though this were the climax of it all, and one didn't *want* it to be the climax yet. It was as if the Top of the Town and Night-Life Knoll (and not the *Wood Beyond the World*) were the central things of the World City.

Perhaps William slept there awhile in the sadness that follows the surfeit of flesh and appetite. There were other doings and sayings about him, but mostly his eyes were closed and his head was heavy.

But then Fairhair had him up again and rushing toward the *Wood* in the still early night.

"It is only a block, William, it is only a block," she sang, "and it is the place you have wanted more than any other." (The *Wood* began at 29th Street and went on, it was said, for the space of *two* full blocks.)

But William ran badly and he even walked badly. He was woozy and confused, not happy, not sad, just full of the great bulk of life in the City. He'd hardly have made it to his high goal that night except for the help of Fairhair. But she dragged and lifted and carried him along in her fine arms and on her dusky back and shoulders. He toppled off sometimes and cracked his crown, but there was never real damage done.

One sometimes enters the *Wood Beyond* in a sort of rhythmic dream, grotesque and comic and jolting with the sway of a strong friend and of the tidy world itself. And William came in with his arms around the neck and shoulders of the girl named Fairhair, with his face buried in her hair itself, with his feet touching no ground.

But he knew it as soon as they were in the *Wood*. He was afoot again and strong again and in the middle of the fabled place itself. He was sober? No, there can be no sobriety in the *Wood;* it has its own intoxication.

But it had real grass and weeds, real trees (though most of them were bushes), real beasts as well as artificial, real spruce cones on the turf, real birds (no matter that they were clattering crows) coming in to roost.

There was the carvan oak figure of old Robin Hood and the tall spar-wood form of the giant lumberjack Paul Bunyan. There was the Red Indian named White Deer who was carved from cedarwood. There was maple syrup dripping from the trees (is that the way they used to get it?), and there was the aroma of slippery elm with the night dampness on it.

There were the famous Muggers from the mugger decades. They were of papier-mâché, it is true, and yet they were most fearsome. There were other dangerous beasts in the *Wood*, but none like the Muggers. And William and Fairhair lay down and slept in the very night shadow of the famous Muggers for the remainder of the enchanted night.

III

"Wonder-bird, wander-bird, where do you fly?"
"All over the City, all under the sky,

"Wand'ring through wonders of strippies and streets,
Changing and challenging, bitters and sweets."

"Wander-bird, squander-bird, should not have budged:
City is sicko and sky is a smudge."
                                                    1st Street Ballad

"Run, William, run in the morning!" Fairhair cried, and she ran while William (confused from the night) shuffled after her.

"We must leave the *Wood?*" he asked.

"Of course *you* must leave the *Wood.* You want to see the whole world, so you cannot stay in one place. You go on, I go back. No, no, don't you look back or you'll be turned into a salt-wood tree."

"Stay with me, Fairhair."

"No, no, you want variety. I have been with you long enough. I have been guide and companion and pony to you. Now we part."

Fairhair went back. William was afraid to look after her. He was in the world beyond the *Wood Beyond the World.* He noticed though that the street was 1st Street and not 31st Street as he had expected.

It was still wonderful to be a world traveler, of course, but not quite as wonderful as it had been one other time. The number of the street shouldn't have mattered to him. William had not been on any 1st Street before. Or 2nd.

But he had been on a 3rd Street before on his farthest trip east. Should he reach it again on his farthest trip west? The world, he knew (being a readie who had read parts of several books), was larger than that. He could not have gone around it in thirty blocks. Still, he came to 3rd Street in great trepidation.

Ah, it was not the same 3rd Street he had once visited before; almost the same but not exactly. An ounce of reassurance was intruded into the tons of alarm in his heavy head. But he was alive, he was well, he was still traveling west in the boundless City that is everywhere different.

"The City is varied and joyful and free," William Morris said boldly, "and it is everywhere different." Then he saw Kandy Kalosh and he literally staggered with the shock. Only it did not quite seem to be she.

"Is your name Kandy Kalosh?" he asked as quakingly as a one-legged kangaroo with the willies.

"The last thing I needed was a talkie," she said. "Of course it isn't. My name, which I have from my name-game ancestor, is Candy Calabash, not at all the same."

Of course it wasn't the same. Then why had he been so alarmed and disappointed?

"Will you travel westward with me, Candy?" he asked.

"I suppose so, a little way, if we don't have to talk," she said.

So William Morris and Candy Calabash began to traverse the City that was the world. They began (it was no more than coincidence) at a marker set in stone that bore the words "Beginning of Stencil 35,353," and thereat William went into a sort of panic. But why should he? It was not the same stencil number at all. The World City might still be everywhere different.

But William began to run erratically. Candy stayed with him. She was not a readie or a talkie, but she was faithful to a companion for many blocks. The two young persons came ten blocks; they came a dozen.

They arrived at the 14th Street Water Ballet and watched the swimmers. It was almost, but not quite, the same as another 14th Street Water Ballet that William had seen once. They came to the algae-and-plankton quick-lunch place on 15th Street and to the Will of the World Exhibit Hall on 16th Street. Ah, a hopeful eye could still pick out little differences in the huge sameness. The World City *had to be* everywhere different.

They stopped at the Cliff-Dweller Complex on 17th Street. There was an artificial antelope there now. William didn't remember it from the other time. There was hope, there was hope.

And soon William saw an older and somehow more erect man who wore an arm band with the word "Monitor" on it. He was not the same man, but he had to be a close brother of another man that William had seen two days before.

"Does it all repeat itself again and again and again?" William asked this man in great anguish. "Are the sections of it the same over and over again?"

"Not quite," the man said. "The grease marks on it are some-times a little different."

"My name is William Morris," William began once more bravely.

"Oh, sure. A William Morris is the easiest type of all to spot," the man said.

"You said— No, another man said that my name-game ances-tor had to do with the designing of another thing besides the *Wood Beyond the World*," William stammered. "What was it?"

"Wallpaper," the man said. And William fell down in a frothy faint.

Oh, Candy didn't leave him there. She was faithful. She took him up on her shoulders and plodded along with him, on past the West Side Show Square on 18th Street, past the Mingle-Mangle and the Pad Palace, where she (no, another girl very like her) had turned back before, on and on.

"It's the same thing over and over and over again," William whimpered as she toted him along.

"Be quiet, talkie," she said, but she said it with some affec-tion.

They came to the great Chopper House on 20th Street. Candy carried William in and dumped him on a block there.

"He's become an ancient," Candy told an attendant. "Boy, how he's become an ancient!" It was more than she usually talked.

Then, as she was a fair-minded girl and as she had not worked any stint that day, she turned to and worked an hour in the Chopper House. (What they chopped up in the Chopper House was the ancients.)

Why, there was William's head coming down the line! Candy smiled at it. She chopped it up with loving care, much more care than she usually took.

She'd have said something memorable and kind if she'd been a talkie.

Violation

WILLIAM F. NOLAN

It is 2 A.M. and he waits. In the cool morning stillness of a side street, under the screen of trees, the rider waits quietly. At ease upon the wide leather seat of his cycle, gloved fingers resting idly on the bars, goggles up, eyes palely reflecting the leaf-filtered glow of the moon.

Helmeted. Uniformed. Waiting.

In the breathing dark the cycle metal cools; the motor is silent, power contained.

The faint stirrings of a still-sleeping city reach him at his vigil. But he is not concerned with these; he mentally dismisses them. He is only concerned with the broad river of smooth concrete facing him through the trees—and the great winking red eye suspended icicle-like above it.

He waits.

And tenses to a sound upon the river. An engine sound, mosquito-dim with distance, rising to a hum. A rushing sound under the stars.

The rider's hands contract like the claws of a bird. He rises slowly on the bucket seat, right foot poised near the starter. A coiled spring. Waiting.

Twin pencil beams of light move toward him, toward the street on which he waits hidden. Closer.

The hum builds in volume; the lights are very close now, flaring chalk-whiteness along the concrete boulevard.

The rider's goggles are down and he is ready to move out, move onto the river. Another second, perhaps two . . .

But no. The vehicle slows, makes a full stop. A service vehicle with two men inside, laughing, joking. The rider listens to them, mouth set, eyes hard. The vehicle begins to move once more. The sound is eaten by the night.

There is no violation.

Now . . . the relaxing, the easing back. The ebb tide of tension receding. Gone. The rider quiet again under the moon.

Waiting.

The red eye winking at the empty boulevard.

"How much farther, Dave?" asks the girl.

"Ten miles maybe. Once we hit Westwood it's a quick run to my place. Relax. You're nervous."

"We should have stayed on the mainway. Used the grid. I don't like surface streets. A grid would have taken us in."

The man smiles, looping an arm around her.

"There's nothing to be afraid of so long as you're careful," he said. "I used to drive surface streets all the time when I was a boy. Lots of people did."

The girl swallows, touches at her hair nervously. "But they don't anymore. People use the grids. I didn't even know cars still came equipped for manual driving."

"They don't. I had this set up by a mechanic I know. He does jobs like this for road buffs. It's still legal, driving your own car—it's just that most people have lost the habit."

The girl peers out the window into the silent street, shakes her head. "It's not . . . natural. Look out there. Nobody! Not another car for miles. I feel as if we're . . . trespassing."

The man is annoyed. "That's damn nonsense. I have friends who do this all the time. Just relax and enjoy it. And don't talk like an idiot."

"I want out," says the girl. "I'll take a walkway back to the grid."

"The hell you will," flares the man. "You're with me tonight. We're going to my place."

She resists, strikes at his face. The man grapples to subdue her—and does not see the blinking light. The car passes under it swiftly.

"No!" says the man. "I went through that light! You made me miss the stop. I've broken one of the surface laws." He says this numbly.

"So what does that mean?" the girl asks. "What could happen?"

"Never mind. Nothing will happen. Never mind about what could happen."

The girl peers out into the darkness. "I still want to leave this car."

"Just shut up," says the man.

And keeps driving.

Something in the sound tells the rider that this one will not stop, that it will continue to move along the river of concrete despite the blinking eye.

He smiles in the darkness, lips stretched back, silently. Poised there on the cycle, with the hum steady and rising on the river, he feels the power within him about to be released.

The car is almost upon the light, moving swiftly; there is no hint of slackened speed.

The rider watches intently. Man and a girl inside. Struggling. Fighting with one another.

The car passes under the light.

Violation.

Now!

He spurs the cycle to metal life; the motor crackles, roars, explodes the black machine into motion, and the rider is away, rolling in muted thunder along the street. Around the corner, swaying, onto the long, moon-painted river of the boulevard.

The rider feels the wind in his face, feels the throb and power-pulse of the metal thing he rides, feels the smooth concrete rushing backward under his wheels.

Ahead: the firefly glow of tail beams.

And now his cycle voice cries out after them, a siren moan

through the still spaces of the hive-city. A voice that rises and falls in spirals of sound. And his cycle eyes, mounted left and right, blink crimson, red as blood in their wake.

The car will stop. The man will see him, hear him. The eyes and the voice will reach the violator.

And he will stop.

"Good Lord!" the man says coldly. "We picked up a rider at that light."

"*You* picked him up, I didn't," says the girl. "It's your problem."

"But I've never been stopped on a surface street," the man says, a note of desperation in his voice. "In all these years, never *once!*"

The girl glares at him. "Dave, you make me sick. Look at you, shaking like a pup. You're a damned poor excuse for a man."

He does not react to these words. He speaks in a numbed monotone. "I can talk my way out. I know I can. He'll listen to me. I have my rights as a citizen of the city—"

"He's catching up fast. You'd better pull over."

"I'll do the talking. You just keep quiet. I'll handle this."

The rider sees that the car is slowing, braking, pulling to the curb. Stopping.

He cuts the siren voice, lets it die, glides the cycle in behind the car. Cuts the engine. Sits there for a long moment on the leather seat, pulling off his gloves. Slowly.

He sees the car door slide open. A man steps out, comes toward him. The rider swings a booted leg over the cycle, steps free, advancing to meet this lawbreaker, fitting the gloves carefully into his black leather belt.

They face each other, the man smaller, paunching, balding, face flushed. The rider's polite smile eases the man's tenseness.

"You in a hurry, sir?"

"Me? No, I'm not in a hurry. Not at all. It was just . . . I didn't see the light up there until . . . I was past it. The high trees and all. I swear to you I didn't see it. I'd never knowingly break a surface law, officer. You have my sworn word."

Nervous. Shaken and nervous, this man. The rider can feel the man's guilt, a physical force. He extends a hand.

"May I see your operator's license, please?"

The man fumbles in his coat. "I have it right here. It's all in order, up to date and all."

"Just let me see it, please."

The man continues to talk. "Been driving for years, officer, and this is my first violation. Perfect record up to now. I'm a responsible citizen. I obey the laws. After all, I'm not a fool."

The rider says nothing; he examines the man's license, taps it thoughtfully against his wrist. The rider's goggles are opaque and the man cannot see his eyes as he studies the face of the violator.

"The woman in the car . . . is she your wife?"

"No. No, sir. She's . . . a friend. Just a friend."

"Then why were you fighting? I saw the two of you fighting inside the car when it passed the light. That isn't friendly, is it?"

The man attempts to smile. "Personal. We had a small personal disagreement. It's all over now, believe me."

The rider walks to the car, leans to peer in at the woman. She is pale, as nervous as the man.

"You having trouble?" the rider asks.

She hesitates, shakes her head mutely. The rider leaves her, returns to the man, who is leaning against the cycle.

"Don't touch that," says the rider coldly, and the man draws back his hand, mumbling an apology.

"I have no further use for this," says the rider, handing back the man's license. "You are guilty of a surface-street violation."

The man quakes; his hands tremble. "But . . . it was not *deliberate*. I know the law. You're empowered to make exceptions if a violation is not deliberate. The full penalty is not invoked in such cases. Instead, you are allowed to—"

The rider cuts the flow of desperate words. "You forfeited your Citizen's Right of Exception when you allowed a primary emotion—anger, in this instance—to affect your control of a surface vehicle. Thus, my duty is clear."

The man's eyes widen in shock as the rider brings up a belt weapon. "You can't possibly—"

"I'm hereby authorized to perform this action per the 1990 Overpopulation Statute with regard to surface violators. Your case is closed."

And he presses the trigger.

Again and again and again. Three long, probing blue jets of star-hot flame leap from the weapon in the rider's hand.

The man is gone.

The woman is gone.

The car is gone.

The street is empty and silent. A charred smell of distant suns lingers in the morning air.

The rider stands by his cycle, unmoving for a long moment. Then he carefully holsters the weapon and pulls on his leather gloves. He mounts the cycle as it comes to life under his foot.

He is again upon the moon-flowing boulevard, gliding back toward the blinking red eye.

The rider returns to his vigil on the small, tree-shadowed side street, thinking, How stupid they are! To be subject to indecision, to quarrels and erratic behavior. Weak, all of them, soft and weak.

He smiles into the darkness.

The eye blinks over the river.

And now it is 4 A.M. and now 6 and 8 and 10 and 1 P.M. and now it is 3, 4, 5, the hours turning like spoked wheels, the days spinning away. And he waits. Through nights without sleep, days without food, a flawless metal enforcer at his vigil, watching, sure of himself and of his duty.

Waiting.

K. M. O'DONNELL

City Lights, City Nights
K. M. O'DONNELL

I

Oswald shoots Kennedy again.

Kennedy, that idiot, has decided for some reason to do this take standing in the car. He falls heavily across Jacqueline, dislodging the roses, which collapse underneath, exploding petals on him, and Oswald, happy for this anyway, throws the rifle down five stories from Municipal and leaves the window as I run out for the mop-up. The rifle is deflected by a third-floor balcony on Municipal and misses my ear by only inches, hitting me a terrific blow on the shoulder. *Lumpen* idiots. They really should know the geometry of this after all the time spent blocking. I fall to the ground in pain and rub the shoulder convulsively until the worst recedes. Perhaps I make slightly more of it than it really is. But they must be taught a lesson. Precautions prevail.

They gather around me quickly: Kennedy, Jacqueline, Johnson, Connally, the security forces. Even though the necessity is to stay in role, I can see fear hammering at the edges of the characterization. Sweat drips; they are frightened. Good. It is necessary that they show me the proper respect. After all, if I am going to perform the auditor's role over and over again, they should take care with my person. "Are you all right?" Kennedy asks. He runs his hand over his jacket, the other hand pumping away in a side pocket. Difficult to believe that he was dying only seconds ago. He has worked himself almost totally out of the role. Discipline. They must learn discipline.

"Get the hell back to the car," I say on the ground, still rubbing the shoulder, then staggering upward. The sun is uncomfortable, the air binding. Manhattan makes a very poor Dallas; I must remind them of that. "What are you waiting for?" I say as they remain around me. "Get back to it."

"We were worried," Jacqueline says, running a hand across my forehead. The fat, stupid bitch; I cannot bear to be touched. How many times have I told her this? I only allowed her to play the role because she begged for it; this is the response I get. She is no actress. Kennedy is no actor. None of them, except for Oswald, have any conception of professionalism.

It is Oswald who joins us now. At a dead run from Municipal he comes toward me, feet clattering. He has seen the rifle, now he sees them gathered around me, the concern on their faces, the way that I am holding my shoulder, and he understands what has happened. He is a man of moderate sensitivity, unlike the rest of them, who are lumps. I do not really know what he is doing in this group but it is probably unwise to speculate: at least he is around. Were it not for him, the re-enactments would be a complete fiasco.

"Are you all right?" he says, stopping some feet from me, backed off from the others, still locked into the role, which is good. He knows he should feel their repudiation, be in flight. At this moment, in fact, he should already be half a mile away, sprinting toward the police car. "I guess you're all right."

"I am," I say, turning from him now to face the others, who are already in scatter, anticipating. "Get on with it!" I shout. "Can't you do anything right? Don't you have any sense, any discipline, any professionalism?" The same old pointless rant. I am sick of hearing it myself but at least it works. They shuffle back to the cars, the grounds, various positions. We are already three minutes behind schedule.

For a moment I think of canceling, telling them off and striking the set until the afternoon, but they have worked so hard up to this point that it is really not fair, and there are also certain notes given them the last time that I must reinforce in run-through or lose forever. The hell with it then. "Let's go," I say, raising my hand, and they see me in the sun; they see me standing there, see the power coming from that hand, and the cars begin to move. Sirens start. Oswald is already gone; it is not impossible that he will retrieve all of the lost time. I pick my pad from the place where I had dropped it and, taking the pen from my pocket, continue my observations. Locked within directorial detachment again it is as if none of this is happening now but has already happened a long time ago, in a Southwestern city, fifty-three years ago next Thursday, already frozen into artifact and how much longer can I put up with their incompetence?

II

Later, with Lara, I try to relax. She is the only one of the players whom I will call by her real name, even in these notes, which are supposed to be confidential and which are to be opened by the Outsiders only decades after the fact, 2050 or something like that, it is difficult to keep track of everything. Under the arrangements I am compelled to keep these notes; actually I would rather not bother. Lara played Mrs. Connally today; I have shifted her to all of the feminine roles, even in an outrage once to Jacqueline, but these enactments do not suit her qualities, whatever they are. She becomes frozen at critical times, postures aimlessly, sometimes lets her sentiments overcome her to the point where she cannot function at all. A bad actress, in short, although she has abilities of another sort. "Don't you ever get tired of this?" she asks, her head now leaned across my legs in a posture of relaxation, her hands rather aimlessly prodding my thighs, slivers of sensation traveling to me that way, although I am not to be moved by any of them. Even by her. They suit limited purposes, is all. "I would think that you're getting bored."

"I am not getting bored. I never get bored. It's work, that's all it is. Don't worry about my feelings."

"All right," she says in a mollifying way, increasing the rhythm of her stroking, as if this could affect me, "you don't have to lose your temper. I was only asking."

"I did not lose my temper. I never lose my temper."

"I don't understand why you want to do this. I can see everything else and what you might be trying to do, but not what you're getting out of it. What could you possible have to gain from this, even in satisfaction?"

Lara is the most intelligent of them and the only one with whom I can manage some informality but she too is disastrously stupid, like the rest, and I perceive, not for the first time, the hopelessness of our relationship. "Stop it," I say. "I don't want to discuss it anymore. It's work, that's all it is, and when the day is over, one can go on to other things. You're here at your own request, you know." This is not a pleasant thing to say but her incessant questioning disturbs me more at some times than at others and the run-through today brought me to a point of understanding I had evaded before; it is really quite hopeless. They will never be able to do it right and we are moving further from true effectiveness all the time. It is possible that on the second run-through, no real preparations, just a set of notes and a quick enactment after their initial familiarization, they did as well as they ever can and from here on in it can only become worse, completely mechanical. Three more days here and out; it will all be over, but what have I learned? I will learn nothing; this is the tragedy. "Go," I say, inflamed by pique and other emotions, "if you have nothing else to say, just go."

"If you want," she says, lolling to the other side, picking herself away from me in one gesture and opening ground. "If you want me to, I will; it's your choice, you know. Why won't you ever talk to us? Why won't you answer my questions? Once I thought it was because you had your reasons but now I'm beginning to be afraid that it's only because you have no answers. Do you really want me to go?"

I reach for her. My cardiovascular and sympathetic nervous systems have been immobilized previously, this being one of the requirements before entrance to the city, but I feel a distant, uncoiling response, more dependent upon memory than connection. "No," I say, "I don't want you to go."

Cunning, cunning, she retreats and holds herself before me with new assurance. "Then you must tell me," she says, "the real truth of why you are here and putting us through these performances. No one Outside even knows that we exist anymore and yet you come here for these rehearsals. You must tell—"

"No," I say, getting to my feet, stalking from her in one motion, "no, there is no more. You must go, Lara."

Stricken, she holds to place. "You must tell me. Otherwise I can't go on—"

"You will go on," I say. "You will go on as long as it is necessary and then further yet because this is what I want you to do. When it is ended you will have your explanation but not until then and I will say no more."

"You think that you can control us," she says quietly. "You think that because you're from the Outside and we the *lumpen* of the city you can make us do anything you want because of your authority but you don't—"

"And can't I?" I say, looking at her. An attractive girl but amorphous at the edges, filled with small shadings toward darkness and dead in the center as all of those left in the city are. She cannot touch me; it means nothing. "Can't I?" I ask again.

She looks at the ground, shakes her head, says nothing. Rumble of stones above; sympathetic collapse of great structures in the distance. The city is falling always as we work through our rituals. Now, leading her from the small enclosed place in the Battery where we have been, I can see the destruction again. Animals whisk invisibly through the park; I feel her hatred as if strung through me by fine wires filled with explosives and the scent of gasoline.

"Yes, I can," I say, answering my question, and so deep am I in the speculation this sets off when I say it that I do not notice when Lara leaves. If she has left. If she is still beside me it makes no difference; I am wrapped in directorial contemplation.

III

I did not think it would be this complex. I envisioned it as a simple process, an assemblage of *lumpen* glad to cooperate with a director from the Outside (because, by inference, it might be the only escape of their own), a few rehearsals, logistics, geometry, line readings and blocking adjustments here and there, and then the crews would be summoned, do the filming in one take and that would be the end of it. I would be out of this accursed place, and on tape would repose my masterpiece or, if not my masterpiece, certainly an interesting idea strikingly put together. Auditors could hardly fail to see the originality of it and would give high marks for audacity if not execution. A grisly historical event—it has been one of my minor interests for some time now—re-enacted and brought back to the sense of its original grubbiness by a cast of *lumpen* playing in the landscape of the city! Yes, it would have all worked out if it had only been that simple. The griminess, the incongruity, the sheer *incompetence* surrounding those bizarre events which become part of our common (unknown) history would have been fully reconstituted through my process, and the insights thus gained would have raised the popular awareness considerably or, if not that, at least the awareness of the Committee through which all projects of this nature must go in partial fulfillment of, etc. But the simplicity of my vision has always been contradicted by an overwhelming breakdown in carry-through; I have had no luck is another way of putting it, or possibly the word I am scrambling for is "foresight," and it never occurred to me, somehow, that the *lumpen* would, most of them anyway, be dismally untalented, some of them barely able to read the lines of the scripts, let alone play them with conviction.

I should have known it! I know I should have known it but

one tends to romanticize, at least in the abstract, these *lumpen* just as all stricken creatures must be romanticized by intellectual types such as myself: sturdy survivors of an era, urban artifacts, lone hangers-on, exiles in torment and so on. Who knew what veins of conviction and energy I would tap? and so on . . . but what I did not see (until it confronted me in all of its wondrous and forthright simplicity) was that the *lumpen* were what they were for good reason; only a tenth of them at best are in the city by choice, the remainder either there by relation- ship or in penalty or for reasons of idiocy (what else could voluntary election of the city be?) and the five to ten years that is the average time spent here has brutalized them all, even the least of them, to the level of little more than pigs who after rooting around in bad grounds for years would not even recognize good hydroponics when they sniffed it. By these terms Lara is *in reductio* as well; my feelings for her are barely more elevated than for any of the others (it is only the instinct for lust that kindled my interest, the desire to function despite the circuitry which blocks this), and what she says to me, stripped of emotional content, comes down to the same com- plaints that I have heard from all the others: weak snufflings of resentment disguised as regret, and beyond that, stupefying incomprehension. I cannot stand it anymore. All of them are getting worse.

Worse: they are not even at the level where I had them two days ago and now time is almost over. Like it or not the technicians will be in tomorrow for the taping and the show will then be struck. Oswald simpering, Kennedy effeminate, Connally palsied and with strange attacks of temper that cause his face to suffuse as he forgets his lines. I refuse to call them by names any other than these; they exist to me only in terms of the roles they have been assigned—or would so exist if things were going satisfactorily—and will not be dignified by any other term. They are *lumpen,* Lara as well, and the worst of them because she has the presumption to think that she understood me.

Miserably: it is going miserably. Oswald levels the rifle, narrows down the sight, and even from this distance I imagine that I can see the lines of involvement working small crosses and hatch marks across his face—the bad actor's method of working himself into a role only through grief or rage recollected—but even as Kennedy huddles in the car, moving darkly toward Jacqueline, a little clot on the cushioning now, burrowing himself into an angle for the shot, I see that it will not work, the synchronization is off. And to compound the disaster, the old car leading the motorcade must throw a piston or something; it comes to a stop with a scream and from that car leap the Secret Service detail cursing. They make hand signals that the motorcade is to stop but the cars behind do not see them or see them quickly enough and the cars pile upon one another with a series of dull thuds, only their extreme low speed giving a certain comic intensity to the performance. Kennedy sways out of the car wiping his forehead, the agents surround him, Jacqueline holds an elbow. From this distance I see Lara, the only one of them with professional discipline, still at rest quietly in the car, her hands folded, locked in the role. She is waiting for the motorcade to resume. The others are gesturing at one another, talking in progressively louder voices, and Oswald disappears from the window to run clattering down flights of the Municipal to join them. The run-through has been ruined. They do not even look at me as I come toward them gesticulating, ranting, slapping the notes in my hands. I am not sure of this but have a certain intimation of laughter, as if all the time they cooperated with me only unwillingly and are now free to show their contempt.

It is the end, the end of it; my last reserve of containment is emptied as I come toward them and I realize—from long knowledge—that I am on the verge of a serious loss of control, something that I should be unable to risk in this context but it is too late to talk quietly to myself in reasonable tones, small whispers of assurance. "Goddamn it!" I scream at them. "Goddamn you all! Can't you do anything right? Don't any of you understand what's going on here? I can't stand it; I can't stand this anymore. We had only three days to get this thing right and now you've ruined everything? Dogs, pigs! You deserve to be in the city! Once I took pity on you but that was before I came to know what you are! You are incompetent; there is nothing you can do in terms of your lives because you are incapable of running them!" and so on and so forth. I am really quite out of control and it is pointless to abuse the *lumpen* so because their condition alone is retribution and abuse means nothing. I know this. Nevertheless, I cannot stop. "Three days to get a simple scene staged and taped and you've ruined it all!" I shout. "You've ruined everything."

I realize that I am not being entirely fair because the *lumpen* have ruined nothing for themselves—their lives are already entirely ruined—but only for me, the director, the scheduling, the necessities. Nevertheless, I cannot control myself, flinging my notes now to the ground, where the winds of the Battery promptly whisk in to scatter them on the ruined clumps of earth. "How," I say, "how am I ever going to get anywhere with this?"

"It isn't our fault," Kennedy says. His eyes are persuasive, at least to me; I still accept him in the role. "Nobody here wanted to do this. We offered our services as a favor to you. We've done the best we can."

"That's right," says Connally. Texan, diffident, he slides a hand into a pocket, looks at me with tormented little eyes. "You made us do this. We had nothing to do with it at all."

"We're doing the best we can," Kennedy says. "We have no idea what you want. It's up to you to tell us."

"Right," Connally says, "that's right. If you don't like what we're doing it's not our fault but yours because we didn't want to do it in the first place."

"They're both right," Johnson says, striding over to us. Of all the principals he is the most poorly cast, being a dwarfish man with stiff hands, and no talent for gesture at all, but the first directorial impulse is often the correct one or at least so I was taught in the final seminars and I was convinced that he would be able to work his way through the part. I was wrong about him, however. I was wrong about all of them.

"I was wrong about all of you," I say. Frustration makes me rash; momentarily at least I must forget where I am, the nature of the people with whom I am dealing. "You're all worthless," I say, "all of you. You pity yourselves and work on your small resentments and hatreds and blame everybody because you're not on the Outside and they call you *lumpen* but the fact is that you are *lumpen,* nothing else but that, and you all deserve to be here. Every one of you. You've made your lives and you have no right to complain about everything because it's all your fault. You disgust me," I say. I am shaking. "All of you disgust me."

Lara is out of her car now, touching me on the elbow and in that touch I feel quivering. "Please," she says to the rest of them. I do not know what she is talking about. "He's not in his right mind. He's very young and there's so much he doesn't understand. He doesn't even know what he's saying. Please leave him alone."

"Leave me alone?" I say, not comprehending. "Why should they leave me alone? They've ruined everything for the taping; why should they desert me?"

"You don't realize," Lara says to me, "what's going on here. You don't understand him," she says to the others. "Please now, let me talk to him. I'm sure that I can make him see if you'll only give me time."

But it is too late for this, and finally I become aware of what is going on. They close about me now: Johnson, Kennedy, Conally, the Secret Service agents. Even Oswald, with a demented look settling into his features, has joined them, and I feel the press of bodies, the beginning of enclosure; scent a high, penetrating smell that can only come from my own glands. I feel their pressure against me. "Now stop this," I say. "This is ridiculous. It's only a play, a re-enactment, a simple run-through for researching purposes and if you don't see that—"

"We see," Oswald says to me. "We see what we need to see." And their hands are on me now. I feel the dread contact of bodies, the actual sense of connection filling me with a revulsion as pure as I have ever known, the *reality* of those bodies, and then I feel myself taken away from there in a struggling kind of fashion but past the first struggles I can do nothing whatsoever.

"Lara," I cry, "Lara, tell them to stop this. It's impossible. They can't do it to me, and anyway, when the crews come in and see this—"

"Our laws," someone says, "are not your laws, here in the city." And then I see where they are taking me. Doors open, I am thrust into a smaller area, a rising stench confronts me, old metal and gates swing open and I am escorted within.

The old Tombs. "I can't do anything," Lara says, "it's all your own fault." My head strikes a bar, I stagger, fall and see no more for a while.

When I return to myself, I am incarcerated.

IV

In the cell, I soon realize that it is useless to struggle and hunch myself against a wall, knees drawn up in a fetal position, staring, listlessly I suppose, although I am mercifully unaware of my own facial expressions, at the small sprays and dots of light that scatter through the one barred window too high otherwise to provide me perspective. In a corner opposite are a cup of water, a few slices of bread, pure food from the city, only slightly marred by dirt, and I suppose that I should make the effort to have some, not only because I must keep my strength up, but because in leaving this they are showing obvious consideration of which I ought, by right, to partake. But it is too much of an effort to readjust myself and go over to that opposite corner, some ten to fifteen feet from here, much easier to simply sprawl and let the impressions overtake me. It is quiet in what remains of the Tombs, quiet and isolated and a good place to do some thinking if one were interested in thought; never a contemplative type, I prefer to leave the impressions subvocal. It was insane to come into the city.

Insane to come into the city from which most of us have been trained from the beginning to flee, crazier yet to involve the *lumpen* in a project of this type—how could they understand it?—but where else was I likely to find cheaply the participants necessary for the project? Professional actors would have been necessary Outside, actors and space, and I did not have the means to hire. The *lumpen* were known to be submissive and would not my quickly acquired cast think that cooperation in the project might be a means of making their way into the Outside? Nor did I ever mislead them; I made no promises. Simply enough, I did not calculate for their strangeness, stupidity and violence, and this makes me a fool.

Lara appears at the gate and, putting her hands on the bars, leans inward, alone. "Are you all right?" she asks. From this aspect she seems more attractive than I have ever seen her but I know their irretrievable corruption now and am not tempted by feeling.

"Leave me alone," I say, "or get me out of here. Nothing else."

"Please," she says, "you must listen to me. You never listened."

"I have nothing to say."

"Please," she says. Is she weeping? "They are very angry. They feel that you have used and manipulated them and they plan to do terrible things—"

"The crews are coming from Outside," I say. "They should be here within a matter of hours now, and when they see what has happened, there will be terrible retribution. I am perfectly willing to wait a few hours. Your prisons mean nothing."

"No one will come. They will turn them back at the docks."

"Then they will circle and come in from the uptown side. You are a fool, Lara."

"No," she says, "you are a fool. I do not even know your name. You never told me your name."

"It doesn't matter."

"You never told me your name or what you planned or what we were supposed to do and now it's too late. You are the one who is a fool." She leans toward me, instinctively trying to put her head against mine but, of course, the bars stop her. Who is in jail? Who is really in jail? "I think I can get you out of here," she says, "but you'll have to make the escape on your own. I can't help you any further."

"I need no escape. It is they who will have to escape when it is seen what has been done to me."

"Oh, you fool," she says, releasing her grip on the bars and fluttering her hands like the wings of a fowl, moving away from me. "Oh, you fool, you fool. You don't understand anything at all, do you?" And I hear footsteps and the footsteps are upon us and *lumpen* come into the corridor and seize Lara, drag her away, leaving the hall very quiet again. In the distance I hear sounds. Then the door down the corridor opens and they come again; I see Oswald, Kennedy, Connally, other faces I do not know, peering incuriously at me through the bars, their faces bland, as if healed over from pain, only the eyes dark and alive in those faces, the hands raised like a network to guide me through. And without necessity to hear what they say, I stand, bracing myself against a wall, feeling the stone moving against my shoulder blades and buttocks or then again the wall is stolid, unshaken, and it is I who am trembling upon it like an insect.

"Come," one of them says to me and I come. Through the corridors of the Tombs, like deep roots from a plant sprawling through the earth, and onto the steps, where I see others gathered to await me.

I would fall gratefully but am held by arms before, arms behind. "Now," one of them says and I am led toward the motorcade.

V

I do not like the *lumpen:* I hate and fear them. But in how many dreams did they move before me, those forms clotted by darkness, shadows against the sprawl of the abandoned city? "We are your history," they have whispered to me in those dreams. "We are what all of you have been and yet could be if you were not part of the city." And I do not know if it was tenderness or mockery but those faces broke open softly, feeling coming out of the planes of those faces like blood, and in those dreams I must have answered, saying, "Yes, it is true. Yes, you are our history, but there must be more to it than that, something that I can extract." And they laughed then as *lumpen* often do in their silly, abandoned fashion and said, "There is nothing you can extract. There is nothing you can learn. We have nothing to say to you, no mysteries to impart, we are mute as stones," and so on and so forth. What intense dialogues I had with them in these dreams! Why I must have been obsessed with them for years, and in terms of that, it made a great deal of sense when it came time for the project in partial fulfillment of, etc., made a great deal of sense to go back to the city itself and confront them in the real. Because if I could use them, could make them part of the project, then—was it as simple as that?—they would be wrenched free of history and import and would become merely actors in my own staging, which was their only function and certainly a far more reasonable way in which to confront the *lumpen* problem. Wasn't it? How did I ever end in this situation?

"Let me do this," I said to the Committee in gravity assembled after I had made the presentation, "and I can bring back to you a genuine reconstruction of an important historical event. What we have forgotten, living on the Outside, is the genuine grubbiness of most of these tragedies. They did not occur in high places among the cleanly assembled but were in fact stumbling events enacted by people very much like the *lumpen.* I can show you this. I can show you something understandable and important that you have yet avoided. Besides, it is going to be fifty-three years since the assassination a few months from now and in terms of the new calendar this is an important anniversary. You can franchise the tapes. Not only will I profit but the Academy as well."

Oh, how they mumbled and grumbled, stumbled and rumbled. "The dangers," the Committee said, "and the known instability of this class of people, and then again, really, how much control can it be said that you will exert over them? They are a violent, unstable class of people; it is a condition of their environment. And furthermore, you would have to sign a full waiver of release not only for yourself but for the crews."

"The crews are no problem," I assured the Committee. "We can use for personnel those who are already on the verge of exile." I must have smiled at them then. "This will assure their total cooperation."

"Of course," the Committee said. They—he, it—inspected fingernails, looked over the small room in which the orals were conducted and then, putting hands on the table, stood ponderously. "Let us think of it," the Committee said, "and we'll let you know. An interesting project, an interesting idea, but minor, we think. Essentially minor. Of course you have made the sensational aspects of it quite clear to us, but it is not merely *sensationalism* that we seek from a major in the histories; rather there must be a certain depth and the idea seems lacking, rather—"

"But remember," I said, rather hoarsely perhaps (I am at times more aware of the tones and tenor of my voice, the sense of my gestures, than the normal person; an extraordinary sensitivity must be the explanation), "the *lumpen*. They will be playing the roles, and the majestic irony, the complexity of the fact that these figures and events are being reconstructed by the filthiest, dirtiest, grubbiest, most dangerous, malevolent, degraded and diseased segments we know—" Choking, I was quite unable to go on. The filthiness of the *lumpen* has always filled me with excitement. It must have something to do with that obsession to which I have already frankly referred. "It will be a fine project," I finished, rubbing my hands. "A fine project, an excellent project, and the tapes will be priceless and become the property of the Academy."

"Well, that is thoughtful," the Committee rumbled and stumbled and grumbled and bumbled and mumbled and went on its ponderous way, leaving me with a promise for decision in the imminent future, and in due course permission came down and I journeyed into the city alone and unarmed (because I had no physical fear of them) to put together my cast for rehearsals, with the crews to come in independently three days later, and everything was to work out splendidly, a remarkable project. And then the rehearsals fell into some difficulty and they would not listen to me when I gave them orders and the blocking became unstuck and the line readings broke down and I had to tell them what they were because this was the only way to shock them into compliance and then they turned upon me and threw me in a cell and then took me out of the cell and—

How did I ever get into this?

VI

I find myself thrust into the third car of the motorcade. Roses all around me; Lara to the left. It is going too quickly for detached observation; the car begins to move. Lara, to my left, sits frozen, hands clasped, looking ahead; in her blank cheeks I can see no reason, no accessibility. They step away from me; the car moves somewhat more quickly. Sea breezes off the Battery waft the smell of fish into my nostrils; I wonder what Kennedy smelled on that day almost fifty-three years ago. Strange, strange, I have never felt so close to him.

"What is going on?" I ask Lara, and again, "What is going on?" And she turns toward me then, her eyes round and open, her mouth sagging. She clutches roses, spills them like blood-drops from her hands, and I see in the slackness of feature that all along I must have misjudged her. She too is *lumpen*. From the beginning, I was surrounded by them. I thought that I was the director and all the time it was they who . . .

The sun comes against my eyes; I squint, raise a hand in a blocking gesture, and I feel the increased acceleration of the car pressing me firmly into the cushions. Amazing that they were able to get this old fleet of archaic vehicles running again somehow; high marks for their animal cunning and ingenuity. I feel increasing speed. "What is this?" I say. "This is entirely wrong. This is not the way it was supposed to be. I am the director. I do not belong in here."

"Quiet," Lara says, "Stay quiet. And keep down. Get down now!" And the rising thread of her voice loops me, causes me to look up at the twinkling sun, at Municipal above me. There is someone in a window of Municipal; I can see the barrel of the rifle moving and retreating through the aperture. "Oh, my God," Lara says, "you fool." And I dive then, beginning to understand what has happened, but as I do so it is with hopelessness because I know that it is already too late and I should have done the diving three seconds or maybe it was three months ago. I feel the impact like a horde of bees around my scalp; it does not hurt very badly.

"The crews!" she cries. "Where are the crews?" And I look up again, trying to sight them. The crews are here at last. They will gauge the situation in an instant and rush in to save me from these barbarians. But then, as I do indeed see them, just coming into view on their slow-moving vehicles at the rim of the Battery, telescopes fixed and pointing at me . . . Well, as I see them, I see everything at last and it is really too much for me. I cannot deal with it. I cannot begin to deal with it. *Why me?* I ask, but no point in pleading. I see the answer. *Why not?* something else says. *Why not you indeed? It could, after all, have been anyone.*

I dive toward the floorboards of the car, hoping that they will support me against impact, and as I do so, in mid-gesture, I feel the second hit, the real one, tearing in through the side of my neck. It must be the windpipe. My breath is cut off; I flutter like a fish against the cushions and then collapse in Lara's lap, groaning. Everything goes away from me. I feel her hands. *It could have been anyone.*

"The crews, my God, the crews! They've shot my husband!" she screams, and this is really the last thing I hear, at least the last during this disgrace, but as I drown in my own series of explosions, I think what it might be like to have confronted the Committee with my knowledge of their treachery . . . and to explain to them that it could have been worked out even more easily and at less expense.

The *randomness* of it all.

Is this why they allow the *lumpen* to live?

The Undercity
DEAN R. KOONTZ

Well, kid, it was a busy day. You might even say it was a harrowing day, and you might be tempted to think that it was somehow out of the ordinary. But you must understand, straight off, that it was perfectly normal as business days go, no better and no worse than ten thousand days before it. And if I live so long, it won't be appreciably different from any of ten thousand days to follow. Remember that. If you want to enter the family business, kid, you have to be able to cope with long strings of days like this one, calendars full of them.

Once, when the cities weren't a tenth as large as they are now, when a man might travel and might have business contacts throughout the world, we were called The Underworld, and we were envied and feared. We are still envied and feared, but now we're called The Undercity, because that is the world to us, and more than we can rightly handle anyway. I, for one, would be happy to roll things back, to break down these hundred-story megalopolises and live in a time where we could call ourselves a part of The Underworld, because things were a hell of a lot easier then for our type. Just consider . . .

Nearly all forms of gambling were illegal back then. An enterprising young man could step in, buck the law, and clean up a tidy sum with a minimal financial outlay and with almost no personal risk at all. Cops and judges were on the take; clandestine casinos, street games and storefront betting shops thrived. No longer. They legalized it, and they gave us bank clerks for casino managers, CPA's instead of bouncers. They made gambling respectable—and boring.

Drugs were illegal then, too. Grass, hash, skag, coke, speed . . . God, an enterprising young kid like yourself could make a fortune in a year. But now grass and hash are traded on the open market, and all the harder drugs are available to all the loonies who will sign a health waiver and buy them from the government. Where's the thrill now? Gone. And where's the profit? Gone, too.

Sex. Oh, kid, the money to be made on sex, back then. It was *all* illegal: prostitution, dirty movies, picture postcards, erotic dancing, adultery, you name it! Now the government licenses the brothels, both male and female, and the wife or husband without a lover on the side is considered a throwback. Is this any way to make a buck?

Hell, kid, even murder was illegal in those days, and a man could buy the big trip for wiping someone off the slate. As you know, some folks never can seem to learn the niceties of civilized life—their manners are atrocious, their business methods downright devious, their insults unnecessarily public and demeaning—and these people need to be eliminated from the social sphere. Now we have the code duello, through which a man can settle his grudges and satisfy his honor, all legally. The once-lucrative career as a hired assassin has gone the way of the five-dollar streetwalker.

Now, kid, you have got to hustle all day, every day, if you want to survive in this business. You've got to be resourceful, clever and forward-thinking if you expect to meet the competition. Let me tell you how the day went, because it was a day like all days . . .

I bolted down a breakfast of protein paste and cafa, then met Lew Boldoni on the fifth subbasement level in Wing-L, where only the repair robots go. Boldoni was waiting on the robotwalk beside the beltway, carrying his tool satchel, watching the cartons of perishables move past him.

"On time," he said.

I said, "As usual." Time is money; cliché but true.

We removed the access plate to the beltway workings, went down under the robotwalk. In less than five minutes, we were directly beneath the big belt, barely able to shout above the roar, buffeted by the wind of its continuous passage. Together, we opened one of the hydraulic lines and let the lubricant spew out over the traffic computer terminal, where it was sure to seep through and do some damage. Before a fire could start, we were out of there, up on the sidewalk again, putting the access plate back where it belonged. That done, just as the alarms were beginning to clang, we went in different directions.

We both had other business.

This bit of sabotage wouldn't pay off until much later in the day.

At 9:30 in the morning, right on time, I met a young couple—Gene and Miriam Potemkin—in a public hydroponics park on the eighty-third level, in that neighborhood they call Chelsea. She was twenty-one and a looker, bright and curious and unhappy. He was a year older than she was, but that was the only real difference between them. They sat on a bench by an artificial waterfall, both of them leaning forward as I approached, both with their hands folded in their laps, more like sister and brother than like wife and husband.

"Did you bring it?" he asked.

I removed a sealed envelope from my pocket, popped the seal and let them see the map inside, though I was careful not to let them handle it just then. I said, "And you?"

She lifted a small plastic satchel from the ground beside her and took another sealed envelope from it, reluctantly handed it over.

I opened it, counted the money, nodded, tucked the envelope into my pocket and gave them the map.

"Wait a minute, here!" Mr. Potemkin said. "According to this damn map, we'll be going out through the sewer! You know that's not possible. Sewage is pumped at pressure, and there's no way to survive in the system."

"True enough," I said. "But if you'll look closely at the map, you'll see that the sewage line is encased inside a larger pipe, from which repairs can be made to the system. This larger pipe is everywhere twenty feet in diameter, sometimes as much as thirty, and is always enough larger than the sewage pipe itself to give you adequate crawl space."

"I don't know," he said. "It doesn't look easy . . ."

"No way out of the city is easy, for God's sake!" I told him. "Look, Potemkin, the city fathers say that the open land, beyond the cities, is unlivable. It's full of poisoned air, poisoned water, plague, and hostile plant and animal life. That's why the air freight exits are the only ones that are maintained, and that's why they're so carefully supervised. City law forbids anyone to leave the city for fear they'll return bearing one of the plagues from Outside. Now, considering all of this, could you reasonably expect me to provide you with an *easy* way out?"

"I suppose not."

"And that's damn straight."

Ms. Potemkin said, "It's really not like that Outside, is it? The stories of plagues, poisoned air and water, monsters—all of that's just so much bunk."

"I wouldn't know," I said.

"But you must know!"

"Oh?"

"You've shown us the way out," she said. "You must have seen what's beyond the city."

"I'm afraid not," I said. "I employ engineers, specialists, who work from diagrams and blueprints. None of my people would consider leaving the city; we've got too much going for us here."

"But," she insisted, "By sending us, you're showing your distrust of the old stories about the Outside."

"Not at all," I explained. "Once you've gone, my men will seal off this escape route so you can't come back that way, just in case you might bring a plague with you."

"And you won't sell it again?"

"No. We'll find other ways out. There are millions of them."

They looked at each other, unsure of themselves now.

I said, "Look, you haven't committed the map to memory. If you want, I can take it back and return half your money."

"No," he said.

She said, "We've made up our minds. We need open land, something more than layer on layer of enclosed streets and corridors."

"Suit yourself," I said. "And good luck."

I shook their hands and got the hell out of there; things to do, things to do . . .

Moving like a maintenance robot on an emergency call, I dropped down to the subbasements again, to the garbage monitoring decks, where I met with the day-shift manager, K. O. Wilson. We shook hands at precisely 10:20, five minutes behind schedule, and we went into the retrieval chamber, where he had the first two hours of discoveries laid out in neat, clean order.

Kid, I don't think I've ever talked about this angle of the family business before, because I'm not that proud of it. It's the cheapest form of scavenging, no matter how lucrative it is. And it *is* lucrative. You see, the main pipes of the garbage shuttle system are monitored electronically and filtered to remove any articles of value that might otherwise be funneled into the main sewage lines and pumped out of the city. I've got K. O. Wilson, of the first shift, and Marty Linnert, of the second shift, on my payroll. They see to it that I have time to look over the day's findings before they're catalogued and sent up to the city's lost-and-found bureau. Before you think too badly of your old man, consider that 20 per cent of the family's gross comes from the garbage operation.

"Six valuable rings, a dozen good watches, what appears to be one folder of a top-quality coin collection, a diamond tiara, and a mess of other junk," Wilson told me, pointing to the good items, which he had set aside for me.

I ignored the watches, took two of the rings, the tiara and

the damp folder full of old coins. "Nothing else?"

"A corpse," he said. "That'll interest the cops. I put it on ice until you could get in and check over your stuff first."

"A murder?" I asked.

"Yeah."

Kid, the code duello hasn't solved everything. There are still those who are afraid to fight, who prefer to sneak about and repay their enemies illegally. And there are also those who aren't satisfied with taking economic and emotional revenge from those not eligible for the duels; they insist on blood, and they have it. Eventually, the law has them. We're not involved with people of this sort, but you should know the kind of scum that the city still supports.

I told Wilson, "I'll send a man around after noon to see what else you've got by then."

Ten minutes later, at 10:53, I walked into the offices of Boldoni and Gia Cybernetic Repairs, on the ninety-second floor, Wing-B, where I acted very shocked about the breakdown in the beltway system.

"City Engineer Willis left an urgent message for you," my secretary said. She handed it to me and said, "It's a beltway carrying perishables in the fifth subbasement."

"Is Mr. Boldoni there?" I asked.

"He accompanied the first repair team," she said.

"Call down and tell Willis I'm on my way."

I used the express drop and almost lost my protein paste and cafa—any inconvenience for a good customer, and the city is the best customer that Boldoni and Gia Cybernetic Repairs has on its list.

Willis was waiting for me by the beltway. He's a small man with very black hair and very dark eyes and a way of moving that makes you think of a maintenance robot with a short between his shoulder blades. He scuttled toward me and said, "What a mess!"

"Tell me," I said.

"The main hydraulic line broke over the traffic computer

terminal and a fire started in the works."

"That doesn't sound so bad," I said.

He wiped his small face with one large hand and said, "It wouldn't have been if it had stopped there. We've got the fire out already. The only trouble is that the lubricant has run back the lines into the main traffic computer and the damn thing won't shut down. I've got perishables moving up out of the subterranean coolers, and no way to move them or stop them. They're piling up on me fast, Mr. Gia. I have to have this beltway moving inside the hour or the losses are going to be staggering."

"We'll do the job," I assured him.

"I went out on the limb, calling you before you could deliver a quick computerized estimate. But I knew you people were the fastest, and I needed someone who could be here immediately."

"Don't you worry about it," I told him. "Whatever the B & G computer estimates we'll shave by ten per cent to keep your bosses happy."

Willis was ecstatic, thanking me again and again. He didn't understand that the Boldoni and Gia house computer always estimated an additional and quite illegal 15 per cent surprofit, more than negating the 10 per cent discount I'd given him.

While he was still thanking me, Lew Boldoni came up from the access tunnel, smeared with lubricant, looking harried and nervous and exhausted. Lew is an excellent actor, and that is another qualification for success in this business.

"How is it down there?" I asked.

"Bad," Boldoni said.

Willis groaned.

Boldoni said, "But we're winning it."

"How long?" I asked.

"We'll have the beltway moving in an hour, with a jury-rigged system, and then we can take our time with the permanent repairs."

Willis groaned again, differently this time: in happiness.

I said, "Mr. Boldoni has everything in control, Mr. Willis. I'm sure that you'll be in business as usual shortly. Now, if you'll excuse me, I've got some other urgent business to attend to."

I went up in the express elevator, which was worse than coming down, since my stomach seemed to reach the fifty-ninth floor seconds before the rest of me.

I boarded a horizontal beltway and rode twelve miles east, the last six down Y-Wing. At 11:40, ten minutes behind schedule, I entered an office in the Chesterfield District where a nonexistent Mr. Lincoln Pliney supposedly did business. There, I locked the outer door, apologized for my tardiness to the two people waiting in the reception area, then led them into Lincoln Pliney's private office. I locked that door too, went to the desk, checked out my bug-detecting equipment, made sure the room hadn't been tapped, then sat down behind my desk, offered the customers a drink, poured, sat back and introduced myself under a false name.

My visitors were Arthur Coleman, a rather successful industrialist with offices on the hundredth level, and Eileen Romaine, a lovely girl, fifteen years Coleman's junior. We had all come together in order to negotiate a marriage between Coleman and Romaine, an illegal marriage.

"Tell me, Mr. Coleman," I said, "just why you wish to risk the fines and prison sentences involved with this violation of the Equal Rights Act?"

He squirmed a bit and said, "Do you have to put it that way?"

I said, "I believe a customer must know the consequences before he can be fairly expected to enter a deal like this."

"Okay," he said. "Well, I've been married four times under the standard city contract, and all four marriages have terminated in divorce at my instigation. I'm a very unhappy man, sir. I've got this . . . well, perversion that dominates the course of my private life. I need a wife who . . . who is not my equal, who is subservient, who plays a dated role as nothing more than my bedmate and my housekeeper. I want to dominate any marital situation that I enter."

I said, "Conscious male chauvinism is a punishable crime."

"As I'm aware."

"Have you seen a robopsych?" I asked. "Perhaps one of those could cure you of your malady."

"I'm sure it could," he said. "But you see, I don't really want to be cured. I *like* myself the way I am. I *like* the idea of a woman waiting on me and making her own life conditioned to mine."

"And you?" I asked Eileen.

She nodded, an odd light in her eyes, and she said, "I don't like the responsibility of the standard marriage. I want a man who will put me in my place, a man I can look up to, admire, depend on."

I tell you, kid, these antiquated lusts of theirs were distasteful to me. However, I believe in rebels, both good and bad, being a rebel myself, and I was ready to help them. Both had come to me by word-of-mouth referral within the past month. I'd researched the lives of both, built up two thick dossiers, matched them, and called them here for their first and final meeting under my auspices.

"You have both paid me a finder's fee," I told them. "Now, you will have sixty days to get to know each other. At the end of that time, you will either fail to contact me about a finalization of the contract, in which case I'll know you've found each other unsuitable, or you'll come back here and set up an appointment with my robosec. If you find you like each other, it will be a simple matter to arrange an illegal marriage, without the standard city contract."

Coleman wasn't satisfied with that. He said, "Just how will you pull this off, Mr. Pliney?"

"The first step, of course, is to have Eileen certified dead and disposed of. My people will falsify a death report and have it run through the city records. This may sound like an incredible feat to you; it is nevertheless possible. Once Eileen

Romaine has ceased to exist, we will create a false persona in the name of Eileen Coleman. She will be identified as your sister; an entire series of life records will be planted in the computers to solidify her false identity. She can, naturally, then come to live with you, without the city records people realizing that there is anything sexual in your cohabitation."

"If you can do it," Coleman said, "you're a genius."

"No, just clever," I said. "And I will do it. In fact, on any date you pick, I'll have a man at your apartment to officiate at a clandestine wedding using the ancient, male chauvinist rituals."

"There will be no psycheprobes, as there are in other marriages?" she asked.

"Of course not," I said. "The city will have no reason to psycheprobe you under the Equal Rights Act because you won't, so far as the city is concerned, be married at all."

At that point, she burst into tears and said, "Mr. Pliney, you are the first person, outside of Arthur here, who's ever understood me."

I set her straight on that, kid, believe me. I said, "Lady, I don't understand you at all, but I sympathize with rebels. You're chucking out total equality and everything a normal human being should desire in return for a life-style that has long been shown to be inadequate. You're risking prison and fines for knowingly circumventing the Equal Rights Act. It's all crazy, but you've a right to be nuts."

"But if you don't understand us, not at all, why are you risking—"

"For the profit, Eileen," I said. "If this is pulled off, Mr. Coleman will owe me a tidy sum." I stood up. "Now, I must see you out. I've many, many things to do yet today."

When I was finally rid of the happy couple, I boarded an entertainment beltway into a restaurant district in Wing-P, and there I had my lunch: a fillet of reconstituted sea bass, a baked potato, strawberries from a hydroponic garden immersed in simulated cream. It was a rich lunch, but one that was easily digested.

A warning, kid: Stay away from greasy foods for lunch. In this business, your stomach can be the end of you; it curdles grease and plagues you with murderous heartburn.

By 1:30, I was back on the street. I phoned in to the offices of Boldoni and Gia and learned that the beltway on the fifth subbasement level was rolling again, though Boldoni now estimated permanent repairs as a two- or three-day job. It seemed that one of the B & G workmen had found a second potential break in the hydraulic line just before it was ready to go. He'll get a bonus for that, however he managed it.

At 1:45, I stopped around to see K. O. Wilson again, down at the garbage monitoring decks, picked up the best part of a set of pure silver dinnerware, an antique oil lantern, and a somewhat soiled set of twentieth-century pornographic photographs, which, while no longer titillating to the modern man, are well worth a thousand duo-creds as prime, comic nostalgia. Kid, the strangest damn stuff shows up in the garbage, sometimes so strange you won't believe it. Just remember that there are thirty million people in this damn hive, and that among them they own and accidentally throw out about anything a man could hope to find.

I delivered the dinnerware, lantern and pornography to Petrone, the family fence, and then got my ass on the move. I was twenty minutes behind the day's schedule.

At 2:15, I met a man named Talmadge at a sleazy little drug bar in one of the less pleasant entertainment districts on the forty-sixth level. He was sitting at a table in a dark corner, clasping his water pipe in both hands and staring down at the mouthpiece that appeared to have fallen from his lips to the tabletop.

"Sorry I'm late," I said.

He looked up, dreamy-eyed, smiled at me more than he had to, and said, "That's all right. I'm feeling fine, just fine."

"Good for you," I said. "But are you feeling too fine to go through with this?"

"No, no!" he said. "I've waited much too long already, months and months—even years!"

"Come on, then," I said.

I took him out of the drug bar and helped him board a public beltway that took us quickly away from the entertainment zone and deep into a residential area on the same level.

Leaning close to me, in a stage whisper, as if he enjoyed the role of a conspirator, Talmadge said, "Tell me again how big the apartment is."

I looked around, saw that no one was close to us, and, knowing that he would just grow louder and more boisterous if I refused to speak of it, I said, "Three times as large as regulations permit a single man like you. It has nine rooms and two baths."

"And I don't have to share the baths?"

"Of course not."

He was ecstatic.

Now, kid, this is the racket you'll be starting out in to get some experience in the business, and you should pay especially close attention. Even when your mother was alive, we had a bigger apartment than city regulations permit; now, with your mother gone, it's *much* bigger than allowed. How was this achieved, this lavish suite? Simple. We bought up the small apartments all around this, knocked out walls, refitted and redecorated. Then, through a falsification of land records in the city real estate office, we made it look as if the outsize apartment had always been here, was a fluke in the original designs. Now, although living space is at a premium, and though the city tries to force everyone into relatively similar accommodations, the government repair robots are far too busy to have the time to section up the large apartment, throw up new walls and so forth. Instead, because this sort of thing happens so seldom, the city allows the oversize apartment to exist and merely doubles or triples the tax assessment on whoever lives there. In a city of fifteen million apartments, you can pull a hustle like this at least twice a month, without drawing undue official concern, and you can clean up a very tidy sum from rich folks who need more than the legal living space.

At 2:38, Mr. Talmadge and I arrived at the entrance to his

new home, keyed it and went inside. I took him on a grand tour of the place, waited while he checked the Tri-D fakeview in all the rooms, tested the beds, flushed the toilets in both johns, and finally paid me the money yet outstanding on our contract. In return, I gave him his ownership papers, copies of the falsified real estate claims, and his first tax assessment.

At 3:00, half an hour behind schedule, I got out of there.

On my way up to the offices of Boldoni and Gia, in the standard elevator, I had time to catch a news flash on the comscreen, and it was such bad news that it shattered the hell out of my schedule. You heard about it. Ms. and Mr. Potemkin, my first clients of the day, were apprehended in their attempt to sneak out of the city through the sewage service pipes. They accidentally ran into a crew of maintenance robots who gave pursuit. They'd only just then been brought to city police headquarters, but they wouldn't need long to fold up under a stiff interrogation.

I canceled my original destination on the elevator board, punched out the twenty-sixth level and dropped down in agonizingly slow motion, wishing to hell I'd used the express drop.

At 3:11, I rode by the offices of Cargill Marriage Counseling, which was the front I used for selling routes out of the city to people like the Potemkins. The place didn't seem to be under surveillance, so I came back on another beltway, opened up, went inside and set to work. I opened the safe, took out what creds I had bundled there, stuffed half a dozen different maps in my pockets, looked around to be sure I'd not left anything of value behind, then set fire to the place and beat it out of there. I had always used the name Cargill in that racket, and I'd always worn transparent plastic fingertip shields to keep from leaving prints; however, one can never be too careful, kid.

At 3:47, I rode back upstairs to the offices of Boldoni and Gia, checked on the beltway repair job with Lew, who had returned to the office. It was going well; the profit would keep

Boldoni and Gia in the black; we're always in the black; we see to that.

I sent a man down to see K. O. Wilson before shifts changed, then dialed the number for Mr. Lincoln Pliney (who is me, you recall), on the fifty-ninth floor in the Chesterfield District. The robosec answered on a cut-in, and I asked for messages.

In a metallic voice, the robosec said, "Mr. Arthur Coleman just stopped in and asked for an appointment, sir."

"Coleman? I just talked to him this morning."

"Yes, sir. But he left a number for you."

I took the number, hung up, dialed Coleman and said hello and identified myself to him.

He said, "Eileen and I want to go through with the deal."

"You've just met each other," I said.

"I know, but I think we're perfect for each other."

I said, "What does Eileen think?"

"The same as I do, of course."

"In one afternoon, you can't learn enough about each other—"

Coleman said, "It's true love."

I said, "Well, it's obviously true *something*."

"We'd like to finalize things tonight."

"Impossible."

"Then we'll go somewhere else."

"To whom?"

"We'll find someone," he said.

I said, "You'll find some incompetent criminal hack who'll botch the falsification of Eileen's death certificate, and in the end you'll have to tell the police about me."

He didn't respond.

"Oh, hell!" I snapped. "Meet me in my Chesterfield District office in half an hour, with Eileen."

I hung up.

I'd intended to see a man who wanted to purchase a falsified Neutral Status Pass to keep him safe from duel challenges. See, kid, there are a lot of people who are healthy enough to have to go armed but who want to avoid having to accept challenges. The government has no sympathy with them and forces them to comply with the system. I'm always ready, however, to give them a paper disability to keep them whole and sane. I sympathize with rebels, like I said. And there's a profit in it, too. Anyway, I had to call the guy who wanted the Neutral Status Pass and postpone our appointment until tomorrow.

Then I ran off to tie the nuptial knots for Coleman and his lady.

You see, now, why I was late getting home. Scare you? I didn't think it would. Tomorrow, you can come along with me, watch me work, pick up some tips about the business. You're fifteen, plenty old enough to learn. I tell you, kid, you're going to be a natural for this business. I wish your mother could have lived to see what kind of daughter she brought into this world.

Well, kid, you better turn in. It's going to be a busy day.

Apartment Hunting
HARVEY AND AUDREY BILKER

"Name?"

"Mr. and Mrs. Charles Reardon," he said.

"Address?"

"West Central Park Complex Seventy-Four, Apartment A21L."

The clerk was a bored woman between twenty-five and thirty. Her fingers were smudged from a morning of filling out forms in triplicate and quadruplicate for computer coding.

Charles Reardon's wife stood by him, her young face bright with hope for their future life together. At last, after five years of applications, the Department of Demography had released new statistics and the result was that the Reardons had been put on the list for a new apartment.

Twice, until now, their approved but contingent license for conception had expired and they desperately wanted a child. But without the complementary acquisition of an apartment with another bedroom the permit was of no use.

When the long form had been filled out almost in its entirety, the clerk asked, "Have you got your Apartment Entry and Possession Kit?"

"No," Reardon replied. "They said we have to have the Potential Tenant Form first."

"I'm sorry," the clerk told them. "I can't complete this until you have the other one."

"But that's ridiculous," Mrs. Reardon complained.

The clerk shrugged her shoulders and put the papers aside. "Those are the rules."

"But we were notified that this is the only day we can look for an apartment," the wife explained. "The fax letter they sent said that if we didn't complete everything today—including taking possession—we couldn't reapply for at least two years. The waiting list is that long."

The clerk gave them a tired smile. "Everybody's got the same problem. There's nothing I can do."

Reardon spoke up. "What do the others do?"

"They get a Residence Interface Form," the clerk said. "Didn't you know about that? It allows you to apply for all your permits in any order."

Reardon began to reply gently, but his wife's loud and now irritated voice overwhelmed his politeness. "There was nothing in the instructions about it," she announced. "I studied them carefully. We were waiting outside this office from 0500 hours —in line. We wanted to have enough time to look for a place. Now we've lost a couple of hours."

The clerk tapped her fingers impatiently, looking behind them at the next waiting couple. "All I can say is get the Residence Interface Form. Then I can put this through."

Mrs. Reardon's expression turned almost animal.

Her husband put a placating hand on her shoulder. "There's no use arguing, darling," he told her softly. "You'll only waste time. Rules are rules." He looked apologetically at the clerk. "Where do we get the Residence Interface Form?"

"It's in this building," she replied, somewhat mollified by Reardon's attitude. "I'm not sure which room, though. You might try 1173."

"Thank you," he replied. He led his angry wife out. The line on the inside had reached the door and continued partly down the hall outside.

They stepped onto the worn plastic vertizontal ped-tred and got off at 1173. At least the wait there wasn't too long. However, they discovered, when their turn came, that it wasn't 1173 at all where the Residence Interface Forms were obtained; it was 1834.

But at 1834, folowing a long delay, they were informed that

2021 was the proper place for what they were seeking.

At 2021 they were sent to 1219. And at 1219 they were given instructions that brought them full circle back to the clerk they had seen originally. This time she directed them to 1416. Fortunately, it turned out to be the correct place.

They were finally seated opposite a scratched and pocked aluminum-titanium-tungsten desk, one of many in a large room that hadn't been surface-coated for years. A man who was prematurely timeworn slowly went about preparing the necessary form. "You young folks," he said, at the same time making notations in various blocks. "So anxious to get a bigger place. What difference does it make anyway? So you'll have your permitted child. So what? What does it all mean?" He looked up. The Reardons could see, deep in his eyes, the many years of dark thoughts. "Then you'll be fifty-five—and it'll be all over." He nodded his head at them somberly. "I'll be fifty-five next year. Then what?" He snorted and bounced his head up and down. Then he returned to his work.

Finally, he tore out their copy and handed it slowly to them.

Mrs. Reardon grabbed it from his hand. "Quick," she said to her husband. "Let's get back." She looked at her watch. "Oh, my God! It's almost 1300 hours!"

"Just relax, honey," Reardon said, gesturing calmly with a spread-fingered hand. "Everything will work out all right."

But she was already on her way out of the office and he was following after, trying to keep up.

When they returned to the office they had gone to in the first place, they were able to get in a shorter line because the Potential Tenant Form had been almost completely filled out that morning. At least they didn't have to start over again; the line they had waited in during the morning was now almost completely around the outside hall.

It was past 1430 hours when they were at last able to present the Residence Interface Form.

The young girl who took it appeared to have just graduated from a government technology school. After about ten minutes, she was still awkwardly checking through the electronic files.

Mrs. Reardon, exasperated, looked at the dusty digital wall clock. "Young lady," she called. "What's the problem?"

The girl walked back to the counter, her facial expression showing signs of confusion in its blankness. "I can't find your Potential Tenant Form."

"It probably hasn't been keypunched yet," the married woman told her bitterly. "That clerk over there is the one who filled it out." She pointed partly down the large room. "Why don't you ask her?"

"I'm not allowed to leave my department," the girl explained.

"But it'll only take a moment that way," Mrs. Reardon shouted. "You're just several meters away from her. Otherwise, you'll be looking all day."

"Now, dear," Reardon intervened.

"But she's wasting our valuable time!" his wife replied irascibly. "Don't you realize we have only a little over two hours now to get the apartment?"

The girl looked at Mr. Reardon. At least *he* understood her problems. "I'll look again," she offered generously.

While the girl searched the electronic files again, Mrs. Reardon, beyond her patience, summed up her feelings by pounding lightly on the counter. Her husband attempted to assuage her anxieties, but to no avail.

At last, twenty minutes later, the girl came over with the familiar form. "Reardon?" she asked happily.

"Yes, *Reardon*," the wife said, her tone stern.

"It was just lying on a pile on the table." The girl giggled. "Now, may I have your Residence Interface Form, please?" she asked routinely.

Reardon gave it to her and she opened a compartment filled with rubber stamps.

After more filling out, signing and countersigning, and stamping, the papers were complete.

"Next," the girl advised, "You have to get your Apartment Entry and Possession Kit."

"It's about time!" Mrs. Reardon exclaimed almost with a snarl.

"First, though," the girl said, "I need your Transit-Ident Cards. And then please stand in front of those scanscreens so I can match up your physiology patterns to these cards."

Mrs. Reardon was at the end of her tether and through her teeth said, "Is that *really* necessary?"

"Yes," the girl replied dully. It was obvious that she had answered that question many times before. "People *do* borrow cards."

After the test checked out, Mrs. Reardon gave the girl a self-satisfied scowl, but it went unnoticed. The youngster just continued her routine procedure.

The girl poised a finger over a machine on the counter; the finish on the terminal was chipped and peeling. "Now," she said, tapping buttons as she entered information from the forms, "I'll put this data into the console." As soon as she had completed the entry, the interior of the machine began to clatter and a print-out emerged. She tore off the sheet and presented it to the couple. "Today's listing," she said, "is entirely of people who have not volunteered to vacate their apartments."

Reardon disappointedly clamped his lips tight and shook his head. "Just our luck!" he said, disgusted. "The one day we get for an apartment and every one on our list is occupied."

"It's better than *no* apartment," his spouse said to him, determination in her voice. "At least we have a chance."

The girl leaned her head over the neatly printed sentences on the print-out sheet, which were upside down to her. "You have to make your choice at this time. I'll put a hold on it until 1700 hours."

Eagerly, Mrs. Reardon perused the list as her husband tried to see over her arm. He pointed to one line. "Look at this one. It's just a few blocks from where we live now."

His wife ignored him until she had found a listing to her own liking. "Here's an apartment that's in the Riverside Park Complex!"

"Do you know how *old* those are?" Reardon asked coolly. "They were built in '25."

"That's just the point," she replied, smiling and excited. "They have two-and-a-half-meter-high ceilings—a quarter meter higher than the new legal minimum."

The girl interrupted. "You have to make up your minds," she said mechanically. "There are others waiting."

"All right," Mrs. Reardon said. "We'll take this one." She pointed to the sheet. As an afterthought, she turned to her husband. "Is that all right with you?"

"Yes," he agreed. "I don't want to be responsible for picking out something you won't be satisfied with."

"Very well," the clerk told them, at the same time punching several more buttons on her terminal. Her voice became a monotone as she reeled off instructions. "You must let us know by the apartment communicator equipment that you've obtained the apartment. And it must be before 1700 hours because of the Geriatric Fair-Play Law. Here's your code." She handed them a card on which she had made a notation. "When the message is received, tenancy will be officially recorded under your name. Try not to do too much damage obtaining the unit—unless it's absolutely necessary. Immediately with your call, of course, a removal team will be sent over."

Once again the Reardons found themselves in the center of the building's activity. They boarded the ped-tred for a trip to, hopefully, the last department that they had to visit. After more waiting, at 1515 hours they were handed a carrying case. The bag's exterior was badly scuffed and the seals were no longer secure.

Reardon grinned at his wife. "Okay, let's go."

"Oh, no!" she replied. "Not until I check this to see that everything is here."

They took the case aside, as the line moved forward, and opened it.

Pasted on the inside of the battered lid was a sheet of paper that had curled away at the corners. Mrs. Reardon read the list of components from it and went through each item in the various compartments. "Aha!" she exclaimed. "Just what I thought!"

She forced her way back into line—in front of the person who was now first.

"The cutter is missing," she told the man behind the counter who had issued the kit.

He took a sheet from one of the piles of papers next to him and gave it to her. "Fill this out," he said.

"No, sir!" she announced. "You're not going to push me around. Give me a cutter from another kit or give me a new kit."

"I can't do that, ma'am," he replied.

"Well, you'd better!" Mrs. Reardon told him. "Or else I'm going to stand right here and not let anybody get in front of me!"

"You can complain to the department head, if you'd like," the employee advised in a matter-of-fact tone.

"I'll do it my way," the woman said adamantly. "It's the only way to get results."

"Look, lady," said the man she had pushed aside. "I want to get taken care of. You gotta follow the proper procedures. That's what *I* did. And the day's almost over."

"Exactly!" Mrs. Reardon told him. "That's why I'm going to stand here—until 1700 hours, if necessary."

A number of people in line began to shout at her, but she stood fast, stone-faced.

The man who had been first in line was exasperated. "Look," he said to the employee, "can't you give it to her? Otherwise, none of us'll ever get apartments."

"I can't" was his reply. "I'm not permitted to. We have to keep exact inventory records."

"All right, lady," said the man whose turn was next. "I'll tell you what. You can have the one from my kit. I'm sure I can make do with the other tools. At least if you get what you want, the rest of us here can have a chance."

Mrs. Reardon agreed to his suggestion, and when he got his kit, he opened it, took out the cutter, and gave it to her.

She smiled to herself with satisfaction, not even bothering to thank the man. "Here," she said to her husband. "Put this in our kit and let's get out of here. We have only about an hour left."

On Traffic Level #3/North they found a cabportation terminal box and signaled.

After almost fifteen minutes, their conveyor railed up. They got in and Reardon gave the address to the pudgy-faced operator.

Traffic was extremely heavy since it was the end of the second daily work period, and they arrived at the apartment house with just a quarter of an hour to go.

The wait for the small, creaking verti ped-tred was agonizing, but it came at last. Finally, they reached their destination—the fortieth floor.

"It's 40K-5," Mrs. Reardon said, rushing down the threadbare hall carpet, her husband padding hurriedly after her. They located the correct door quickly.

Reardon knocked. "Open up, please."

"No," came a shy, weak female voice. "You're not getting in."

"Break it down," Mrs. Reardon ordered resolutely.

Her husband stood back, then ran against the door several times with his full weight. But he wasn't successful. In the meantime, Mrs. Reardon had opened the kit and was rummaging through the equipment. "Here, try these," she instructed, handing him a large ring of keys.

He looked quickly through them. "There just isn't enough time to find one that might work."

"Yes." His wife nodded. She checked her watch. "If we don't call in by 1700 hours, we're disqualified. You'd better shoot it open." She took the gun from the kit and gave it to him.

He put the weapon to the lock and fired. Metal and wood fragments clouded back in a slight haze. He pushed the door, but it stopped slightly ajar. "She's got one of those real old chains on!" he said desperately.

"Only five minutes!" his wife warned. "Hurry!"

"Give me the cutter," he said to her.

With a smirk, she handed it to him. "See, I was right when I put up a fight for this."

Reardon hooked the cutter around the chain and turned it on. Slowly, the instrument began to penetrate a link. Then, finally, the chain separated and its severed ends clattered apart.

"Thank God!" Mrs. Reardon breathed.

Now, with ease, they both pushed the door completely open.

In front of a window, in a soft chair of ancient vintage, its padding worn and faded, sat a woman with grayish hair. She must have been young not too long ago, it seemed. In fact, her features weren't really that aged. A fair semblance of her youthful past was still evident; in its extreme youth, her appearance had no doubt been sweet. However, at the sight of the intruders her lips twisted and, in an instant, years were added to her demeanor.

Mrs. Reardon looked at her watch again. "Only four minutes. Get it over with."

The tenant nodded her head with resignation. "Some day *you'll* be old, too," she said, "and strangers will do this to *you*." Then, strangely, her expression changed, softened. The instinct of self-preservation appeared to have broken through. "Please," she pleaded. "Let me have one more day." She turned her head slowly to the window, where the dying sun streamed in. The city below, its distant white towers and buildings on the New Jersey side were streaked orange as the sky gave up its full energy. She continued to look at the sight before her as if she wanted to absorb it into her entire being.

"For God's sake!" Mrs. Reardon said to her husband. "Don't waste any more time." She anxiously eyed the communicator.

Reardon raised the gun and aimed it across the room as precisely as he could at the woman's temple. A calm had now come over her as she continued to view, almost hypnotized, the brightly illuminated scene outside her apartment. Her expression was placid yet enthralled, as if she were beholding a treasure.

Reardon's eyes suddenly brimmed with tears until liquid lenses so thick were formed that he had to clamp his lids closed to release the fluid; it ran in warm rivulets down his cheeks to his chin, where he could feel the stream, suddenly cooled, dripping to his shirt. But his eyes quickly refilled and once more he had to blink hard to clear the vision. It was important for him to see accurately—for the woman's sake.

"It's almost 1700 hours!" Mrs. Reardon screamed. "We've got to call in on the communicator!"

As Reardon continued sighting the woman along the barrel of his gun, scenes of his past and fantasies of his future suddenly flashed before his unsquinted eye and he felt his taut shoulders collapse. "I can't," he told his wife listlessly, aiming the gun halfheartedly now.

"If we don't get the apartment," he heard his wife cry, "someone else will!"

Readon pulled the trigger.

As a Drop
D. M. PRICE

as a drop
out, i like skies;
they're beautiful
things to have hanging a
round.

i was in one
once. at least,
part of me was, drifting
about the osmostic cosmos, probably

spat out (like much
of population II everything) from some
dyspeptic star who had gargled
too much helium.

sometimes i wonder who
i shined upon, bi-, sex-, or quadruped,
but i never wonder
before dinner.

i was in the sky once, might be
again,
imparting my light soon
on my calcium wave
length as white as before, some
where between here and

Algol's

fiery

suburb.

Abendländes
VIRGINIA KIDD

Decline of formalism save for stylized decay
Saves nothing; only nips the heels and harries on
Our shambling end.
  There has been time since when
A social rite attended on beginnings, there has been time
For termites and for rust. Old structures
Crumble, but the new-and-large like thunder-lizards
Pay the price of size before the skeletal
And complicated steel can realize fatigue.

Chewing on doled bread, sidewalk watchers
Cheer gladiators in the wrecking crew
Or–fewer since the band is out of key–
And dull-eyed if the speech is overlong
Applaud a final cornerstone appended to a finished church.

Nominal commencements when the thing is done
Mark subsidence of culture; return to shapelessness
While the towns still empty, and the cities rot.

The Weariest River
THOMAS N. SCORTIA

. . . old men must die, or the world would grow mouldy, would only breed the past again.
> —ALFRED, LORD TENNYSON, *Becket*

In the middle of the already decaying city, he screamed.

It was a quiet scream, filled with an anguish that spoke of centuries of pain to come. It tore at his throat, ripping its silent pain through his larynx and venting its violence on a frozen air, expending its energy in a terrible internal spasm of sorrow for the thousands of robot creatures about him.

They were human—these creatures in the city—and that was the terrible thing about it. They were flesh and squirming viscera and pulsing blood and lymph and they were totally . . . completely . . . agonizingly unaware of him, of what he had done to them.

Unaware that in their newfound centuries of life, they were destroyed—as was he.

He moved through their midst, positioning each foot carefully in front of the other, painfully aware of the effort to coordinate this simple, unelaborated, primitive complex that was his body.

How terrible, he thought, to be trapped forever in this thing with two legs and two arms and quivering gonads and peripheral functional parts that stir like the passing fantasy of fern fronds before the winds of the most casual physical impulse.

How terrible, how terrible, how terrible.

How terrible to be trapped in this body, this husk with fingers that articulate with a clumsy intent, with legs that flex at the slightest effort, with stomach that churns and growls and aches, with head that swivels idiotically on corded neck and eyes that peer and burn and water and blink and see little beyond the images a few feet from them. Forever? Surely not forever?

"Hey man," his mortal friend said. (What was this word "friend."? He wasn't quite sure that it fitted the semantic content of the present situation.) "Hey man, you look spaced out. Real spaced out."

"I am," he said. (Was that his voice? Did it belong to him? Was it a part of his total structure? The resonance, the vibration, the feeling of articulation? Am I what I say—me? Was that Hopkins? No, "What I do is me; for that I came.")

Truth, undying truth . . . "I caught this morning morning's minion, kingdom of daylight's dauphin . . ."

"I am in a bad way," he said slowly. "I am remembering."

"That's a bad scene," his friend said. "Can't have that."

"It's too terrible," he said. "I remember. Oh, God, I remember."

"We gotta fix that. That's the word. Fix and the world fixes you."

True, true, true. Paradissium Ammisam. But who knows what things in the chemical delirium of life may come? It is the end, it is the end.

"I gotta go," he said. It was an intense demand, a full and compelling thing. He shouldn't have had the beer. The beer was all wrong. The beer was yin and not enough yang . . . pang . . . it had invaded his turgid loins to . . .

"Gotta urinate," he said.

"Merry, sir. Drink is the provoker of two things, sir. Urine and lechery, sir. It both giveth the desire and taketh away the ability." That was . . . that was . . . the porter. The mad porter. Macbeth and "Tomorrow, and tomorrow, and tomorrow, Creeps in this petty pace from day to . . ."

"I gotta go," he repeated. "This fragile, clumsy, intangible, awkward, painful, lewd, disorganized body has generated excessive fluid as a part of its purine metabolism and out of *all this I must void a certain discrete amount of urea. I did not say uric acid since uric acid is exclusively the end product of the purine metabolism of birds and of the mammals; only the noble Dalmatian–the dog, that is–has uric acid as the end product of its purine metabolism. That, of course, is exactly, precisely the way it should be."*

"In the alley, babe. In the alley and we're away like the b. a. bird to the pad, the living machine."

They went and he did and they did.

In the end by devious routes . . . by hyperspace tube? By walking? By teleportation? By finding the yellow brick road into the center of the simple intricacies of a Klein bottle or perhaps only a prosaic tesseract, they came to the palace, the place, the pit, the pad, where they lived, the non-Policyholders, fleeing from reality.

And Gloria said "Hello" and Glenda said "Hi" and Geraldine said "Far out" and Gervais said "You freaks" and he wondered . . . here is the family and the family is all g, completely g, they glory in g and the final g is . . . must be God.

"And here's the hepatitis express," somebody named g said and there was a wonder in the constricting live rubber thing on his arm and the bite that pierced the blue veins surrounded with a wealth, a tapestry, a blue-and-black universe of hematomata.

And . . .

And . . .

And . . .

"For a time," he said, "I was possessed by a completely irrational fear."

"It's all right," Gloria said.

That was the way it was in the first century, in the formative century, when he—fabricator of immortality—fled like the rest to an endless fantasy of drugs. For them, it was boredom. For him, the heavy weight of guilt.

Now, two and a half centuries later . . .

Malcolm, who was now nearly three hundred years old and

looked—for the evening at least—perhaps forty, sat at the center table in the Meatrack, waiting for his female customer. The small vial containing the single amber capsule of death felt like a pound weight in his pocket. It was one of his few remaining ambers until he could see Nordling again.

Nordling, he thought wearily. Nordling, death's deputy, right hand of the Angel of Death; Nordling, who brewed the one sure exit in this life of pain and endless decay. Malcolm really didn't need Nordling, he told himself. After all, he could make the rather simple polynucleic acid endotoxin himself, but there was still the emotional reluctance to have anything ever to do again with that deadly science of creation. Hence Nordling, and before him what seemed an endless line of suppliers, all dead or immobilized in the Kraals now.

Malcolm had told Bobby, his runner, that he did not like making the contact in such a public place as the Meatrack, but the man had refused to see him elsewhere. He badly needed the money to pay the interest to the barracudas for the money he had borrowed. *Funny,* he thought. *It's the young ones who come to me now.* Well, not so odd actually, when you considered the meaning of life after fifty in this decaying city that existed under the benevolent tyranny of the Company.

He lifted the coffee cup to his lips and sipped cautiously. It was much too hot, as though the waiter thought the temperature might disguise the harsh taste of roasted grain. He sat the cup precisely in its cracked saucer to the left of his plate and stirred it patiently, thinking of Eliot's Prufrock, "I have measured out my life with coffee spoons."

He sighed, remembering when there was a time for poetry and even love in the days before the world had filled with the aged and the fierce young ones treading hotly on their heels, before the drug scene, before the passion of the gorgons. There had been fine dining places in the city—he remembered them from two centuries before—where one might enjoy the pleasurable graces of a culture that still held itself a few footsteps above the survival level. Now . . . ?

THE WEARIEST RIVER

The muttering retreats
Of restless nights in one-night cheap hotels
And sawdust restaurants with oyster-smells . . .

Only the smells here were of burned food and the stench of decaying garbage drifting in from the open alley door. He had become obsessed with Prufrock lately. He wondered if anyone else even remembered Eliot's aging drab. Prufrock, he thought, seemed the perfect anthem for the city and the people in it.

He nervously scanned the faces of a new group that entered the curtained door, searching for some sign of recognition on the faces of the women. They were all high on alkaloids, he saw. The Meatrack was one of the few remaining public restaurants in the city and existed perilously by virtue of a platoon of bullyboys who policed the immediate area and warred with the indigenous gangs. The extra expense of protection found its reflection in their prices.

He was contemplating the limp vegesteak on his plate (fifteen dollars for eight ounces) and idly pawing through the soya gravy when the waiter behind him, obviously high on some psychedelic drug, slipped on a piece of discarded food and dumped a pitcher of precious water on him. Malcolm jumped to his feet, realizing that in seconds he would be compromised.

His make-up ran in an instant. The smooth thirtyish face that he had so carefully built up earlier that evening dissolved in running primary colors and the protein-based tissue firmer lapsed into a semigelatinous liquid that slumped down his cheeks. In an instant, amid the young and not-so-young diners, he dissolved and became what he was, one of the old ones, the hated, feared and loved old ones and . . . worse . . . several youngish people at the near table recognized him.

"Look, look," the girl at the next table said. Her pupils were widely dilated, magnifying her eyes.

"Malcolm," the girl next to her breathed and then squealed a high ecstatic squeal.

The mid-thirties blond man next to her glared and half rose, his biceps in the clinging gauze-thin shirt bulging with the unconscious need to attack.

"It's Malcolm, Malcolm, Malcolm," other female voices around the room breathed and he knew that he had been found out.

He pushed from the chair quickly. He threw a wad of credits onto the table, scarcely noticing the wide contemptuous eyes of his waiter, who had moments before been relatively deferential. Malcolm looked wildly about the dusty dining room, seeing hate-filled male eyes, lust-filled female eyes, dull eyes, abnormally bright eyes. Only one understanding glance met his and he recognized Felice, a dancer at his club, her dirty yellow-white hair framing sagging jowls and a pain-filled expression. The drunken young man with her reached out to touch her liver-spotted hand and she turned away, withdrawing her sympathy from him in the instant. The young man glared at him. Malcolm guessed from his youth that he was not a Policyholder, that he had not yet received the Heinholtz treatment. This, of course, made him very vulnerable and overly cautious in his reactions. Malcolm had little to fear from him.

The waiter snapped, "Take your money, damn it."

Malcolm stared at his six-foot bulky body, with the tight muscles and the first signs of a bulging stomach. The young ones didn't keep themselves in shape anymore. Well, why should they work at it? There were so few of them and little competition. Besides which the standards had changed dramatically in his time so that the lame and the halt and the disfigured became invested with a special beauty all their own.

"Keep it," he said. "You earned it."

"Look, mister," the man said, "get out of here fast. I'll show you the back door. We don't want any more trouble with the constables. We got enough trouble now on the streets."

Malcolm paused to consider his offer. Yes, it would perhaps be better to leave by the rear entrance now that he was unmasked.

"Show me the way," he said tiredly, throwing down his napkin and placing his hand unconsciously on the younger man's arm.

"Don't touch me," the young man said with distaste. "I'm trying to save your life. So don't touch me."

Malcolm followed him to the rear of the small café while the girls ohed and ahed at his shambling figure and the men held themselves in tight reserve. Had he been a woman, he thought, the situation would have been completely reversed. He felt the physical texture of the young men's hate and he thought, *Never mind, in another thirty or fifty years you will join me and the young men who are left will hate you and loathe you and I will be here in the fading vigor of my fourth century to mock you and gloat at how the world has turned and the prince has become the frog.*

Once through the kitchen and into the cloying darkness of the alley, he paused and rested against the decaying brick of the building. The waiter turned in the yellow glow of the doorway and snapped, "Old man, you move on. If you want to get yourself killed, do me the favor of doing it a few blocks from here. You owe me that much."

"Yes," Malcolm said tiredly, "yes, I owe you that much." He started slowly down the alley.

At the opposite end of the alley he heard excited voices and a sudden whooping sound. *Like hounds after the aging stallion,* he thought.

Or wolves.

They thought they had been wolves—Gloria, Gervais, all the rest. Just because they were mortal and did not fear death. Instead they embarked on a kind of spiritual immortality, taunting physical death.

"Have you ever felt that way?" Malcolm asked. "That sense of panic, of complete disorientation?"

"We all get it," Glenda said, embracing him. "I wonder that you don't get it more often." (They didn't know about him, that he did not share their cherished mortality.)

"I don't like it," he said.

"None of us do," Gervais said. He was the big one, the strong one of the family, and even when he wasn't trying to

show off, his most casual move brought great biceps bulging against his knit shirt. He was reddish blond and in the open throat of his shirt a crinkly mass of red-blond hair writhed on his chest like the snakes of Medusa's head. His arms were peppered with freckles and freckles spotted the backs of his fingers. He had a turned-up nose and nostrils wide and flared and he looked into distances not easily perceived by the others.

"We are," Gervais said, "an enclave of wolves. In the midst of the sheep flocking to the Company and its immortal pablum, we are wolves."

"I have a confession," Malcolm said. "I've run from it too long and there's no respite in the family. The weight of guilt is too much."

"You're spaced out," Gervais said. "Why should you have more guilt than I have guilt or she has guilt?"

"Because," Malcolm said, "I am a stranger and afraid in a world I surely made."

"I like you," Gloria said. "You're a classicist and I've always liked classicists. How old are you?"

"Much older than you," Malcolm said.

"How old?"

"A century, at least."

They drew back from him then, the whole family, and Gervais said, "You didn't tell us."

"I couldn't," he said plaintively.

"You took a policy?" Gloria accused.

"Long ago," he said. "Rather, I wrote the policy."

Glenda said, "That's impossible. Heinholtz wrote the policy and he gave his formula to the Company and the Company has come to own the world, but Heinholtz is dead or worse . . . in the Kraals."

"If it were only true," Malcolm said.

"You can't be that old," Geraldine said.

"I am, I am," he said.

"You sicken me," Gervais said. "We'll all die soon."

"But you won't," Glenda said.

"I've tried to," he said. "I've gone your drug trip and I've *swallowed your own private brand of immortality and I've tried."*

"But you'll still live," Gervais accused.

"Forgive me, forgive me, forgive me," Malcolm pleaded.

"I sicken unto death at the sight of you," Gervais said, posturing.

Malcolm felt a dull sense of futility. He was getting high again as they all were. It was no use, no possible way of assuaging his guilt for what he had brought on the world.

Outside, the first signs of decay were creeping over the city. The Company existed, the single most potent financial force on the globe, and there was no hope, not so long as humans held to life and other humans disavowed life. It was all a dead end, the people outside embracing the treatment and these poor creatures fleeing into a dream existence in which they fancied themselves wolves among sheep.

Enclave of wolves, he thought bitterly. Everyone knows that on the North American continent wolves are extinct.

A sad good-by to the family of *g's*, he thought. It was a lost period of his immortal life. But now there were other wolves . . .

Malcolm ran down the alley behind the Meatrack as fast as his tired legs would carry him. If only he could come on a patrol of the Company constables, he thought.

"There he is," a bull voice yelled.

"Get him and let's do him," another yelled, his voice chemically blurred.

He tried to run faster. The alley's mouth was a thousand miles away and the searing breath was already tearing at his throat. He had been in such situations before and had managed to escape. Thank God, he was not that attenuated. Not like the rank on rank of oldsters in the Kraals on the edge of the city. The endless rows of weak and pulsing oldsters who could not die, who could not be killed. All because of him, that being who was Malcolm in an avatar long ago, before the world had sunk into the corruption of the present, the decay of now.

He broke from the alleyway and looked to the right and

left. They would soon be upon him and he had no more strength. (What demands can you make on a body nearly three centuries old? True, he had preserved it in a fashion that the other oldsters without his specialized knowledge had not been able, but it remained a three-century-old body and the end was in sight . . . distant and prolonged but definitely in sight.)

At the alley's entrance, his foot caught in a chuckhole in the macadam and he fell sprawling. His outthrust hand skidded across the gritty pavement, leaving layers of skin behind. He felt the sudden tingling as the friction wound gathered quickly and began to heal. Then the five men tumbled from the alley's mouth and were upon him. He raised his arm to ward off the blows. They would have knives. Everyone had knives, knowing that they would wound and rend and cause pain but would not kill.

The young ones did have knives and they used them. His outstretched hand took one that pierced his palm. Another thrust at his chest and buried itself an inch deep. A third in a grimy hand buried itself in his belly as he screamed with pain. The attack had been silent to this point. His scream alarmed them.

"He'll bring the constables," one yelled. A second aimed a kick at his ribs and he fell back gasping. He heard a distant grinding and suddenly the attack was over.

The twelve-wheeled lorry came from a side street, its hard plastic wheels grinding at the scattered litter of the street. Its multiple red lights plucked at the decaying buildings on either side. They saw him even before he saw them and pulled toward him. *Thank God*, he thought, *constables*.

"Damned old fool," a voice said. "Know better than to come downtown."

A bulky body leaped from the lorry, scattering garbage before a booted foot, and grabbed him. "Inside, gran'pa," the man snorted. "Inside or we'll let them spread your immortal guts over the pavement."

He needed no second urging. He bustled into the lorry and

the armored door closed behind him. Seconds later, the lorry turret ground out twenty degrees to face the gang of young-sters.

"Back," an amplified voice said. "The Company is marshaling the block."

"Give us the raunchy bastard," a voice yelled from the group.

"Back," the lorry's amplified voice shouted again. A thick tubular structure emerged from the turret and seconds later the chemical match of the flame thrower ignited. The young men saw the first glow and broke in frantic retreat.

"Thank God," a voice from within the lorry said. "I don't think I can torch another one this evening."

"Mary-waist," another voice snorted in contempt.

The sergeant in charge of the lorry turned to Malcolm. He wore a heavy grenade launcher as a side arm. "How are you, old man?" he demanded.

Malcolm inspected his body. The wound on his hand was now only a faint pink scar. The one in his belly still ached but his exploring fingers told him that it had closed cleanly. The pain was another matter from this and the shattered ribs. It would abate eventually, he knew, but it would probably never completely disappear. For every wound the fast-healing scar tissue developed tiny points of pressure on nerve endings. He could not be wounded or killed but each breach of the quick-healing walls of his body left its legacy of unending dull pain.

The lorry began to move, gaining speed to thirty miles an hour as they threaded their way down the boulevard past the shattered walls of abandoned high-rises and piles of debris stacked beside the curb. Of all the streets in the city, the boulevard was still relatively clear.

The constable sergeant took his name and asked his resi-dence. Malcolm attempted to thank him.

"I get paid," the man said in complete disinterest. "Besides, they couldn't have killed you."

"It wouldn't have been worth living afterward if you hadn't arrived in time," Malcolm said.

"But you would have," the man said in complete detachment. Then, "Stay home at night. Don't go out like that. Next time, we may not be able to rescue you."

"All right, all right," he said. "The young ones haven't got me yet."

"How old are you?" the sergeant asked.

"I'm not ready for the Kraals yet," he snapped, knowing full well that many men a hundred years his junior were already a part of that living death.

"You will be," the sergeant said.

"So will you," he snapped irritably.

"I'll take my chance," the sergeant said. "What do you do?"

"Do?"

"For a living."

"I'm an entertainer," he said. "A dancer."

"Oh," the sergeant said, not bothering to hide the distaste in his voice. "One of those."

"One of those," Malcolm said.

They drove him down the dark and dangerous streets to the club in the Village. He checked the time and thought that if he made it through the show, they might be able to get back to their apartment before the barracudas caught him. He had borrowed the money at Britt's insistence. She loved the precious luxuries of this sad world and who was he to deny her? Now the barracudas were pressing him. If he didn't pay up soon, they would certainly take action against him. What action made him shudder. He cursed himself silently for his weakness, his pathetic need to please Britt, who, after all, would be with him regardless of the favors he lavished on her.

At the alleyway entrance to the club, the sergeant said, "You're clear. You can make it."

"Thank you," he said tiredly.

"What do you do there?" the sergeant asked idly.

"As I told you, I dance," he said.

"I just bet you're light as a leaf on your feet," the man said.

"It isn't that kind of dance," he said.

"I didn't think it was," the man said contemptuously.

Malcolm swung heavily from the lorry, dropping the last foot from the steps in false bravado. The shock of alighting twisted his ankle slightly, but he would be damned if he would let the sergeant see it.

"See you sometime," he said mockingly.

"Not bloody likely," the man's voice came to him. The lorry started, spun its wheels and lumbered down the street, leaving him at the head of the alley. He turned and walked into its shadows.

He entered the stage door and moved through the dim lights to his dressing room, pausing to eye the stage. He was surprised to see that Felice was on and he wondered how she had made it back from the Meatrack in time for the performance. He watched her clumsy movements that contrasted so grotesquely with her partner's, a lean young man with jet-black hair and stringy young muscles. He was clad only in a ragged loincloth and she wore a musty lion's mane. The act was quite trite, but the sadomasochistic overtones appealed to the young males in the audience.

He looked out over the club floor. The younger men clustered in the rear, most of them unaccompanied. He watched several sprawled out in the dimness, the young thighs jerking nervously to the music. Several of them had their hands thrust deep in their pockets and he could see the cloth that covered their abdomen squirm with the violence of their parallel play. The aphrodisiac smell of amyl nitrite was oppressive.

"The dead are dancing with the dead," he thought wearily and tried to remember where that had come from. Wilde? Yes, Wilde, he thought.

He made his way through the dusty scenery, past tables of empty bottles that exuded a rank odor and to the rear curtained area that was their dressing room. Britt was already there, changing to her costume. It was a wispy thing of green-and-blue gauze with small starfish clustered about the breasts and pubic region. Under the blue and green lights of the floor, the drinkers of the club would get the illusion of garments floating on vagrant ocean currents. Her long blond hair she had carefully matted with spray so that it drifted like a damp halo about her head. She looked up as he entered and her thick sensuous lips parted moistly.

Her eyes were excited, those marvelous blue eyes that seemed to have a separate existence from her superb flawless skin and straw-blond hair.

"What happened?" she asked.

He told her, watching her eyes grow wide with excitement as her small kitten's tongue extended and licked her lips with a sensuousness that still excited him. During their club act, she quite frequently used that gesture, but then it was for effect . . . studied, carefully structured. Now, it was unconscious as she savored vicariously the terrible danger of being maimed and living on, helpless and shattered in body.

He began to change to his costume. It was equally brief, consisting of a loincloth and a pair of sandals over which plastic scales and long talons had been glued to give the appearance of a monster's feet. He divested himself of his clothing and donned the loincloth, the sandals and finally the chilling sea-creature mask that he wore in the act. Britt came over and helped him position the dorsal fin that protruded from between his shoulder blades and ran down to the base of his spine. He stood in front of the mirror. Of course, under the lights the effect was more exotic.

He secured the net and trident from beside the dressing table and turned as one of the lighting men stuck his head through the curtain to yell, "Get a move on. You're up in five minutes."

Britt came over to him and touched his belly where the scars were still an angry red. She leaned forward and kissed each mark, her eyes suddenly intense. He wondered if she had been taking anything. It was very hard to tell and she had promised him that she wouldn't.

When their music started, she left the dressing area while

he made the final adjustments to the mask. Then he walked through the cluttered passageway to the curtains that separated the stage from the back. He peered through the slit in a side hanging and noted that the crowd had increased in the last hour. Whereas the front rows had been largely women, the sexes were now equally mixed, although there was some tendency for the older men to sit to the right of the club with their dates while the older women with their young men were to the left. He supposed the maître d' had arranged this to avoid the friction that had marred the performances in the past.

The music started then, an eerie atonal theme of flute, wood winds and a theremin. It had been mechanically synthesized a year before for their act and the tape was beginning to show signs of wear. It remained, nevertheless, a very effective background. He looked out to watch Britt's first sinuous, gliding steps across the small stage, her hair drifting in the cold blue-green light as though she were underwater. She was a sea thing, sinuous and exotic, her breasts rising and falling with the slow exertion of her body. The dance was deliberately sensuous, showing the fine muscular development of her body. Her near nudity was more suggestive than any more bold show of flesh.

He waited until the flute gave a shrill trill and entered from stage right. He was a sea creature himself now, a thing of grotesque lust, twisting through the stage fronds, his stance a clear menace to the more delicate figure of Britt. He made swimming motions toward her, brandishing his trident, as she fell back in mock terror. He was conscious of the clumsiness of his movements, the lack of grace in his aging body. As the audience leaned forward expectantly, he deliberately exaggerated the clumsiness. He threw the net now, tangling her in its coils and she writhed sensuously. In the next instant he had carried her back against a papier-mâché rock and had imprisoned her in the coils of the net.

Now the erotic play began for which the audience had waited.

Slowly with the end of the trident he divested her of her gauze costume, stripping it from her in shreds and scattering the concealing starfish to the floor of the stage. In minutes she was pinioned against the rock, completely nude, her body cringing in mock horror. He continued his slow clumsy dance about her, thrusting out with his trident at intervals to draw a tiny patch of blood. With each rivulet of blood, he heard a whispering gasp from the audience. The women were watching him with bright eyes, the men leaning forward. He caught sight of a white young male face with glazed eyes and a tiny tongue wetting white lips as he stepped back to eye Britt's blood-dotted figure. *Ah,* he thought, *Medusa and the other Gorgons—I am one with you all.*

He was preparing for the final thrust of the trident. To this point the blood had been very real, but secreted in a taped pocket under one arm Britt carried a vial of thick red dye for this final movement. As he drew back for the mock thrust that would penetrate the plastic vial, the feverish young man jumped to his feet and yelled, "Make it real; make it real!" Before Malcolm could recover, the young man had leaped to the low stage and was trying to wrest the trident from him. Club security guards ran from either side for the stage but the whole audience seemed to dissolve suddenly into groups of struggling people.

Malcolm fell back from the young man and aimed a heavy kick at him. The man shrugged it off. He was a Policyholder, Malcolm realized, and almost invulnerable. Any assault—no matter how lethal—would incapacitate him only for minutes during the nervous spasm of regeneration. The security men saw this and fell on him with the electrostingers that they carried in their belts. He writhed under the spasms from the stingers and fell to the stage as Malcolm ran to Britt and freed her from the clinging net. Her eyes were wild and excited at the turmoil over the footlights.

"Let's get out of here before the constables come," he shouted and forced her backstage. The noise of the conflict faded behind the heavy curtains. He forced her into a robe and found a shirt and pantaloons for himself. Once out into the street, he dragged her into a stumbling run. They reached the head of the alley as the lorries loaded with constables approached down the main street.

The seven blocks to their tiny apartment was a time of continuing panic for Malcolm. Had they come upon a street gang, he would not have known what to do. She was so vulnerable, he thought, in her young mortality and so enthralled with the thought of violence.

At the door, he whistled the combination that activated the lock and propelled her insward. She sprawled on the bed while he found quick-healing unguent and touched the wounds his trident had left. They healed quickly as he watched.

She sighed and said, "Take off your clothes."

He eyed her tired flesh and removed his shirt and her eyes brightened. He finished undressing and stood nude before her, his belly drooping with the corduroyed ridges of expansion marks where he had gained and lost weight again and again. His legs were intricate laceries of blue and red capillaries slashed by scars. The flesh of the calves sagged while the heavy muscles of the thighs bulged through the thin skin in stringy masculinity. His chest remained remarkably firm although the nipples had expanded and the fatty deposits about the pectorals were sagging. The scar tissue on his belly was still an angry red mass.

She groaned when she saw his body and threw the robe from herself, positioning herself on the bed, arms and legs akimbo. He thought, *Oh, please, do I have to go through this insane charade?* Only, this was what she wanted, and he was much too old and too tired and too corrupt to argue against it.

In the cupboard he found the ropes and tied her arms to each end of the headboard, feet spread-eagled each to the foot of the bed.

"Make love to me, Mal, Mal, please, baby," she breathed.

He found the belt, old and supple black leather, massaged to the delicacy of human skin by a hundred oily hands, and doubled it in his fist as she squirmed below him. He raised his arm and the black thing struck out like a snake. The soft smack of leather against skin was almost a caress. She squirmed in ecstasy as he brought it down again and again. Red welts appeared on her back. Not raw welts but light ones that would fade with the morning. He growled at her because she wanted him to do so.

Then he made love to her, violating her as she squirmed and struggled and climaxed again and again. Later they lay silently in an embrace that was the nearest they ever got to tenderness.

"I wish . . ." she said dreamily.

"Wish what?" he asked.

"I wish you were . . . well . . . different."

"Different?" he asked, knowing well what she meant.

"I mean, not so perfect," she said. "You know, except for age, you're too perfect. I remember Martin. His face was badly burned, the whole side twisted up so that he couldn't smile. There was something so beautiful, so exciting about his face."

"I'm sorry," he said.

"No matter," she said dreamily. "But it would be nice . . . you know, if maybe you had lost an arm or maybe been badly scarred tonight. Oh, I don't know."

"I'm sorry," he said again, beginning to drift off to sleep.

"It's all right; it's all right," she said dreamily. "I still love you." After a long moment, she said, "It's a long time ahead. Maybe something will happen."

"Maybe," he said tiredly as her hand dreamily massaged the decayed mass of flesh about his biceps.

He lay with her breathing heavily in his arms and thought that he would have to find some other way of getting money soon. Customers were hard to contact for the amber capsules. Besides, he thought, there were few enough of the capsules left . . . the one he always carried hidden in his boot heel against the time he might be too badly maimed, the one he kept here in the room and the box of perhaps five he had cached in the cellar of the club where they worked. It was only a matter of time before the Company finally caught up with Nordling, he supposed. That ancient decrepit could barely function now and he took useless chances.

God, he thought, how many had there been before Nordling? He had known them all, helped them begin their operations to synthesize the deadly toxin, the only material that could bring death to a Policyholder. One by one they had been caught and sent to the Kraals' living death. Eventually, Malcolm thought, he too would be caught and there would no longer be any release from the Heinholtz treatment. He would lie in the Kraals as the world decayed and the Company, mindless in its corporate need to hold power, would flicker out with the world, like some smoky candle guttering in the wind.

Yes, it was inevitable that the Company would find Nordling someday. At the moment he was merely a thorn in its corporate hide, certainly not a major force menacing it. His operations were too restricted, too limited in the number of people he might affect. He had encountered increasing difficulty in getting the raw materials for the synthesis and his production had dropped alarmingly in the last two months. Besides Malcolm there were perhaps a dozen pushers in the city who depended on him and their supply of the amber capsules had become very limited recently, driving the price up severalfold. It was just as well, he thought. With the increasing pressure of the barracudas on him, he needed every extra dollar he could marshal.

Still, he thought dreamily, he would always keep the two capsules in reserve. One for him—he shook his head sadly on the pillow—one for Britt if indeed she should decide to take a policy with the Company. He had tried to talk her out of it, but it seemed certain that she would do it eventually as she neared her traumatic thirtieth birthday. Then, of course, she would eventually want one of the ambers and, no matter how badly now he needed money, he would always keep one in reserve for her.

He drifted into sleep, his mind's eye imaging that last moment when she too would join him in that death that was denied to all of the oldsters. It would be a tragically beautiful thing, he thought. Exciting in its own way. A part of him twisted at the thought and at the physical evidence of excitement it evoked from his sagging body. Still—he licked his lips dreamily—still it would be an experience the like of which they had never shared in their childish games of ropes and belts. All of that, he thought, was a mimicking of the pain of death prompted by fear. Fear of death. Well, he remembered that emotion very well . . .

In the beginning his sole motivation was fear. How do you characterize the fear of living? You look at your body and you see it mature, lengthen its bones, grow full and mature, see groin hair form with puberty, the growth of genitals and with them desire, and having reached this point of full and complete development . . .

You feel that you are growing old.

What a terrible, frightening feeling at eighteen to see the inevitable touch of death on your body. For Malcolm the fear of death came very early, much too early, neurotically and compulsively early. Which was why his whole life became deformed. He knew before he went to college what he must do. The state of biochemical and particularly molecular biological knowledge had reached the point where one might conceivably do something about this inevitable death sentence.

So he studied. He raced quickly through his undergraduate work in barely more than two years and entered graduate school, impatient, filled with the need to know, to garner information, to fit all the bits and pieces together, to find the ultimate answer to this terrible compulsion that obsessed him.

After his Ph.D. (that robot period when he crammed knowledge into his head and recited it back like some giant white-skinned parrot, while he pursued his carefully directed doctoral research) he was free at last, free to do what he wished. Provided, of course, he could find the funding. Well, there was funding, a mass of funding from the pharmaceutical companies that at that moment were swallowing Ph.D.'s like the whale swallowing Jonah. Brakeley Pharmaceuticals (famous for Argomycin) swallowed him but fortunately he found himself in the right compartment of that multiple stomach. They were working on synthetic viruses in the laboratory in Brooklyn where he found himself. Imagine a pharmaceutical company, devoted to fun and profit (oh, yes, very much for profit), manufacturing viruses. Well, of course, it makes sense if one considers that viruses are potential information carriers, as are RNA and DNA. A suitably tailored virus may take its place as a part of the genetic chain, indistinguishable from the natural nucleic acid chain, if one could suppress the naturally generated control factors.

They had the idea of using an artificial virus to counter the natural virus that everyone now knew caused all of the varieties of cancer. The cancer virus was endemic to the cell from birth, suppressed by factors in the body until failure occurred and the virus entered the cell's reproductive mechanism. After this point the cell ceased to follow the ordained plan and grew cancerous. The plan was to balance the natural virus with a tailored one that would unite in the cell with the natural genetic material and cancel out the cancer virus.

Clever. It gave him the chance he needed, the tools he needed. He became interested rather in a virus that would carry the genetic pattern for instant renewal of tissues, for selective acceleration of metabolism, for the removal of all the degenerative processes that collectively spelled old age.

He succeeded. How well he succeeded was truly astonishing. The laboratory animals did not age at first. More . . . they could not be killed. They repaired themselves at a fantastic rate. They were immortal. The Company brass came down from the glass tower in which they lived and marveled at what he had wrought.

It turned out that Brakeley was part of a conglomerate that had been assembled by a manufacturer of industrial cleaning compounds. More, the major stockholders of the parent corporation were also members of the board of a major insurance company in Connecticut. There was a subtle shift in financial alignment. The parent company divested itself of Brakeley by a complicated exchange of paper (completely and piously approved by the SEC) and Brakeley became a part of the Company, the Universal Surety Company.

He was baffled at these maneuvers. He wanted only to pursue the thing he had made. By now the problem had become apparent to him, though not to the enthusiastic corporate officers. (If they recognized the problem, they chose to ignore it in the sugar-plum visions of profit and power.) Still, the laboratory animals–the rats, hamsters, rhesus monkeys–were truly immortal or at least capable of life-spans many multiples of the ordinary. Only, after a stasis period, they didn't stop aging. They aged and they aged and they aged, growing more decrepit, more burdened with the accrued wounds of living, less agile, more needing of attention, but still living. Always living.

Which mattered not a damn to the Company. There was a new type of life insurance. It took time for all the states to approve it. Arkansas was the first. Then Washington. Surprisingly, California (the center of the national youth cult) was next to last. By this time foreign subsidiaries were busy with the new technique. Pay your monthly premium or sign over a certain percentage of your present and future resources– become a Policyholder (now it was always capitalized)–and life perpetual or at least very much extended became yours.

Malcolm wondered and marveled and feared at this. Surely, there was someone at the top who could see the danger, the terrible danger of this burgeoning policy. But no corporation is ruled by a single man. There is no continuity of personal power even in a near-immortal corporation. One director gave way to another and always there was a board to answer to, innumerable anonymous stockholders to placate, the various *autonomous governments whose economies became increasingly immersed in the workings of the Company. Like Juggernaut, the whole process rolled, accelerated and could not be stopped by men of good or ill will.*

In due course the Company dominated the world . . . and stagnated it with a vast population of near-immortal but constantly aging men. No one knew how to stop the complex economic machinery that had been started. There was finally an immortal Director and Malcolm took the new toxin to him.

"This is how we end life," he said sadly, tiredly.

"Who are you?" the Director demanded.

"I'm the one who gave you the treatment," Malcolm said.

The Director sneered. "Something as world-shaping as this the product of a single man? Don't be silly. No one man could conceive of the Heinholtz principle and carry it to completion."

"I did," Malcolm challenged.

"Please don't waste my time. I'm very busy," the Director said. "Besides, who wants a toxin that kills when we have eternal life?"

They ushered him out and that day he left the elaborate quarters in Brooklyn that his status in the Company gave him. He left and disappeared and gave up all that he had ever wanted. For a long time he disappeared in the new drug-drenched subculture, trying to forget, trying to drown the sorrows of his aging body (yes, he had been one of the first) in the useless flight from psychological reality.

Eventually he saw that this too was a dead end.

Malcolm was awakened by an insistent pounding on the door. Britt still slept, her body curled into a loose fetal position while her wealth of blond hair sprawled in thick locks over the faintly soiled pillow. He gathered a threadbare seersucker robe about his body and opened the door on its chain. Through the partially open door he recognized Bobby, his runner, fidgeting nervously on the doorstep.

"Sure death," Bobby swore, his teeth chattering against the morning chill. "I ain't gonna stand out here all morning. Why in hell don't you answer your door?"

"I was asleep," Malcolm said irritably.

"Well, I got business for you. Big business."

"How much?"

"Five caps," Bobby said, "and by ten tonight. There's ten thousand total in it."

"Fifteen," Malcolm countered. "You know how short the supply is. I must have that much."

"Twelve," Bobby snorted. "That's all my clients say to settle for."

Malcolm thought. With the barracudas pressing him on the loan interest he'd have to settle for that he decided. "Twelve it is," he agreed finally, "but not the Meatrack again. Say back of the show after the last performance."

Bobby nodded. "I'll be there. Take it easy on the streets this morning. Things are getting tight even this early."

"Thanks," Malcolm said and shut the door. He leaned back against the door and shuddered. He didn't like to get on the streets until afternoon, but he'd have to get to the club and rescue his cache before any of the other personnel showed up. It was bad enough getting to it with only the cleaning women present but later it would be almost impossible. If he could have thought of a better place to hide the capsules, he would have long ago. As it was, the club was about the best place.

As Britt stirred and slowly came awake, he prepared breakfast. He used their last egg with some soya paste and spinach to make an omelet. It was lean enough fare to begin a trying day but until he could get some more money they'd have to make do. The tips at the club had been sparse enough lately and they still had a week to run before payday.

He flipped the omelet expertly with long years of practice, divided it in portions of one-third and two-thirds. The larger portion he carried over to the bed, where Britt was now sitting up, blinking at the light that streamed from the barred window. "Good morning, love," she said between yawns. "Oh, that's nice of you. Only"—she wrinkled her nose—"I'm getting tired of soya omelets."

"There won't be any more for a while," he said. "That was our last egg."

"Oh," she said, looking as if she were about to cry.

"I've got a customer," he said quickly. "Bobby came and they want five caps."

"That's dangerous," she said. "You know how close the constables came the last time you supplied a party. One is bad enough, but a party gets a lot of attention."

"I don't know that it is a party," he said.

"With that many ambers, it's always a party," she said, downing the last of her omelet and making a faint gesture of distaste as she shoved the empty plate across the bed. "Any coffee?"

He shook his head. Her face formed a distinct pout. *Well, hell*, he thought, *what does she expect? I can't keep the place in food when she spends it all on clothes and make-up. Who notices in the dim lights of the club?* But she had to have the best, as though she were under the closest scrutiny.

"We've got some tea," he said. He didn't tell her it was synthetic, hoping that she would not notice. Fortunately she didn't and sat sipping the hot brown liquid as he dressed.

"You're going out?" she asked in sudden alarm.

"To get the caps," he said. "I have to get to the club before the day personnel show up."

"Take care," she said. "If you run into anything, forget the caps and come home."

"We need the money," he said.

The morning sunlight was blinding when he stepped from the apartment onto the street. He looked carefully to the right and left but the alley was deserted. He turned from the alley onto the littered thoroughfare and walked for three blocks before he became aware that the street was peopled largely by oldsters. There were several groups of constables along the way. He wondered what this might signify but he felt relatively safe in such crowds.

He covered the seven blocks to the club in an hour, pausing periodically to rest. He walked quite regularly, but as he grew older, the fatigue of covering even two blocks weighed heavily on him. At the club, he paused and leaned against the side of the building to get his breath. He was quite unprepared for the appearance of the constable in the door of the club.

"What are you doing here, old man?" the constable demanded.

Malcolm thought of telling him that he worked there, but a sixth sense warned him to be silent. "Resting," he said breathlessly.

"Well, you just move along," the constable said.

He nodded silently and moved away. At the alley, he considered going in the side door, but he saw that there was another constable posted there. His heart sank for a moment. What were they doing? Was it possible . . . ?

"Malcolm, get the hell away from here," a woman's voice said near him. He turned as Felice grabbed his elbow. Her yellowing white hair was badly disarrayed; her bloodshot eyes buried in innumerable folds of flesh were wide and excited. "Them constables is roughing everybody up," she said. "Better get away."

"What's happened?" he demanded.

"They found a bunch of ambers in the basement. One of our people must have hid them there."

"Ambers?" he asked. "Not in the club?"

"Oh, God," she said. "I wished I'd known. What I wouldn't give for just one."

"You don't mean that," he said.

She sighed. "You just don't know how badly I mean it." Her eyes began to mist and in a second she stood blubbering like a small child. "Just that close and I didn't know. I'd never have enough money to buy one and they was that close." She eyed him then with suspicion dawning in her eyes.

He fled, leaving her sobbing like some mechanical doll who had been programmed to endless repetitive sorrow. On the street he was caught up in the flow of traffic. Surprisingly, there were still a large number of oldsters hurrying along and he suddenly realized that a demonstration must be forming. He turned, thinking that he must get away from here. At the opposite end of the street a line of constables was forming, their riot batons linked electrified tip to electrified tip as they moved forward. All of them carried hand-grenade launchers on their belts and several labored under the weight of flame throwers.

He looked to the right and left, hoping somehow that he could evade the cresting flood of humanity. If he could get away, he could still find Nordling. He was only a few blocks away; he never ventured forth now, depending on friends for what food he consumed, living only for the stinking basement under his shack where the filthy glassware sprawled to the ceiling, the Soxhlet extractors gurling, the calcium-encrusted condenser dripping out its slow amber drops.

The streets were filling rapidly now with the oldsters, many of them lame and hobbling. Most of the men were accompanied by younger women, many of these half supporting their escorts as they converged on the plaza fronting the Company's downtown headquarters. Malcolm could see that another line of constables, armed with grenade launchers and several portable flame throwers, had drawn up in front of the plaza, backed by several armed lorries. The tense group of constables ringed the great obsidian statue in the plaza, its golden-black hands stretching outward over the plaza, cupped to bear the small simulacrum of a limp human form. The Company called it *Succor*. Malcolm hated its perverse symbolism. Behind the statue two turreted heavy flame throwers crouched menacingly.

Malcolm found himself suddenly halted in a crush of bodies. The square before the plaza was filled with old people, many of them carrying the tattered yellow banners of the Retrenchment Party. They stood silently, waiting. A dreadful menacing silence settled over the plaza.

"Your right to assemble will be protected; now, go home," a voice boomed out from a public-address system. It was the Director's voice. Malcolm had not heard it in years but he recognized it.

Several of the old people hoisted a banner. The wind whopped at it, rippling the words. They shouted: "The World Is Starving. POLICY RETRENCHMENT NOW!"

Go home," the Director's voice boomed. "You've had your say. The Company's policies are open to everyone."

A ragged wave of voices flowed from the crowd, old throats crying threats and protest.

"Go home or the constables will take action," the voice shouted.

"Retrenchment now," old voices screamed and withered fists thrust above the crowd like a sudden stand of ancient wheat. The line of constables began to move forward, electrostingers at the ready. From somewhere in the forefront of the crowd a paving brick sailed out and struck one of the constables on the temple. He folded slowly to the pavement. Others were ripping up paving blocks and pieces of macadam. The line of constables faltered before the sudden assault of missiles, then the line hardened and it began to move forward again. Malcolm saw their young eyes, bright and greedy beneath their visors, their faces grimly joyous in anticipation of the attack. Many drew their launchers.

The crowd began to disperse, the old men moving back painfully. How often had he seen this, this silent gathering of misery? The constables began to relax. It was all over, he thought, moving back and trying for a side street that suddenly opened to his left. It was all over, a completely ineffectual, thoroughly futile protest without leaders, without an statement of need. Old men did not make demands, he thought; they merely stood pathetically and waited for someone to succor them.

Pathetic men, he thought. Dead men whose bodies still somehow carried the spastic fire of life. *Like myself*, he thought.

"*I am Lazarus, come from the dead*," he thought. "*Come back to tell you all, I shall tell you all*." *I am Lazarus and Prufrock, his mind said, and Joseph of Arimathea and the ghost of Caligula and Alastair Crowley, clutching decay to my breast saying, "Look what I have wrought*."

He started to move away, conscious of the black mood of

defeat settling over the old men. The first hint of trouble yet to come was a distant murmur that grew louder. He turned to see a crowd of young men spilling into the plaza, their eyes bright with hatred. *Oh, God,* he thought, *I've got to get away from here.*

Too late. The young men converged on the crowd of dispersing oldsters. He heard shouts of "Parasites" and "Leeches" as the two forces converged. In an insane corner of his eye, he saw the constables drawing back. Their faces glowed with anticipation; their eyes were bright with the anticipation of the conflict. He heard the *pop* of a chemical match and knew someone had armed a flame thrower.

Malcolm knew he had to get away. The only channel of escape was the edge of the plaza but this would bring him close to the outer ranks of the constables. He paused in indecision and then decided that he would have to risk it. From the far side of the crowd he heard shouts of rage and cries of pain and he knew that the two mobs had joined in combat. Frustrating, useless carnage but he could not get involved. He began to sprint along the edge of the crowd, his ancient heart laboring with the exertion.

He was abreast of the constables now, passing around their ranks. "You, stop," an officer yelled and he realized that he had been seen. He tried to increase his speed but the young officer almost contemptuously caught up with him and in an instant grabbed him, pinioning his arms to his side.

"Damn, I told you to halt," the officer said and then yelled, "Sergeant, take care of this man."

A constable sergeant ran from the rear ranks and the officer released him as the sergeant menaced him with his electrostinger. He heard screams as the constables opened fire on the mob with launchers. Again and again he heard the *whoosh* of flame throwers. Over all this came wave on wave of anguished screaming.

"I haven't done anything," Malcolm whined. He tried to appear weak and ineffectual but a part of him was surprised to discover that his cringing stance was not completely an act. He was frightened and the potent muscularity of the sergeant intimidated him.

"Brace," the sergeant said and began to search him. He suddenly remembered that he could not be searched. The man's hands drifted over his body and he bolted, hoping for one insane instant that he might escape. The man launched himself in a low tackle and brought Malcolm to the ground. The impact drove the breath from his body. Hands pulled at his clothing, turning out his pockets, and then the sergeant had the plastic box that he still carried, the box that contained the amber capsule for his client. He shuddered, hoping that the man would not find the one secreted in the hollow heel of his boot.

The man had found what he wanted, however. He shouted and the officer hurried over. "An amber." The officer laughed. "That means a leave for both of us, catching a pusher." He slapped the sergeant on the back and then self-consciously recovered his dignity.

"I'm not a pusher," Malcolm protested.

"Where did you get the amber?" the officer demanded.

"I stole it," Malcolm answered. "One of the men in the crowd dropped it. I picked it up and ran."

"Frankly, old man, I don't believe you," the officer said. "We'll see if the colonel does." He addressed the sergeant, "Take him along."

The sergeant pinioned Malcolm's arms behind him and half dragged him, skirting the strife-torn plaza, to a small compound where there were already several prisoners. Malcolm was thrust behind a fenced and guarded wire barricade that had been thrown up in the last hour. From there he could see the final scenes of the battle between the youngsters and the old men. The constables were breaking it up now and the plaza was dotted with writhing bodies of young and old men, many of them horribly burned in the cross fire from several turreted flame throwers. Some of the bodies were still and he realized that part of the attacking force had been young men who were not Policyholders. Strange that they would risk their lives in such a senseless fight. He could understand the motivation of the young Policyholders. There were few enough resources left in the world with the work force so diminished and the oldsters represented a large unproductive segment. Better in their eyes to carry them all off to the Kraals, where at least in their suspended existence their consumption would be reduced to a minimum.

Guards came now and began to remove prisoners one by one for disposition. He waited his turn impatiently, wondering what would happen. Would they banish him to the Kraals or simply impose a lien on his basic ration? God knows, it was hard enough to exist in this decaying mass of stone and brick that had once been a city but he could survive that with the help of Britt.

When the guard came to the gate and beckoned for him, he came forward hesitantly. He was led through the wire and down a line of constables, now at ease and relaxing, to a camp table where a man with eagles on his fatigue jacket looked soberly at him. "The lieutenant says you're a pusher," the colonel said tiredly.

Malcolm repeated his story. The colonel looked at him as if he didn't exist. Then he leafed through the forged identification papers the lieutenant had taken from Malcolm. "No previous record," the colonel said. "What the hell made you steal this?"

"Wouldn't you have done the same thing?" Malcolm demanded tiredly.

The colonel pursued his lips. "I'm not that old, old man."

"You will be someday," Malcolm said.

The colonel held a whispered conversation with the lieutenant. Finally he looked up and said, "We've had enough trouble today. Your record is clean. I'll make an entry and let you go. The next time you'll be in serious trouble."

"Thank you," Malcolm said. The colonel said nothing.

The lieutenant detailed a man to take him back through the ranks of constables and on the edge of the plaza the man released him. Malcolm sighed, realizing that he had somehow escaped. The forged papers still held up. Well, they had been done by an expert many years ago, just after his surgery, and he had been sure that they would pass. The possession of the amber was another matter and the colonel was too tired of the whole mess apparently to pursue that. He felt a vague unease at how easily he had escaped but he turned and retraced his earlier steps. He still had to see Nordling. Without the money from the order Bobby had brought, he thought fearfully, he would be unable to meet his weekly payments to the barracudas.

It was over a mile to Nordling's house, a decaying brick shack that opened on a street whose walks were piled high with festering garbage. He climbed the splintered steps that popped and creaked under his weight. They had long ago lost any trace of the paint that once protected them and each step Malcolm took caused a cloud of dust and wood powder to puff from the joints of the steps. He tapped the coded tap and saw Nordling's withered hand pull aside a rain-streaked piece of canvas to look out. When Nordling recognized him, he pulled the door half open and spoke. "Inside, inside, don't camp out there. You know how dangerous the streets are."

He led Malcolm through a dank-smelling hall, half denuded of plaster. The walls canted at a distinct angle as though part of the foundation had collapsed. At the head of the basement stairs, Nordling paused and shivered. "I had three young'uns break in last night. Thank God, the locks on the basement are good."

"I need five caps," Malcolm said impatiently.

"I just let you have five a week ago," Nordling whined. "What happened to them?" Malcolm told him. Nordling led the way down the stairs to the basement. He adjusted a mantle light and Malcolm looked around. The place was webbed with cobwebs except for the area where Nordling had set up the apparatus. Malcolm noted the arrangement of glassware—the molecular still, with its rusty vacuum pump; the Soxhlet extractor near at hand, its flask filled with bubbling green-stained ether; the three-necked reactor that produced the final amber material that went into the molecular still. This last step was necessary since secondary contaminants from the reaction canceled the effectiveness of the primary toxin.

"I've got to have the caps," Malcolm insisted.

"Well, if it was anybody but you . . ." Nordling sniffed. "The danger of getting the materials, not to mention the cost . . ."

"You've always gotten your money," Malcolm said. "Besides, who set you up in the business to start with?"

"You had your reasons," Nordling said. "Only what if the constables ever—"

"The worst they would do would be to put you in the Kraals and you've been expecting that for years."

"Would too, if it wasn't for the special formula," Nordling said.

"Well, that's payment enough," Malcolm said.

"Sometimes I wish the hell I'd never met you," Nordling said.

"You'd have been in the Kraals long ago if you hadn't," Malcolm said.

Nordling sorted through the contents of a drawer in the rickety table under the still. "Here," he said. "I've got just five. You'll take all I've got and I bet you didn't bring any money."

Malcolm took the five amber capsules. "You'll get your money," he said. Nordling smiled sourly. "I'll see you to the door," he said.

They ascended the steps from the basement to the hall. Malcolm pushed open the door and stopped. Before he could pull back, the door flew against the wall and a large hand grabbed at him. Behind him, Nordling cried out a high, womanish cry. The hall was filled with constables and the hand that grabbed at Malcolm belonged to the sergeant who had seized him earlier in the day. Felice was with them, screaming, "See, see, I told you he was the one. I followed him. He's the one."

Behind the sergeant, the lieutenant grinned knowingly. "We thought you'd lead us to the supplier," the lieutenant said. "Like a damn fool, you came right to him."

They took them back to the aluminum-and-glass headquarters of the Company, past the torn and blasted plaza where scavengers were still gathering the wounded and the dead. In the subbasements where prisoners were held and interrogated they made both of them strip to their shorts and they were separated. Malcolm found himself imprisoned in a narrow cell with white poured-concrete walls. It was without windows and a merciless white fluorescent light beat down on him, prying its way under his eyes when he lay on the cot suspended from the wall and tried to sleep.

He lost track of time. He might have been there hours or days. He knew only that he was cold and that the single fragile coverlet was insufficient to stop his shivering. Part of the shivering, of course, was reaction. He felt a dull dread oppressing his mind and he knew that it was only a matter of time before they would come for him. He had heard the stories of Company interrogations. In a world where physical damage to the body was repaired in minutes, there was no particular moral onus to torture and the Company had, he heard, developed some very refined ways of handling those from whom it would extract information.

He hoped that they would consider him small fry. Nordling was quite another matter and he imagined that they would expend their best efforts on him. Nordling was not a strong man. It was, therefore, inevitable that he would compromise Malcolm. When they came finally for him, Malcolm supposed that they would have the whole story. They could not afford to release him and he was sure that the Kraals were not for him.

He thought of the alternatives and realized that only his death would satisfy them. So be it. In this terrible world of which he was a part, in which he had played too much of a formative role, it was just as well. He knew now at long last that he would welcome the end of consciousness. Indeed, he should have chosen that way long ago. Now that they had the amber secreted in his boot and he was unable to get to the one in his and Britt's apartment, he was wholly dependent on them. They would give him what he wanted.

He was dozing uneasily when they finally came for him.

The lieutenant and the sergeant lifted him from the bunk and dragged him unprotesting along the sterile corridors to a large room. The colonel sat at a table at one end of the room looking stern and just. They threw him to the floor before the colonel and he raised himself and looked around. When he saw what was affixed to the wall, he retched, shuddering in fear and horror.

It was Nordling, of course. They had been very imaginative with him. Since any physical damage to a man who had received the Heinholtz treatment was quickly repaired, they had found a unique solution.

They had flayed Nordling alive.

They had carefully incised the flesh of his arms and thighs and abdomen and pinned the flesh back with heavy pins to the wall so that the flesh could not close with the tissue underneath. Nordling was pinned like an insect to a drying board, the raw tissue and musculature of his body red and oozing. He lived still and would continue to live but his flesh must be a burning agony.

"Why don't you kill him?" Malcolm demanded.

"No," the colonel said. "We will release him in due course and he will heal."

"Why, why?" Malcolm said.

"Because he had information. He was incapable of developing the process for the toxin in the ambers. No more than the others we have captured. We had to know where he learned the technique."

"Did the others tell you?" Malcolm challenged.

"No," the colonel admitted. "They did not know enough, but Nordling did. He has told us all we want to know."

Malcolm slumped in defeat. Finally he looked up and said, "Take me to the Director."

"The Director knows you are here," the colonel said. "He does not wish to see you. He has given us his orders."

Malcolm began to sob quietly. "To think," he said, "to think that I created all this."

"I don't understand why you should have decided to renounce your identity, to hide and live the way you have done."

"Don't you see the horror?" Malcolm said. "Can't you see why I would be ashamed, feel guilty?"

"You?" the colonel said. "Heinholtz? The man who gave us the treatment, on whose efforts the very existence of the Company is based?"

"There was a time when I wanted that recognition," Malcolm said, "and I couldn't get it."

"But guilt?" the colonel said. "That's a stupid word."

The most terrible invention of Western society, Malcolm thought, is guilt. No Easterner understands the term in the terrible, personal, God-related sense that a Westerner does. He remained afflicted with guilt.

Guilt for what he had done. Guilt for the pride in what he had done.

For in the center of world decay, the final destruction of all that was good and kind and gentle and beautiful in a world webbed with the cobwebs of neglect, what man cannot perversely glory in the knowledge that he had brought the proud race of man to this impasse?

The end objective of power is power. Orwell had said that. The end objective of destruction is destruction; the end objective of decay is decay. It was so simple, so obvious, so terribly real.

And he had brought it to pass. Innocently, naïvely, he had brought it to pass. He had moved among the tattered remnants of his culture and a part of him perversely gloried in what his ego had wrought. Surely, he thought, they will remember that I have passed this way.

Only he remained and remained and remained. He lived a dozen lives, watched the subtle intrusion of new mores, new needs in the culture that became fragmented between the naturally aging and the aging deathless beings he had created. He watched the ones too debilitated to care for themselves taken off to the Kraals, where they were sustained, washed, urinated, defecated, swabbed and allowed to live and live and live. He watched these and saw the terrible economic drain on the faltering society. Surely, it would be simpler to kill them or let them somehow die. Only power had bred power and the Company was a mindless thing that had tasted power and thirsted for power and would not let power go. There was no end, only the continuing pattern of desperate people paying for life and the Company existing, nurturing, faltering, watching the slow, inevitable decline simply because no one had the power or the inclination to cry "Halt."

In the end he began again to make the toxin. Later he taught others. Someone had to cry "Halt," he decided. Only by this time the cries of "Halt" were feeble and hardly effective.

There was only one way that the machine could run down and he saw that within his lifetime it would. After that, there was little left that even he, perverse and involuted as his emotional processes had become, could be proud of.

How to be proud of the slow destruction of a culture?

He recalled the character in a mid-twentieth-century novel—Priam Kurz, he thought—who in one scene broke a rare Han vase, proclaiming that the power of the destroyer was equal to the power of the creator. A wretched, twisted notion. Only, his secret mind whispered, perhaps it was true.

In his own unique way he continued to be a destroyer. Though one cannot truly be said to be a destroyer when what one destroys is destruction itself.

Only it was over now. They had twisted the last truth from Nordling in his agony and . . .

"I'm sorry, Malcolm," Nordling sobbed from his wall of pain. "I tried. I had to tell them."

"It doesn't matter,' Malcolm said tiredly. "What will you do now?"

THOMAS N. SCORTIA

"The Director has ordered that we take you to the Kraals," the colonel said.

"Very well," Malcolm said.

The lieutenant helped him to his feet. The sergeant handed him his clothing and he donned it slowly, painfully. He turned to look at Nordling. Mercifully, he had fainted. "Take him down from there," Malcolm said.

"In due time," the colonel said with no particular interest.

They left the subbasement, the lieutenant leading the way up the dank concrete corridors to the first floor. They took a side entrance and skirted the plaza. Its broad expanse was now mercifully free of the wounded and the dead, but the dirty black slick from the flame throwers stained the plaza and the turrets with the flame throwers were still manned.

At the edge of the plaza a single vehicle waited for them. The sergeant straddled the driver's mount, hand on tiller, and the lieutenant grabbed Malcolm by the loose cloth of his sleeve. "Come on, old man," the lieutenant said. "We've had about enough of you."

Malcolm shivered. After this only the Kraals, the endless imprisonment in a coffinlike cell with liquid nutriments pumping food and oxygen through his dreamless body. Total dreaded immobilization forevermore without even the salve of unconsciousness. He had sworn this would never happen to him, that the single amber he carried with him would give him the release from this nightmare. If only he could get to the one hidden in the apartment. It was the only way.

He whirled in the last second with all of the energy he could marshal from his aged body. His hand darted out and pulled the lieutenant's launcher from its holster. If the lieutenant had not been so careless he could not have done it. Malcolm fell back, the launcher raised. The projectile blew a hole in the sergeant's chest and he fell over the tiller, his body convulsing with the nervous discharge of healing. In ten minutes he would be whole and . . .

The lieutenant fell back, fear distorting his face. Malcolm

145

fired, and in the instant he fired, he suddenly knew why the lieutenant was so afraid. The projectile shattered his body and blood spurted from a dozen wounds as the man died. He was not a Policyholder, Malcolm saw. He had killed the man and he would not rise again.

Constables were yelling and running toward him. He had to get away. He pushed the convulsing body of the sergeant from the saddle and mounted. A projectile struck his shoulder, the explosion shattering it. Somehow he managed to start the motor and throw it on automatic as another projectile nearly tore off his leg. The carrier was roaring across the plaza now and heading into a side street. In the last instant one of the flame-thrower crews managed to get its turret turned in his direction and a great rolling ball of flame marched smokily down the street. It engulfed the carrier and Malcolm screamed in the searing agony. Somehow, miraculously, the carrier kept moving swiftly up the street.

The carrier ran for several blocks before it struck the pile of debris where an ancient stone-and-concrete curtain wall had slid from the face of its parent building. He was dimly, painfully aware of the carrier tipping wildly, of his body flying out and over the pile of debris. He struck the ground and his impact dislodged the pile of stone poised precariously over a deep trench. All light faded as he was buried under the rubble.

He lay for hours under the debris, hearing the sound of shouting men and the roar of searching lorries. Somehow, no one thought to investigate the pile of rubble. Several constables mounted the pile and looked about but no one thought to look underneath. He lay, burning, feeling the agony in his body as it slowly healed. It healed so much more slowly than ever before because the damage had been so widespread. After darkness fell and light between the interstices of the stone had faded, he knew that he was well again.

He tried to wiggle under the debris and heard the rattle of brick fragments striking the pavement. He must get back to Britt. They would be searching for him and he must get to the amber before they found him. He might escape with her, hide and start another synthetic existence, but he was too tired. He would rather escape by the only sure path available to him.

He tried again and heard the sliding sound of debris. Suddenly an arm was free and painfully he found purchase and pulled his torso free. Now he could move bricks and stone and mortar fragments with his horribly scarred hands. It took him another fifteen minutes of panting effort to free his legs, the right and the horribly twisted left. Charred clothing fell away from his body as he moved.

He stumbled down the alley. The flesh of his face was puckered and scales of dead skin fell away as he wiped his hands across his eyes. Somehow he identified the intersection leading to the apartment and turned, falling back against a wall as a patrol of two constables passed.

He moved painfully toward the alleyway and stood finally before his door, praying that Britt was not home. He didn't want her to see him this way. He keyed the door and stepped over the sill, pushing the heavy drapes aside. Then he leaned back against the wall and sighed. She wasn't there. He stumbled across the room and pawed through the clothing in the bottom drawer of his bureau. The small plastic box with its single amber capsule was there where he had left it, tucked deep into the sleeve of a shirt.

He whirled as the door opened behind him. She came in as he feverishly pried open the box and picked at the capsule in its bed of cotton. His fingers were puckering with new scar tissue and in his clumsiness he dropped the capsule. It fell to the carpet as Britt pushed through the canvas curtains and saw him.

"Oh, Mal," she cried and ran across the room to him. He was struggling with his hand but the muscles would not obey. Finally he managed to pick up the capsule with his other hand.

"No, don't," she yelled, and before he could move, she was beside him, prying open his fingers. The capsule dropped into her small hand. "No, not that way," she cried. "I know what happened. We can get away, buy new papers. They'll never find you."

She rose and ran across the room to the curtained commode. Before he could stop her the amber disappeared in a vortex of water.

She was back beside him now, her hands caressing his body, pulling his remaining clothing from him. "I love you," she sobbed. "I love you."

She pulled him to the bed, heedless of the litter of costumes sprawled across it. She was in his arms, kissing his body, caressing him. His eyes saw the gauze and the sea things littering the bed and the monstrous sea-creature mask at one corner.

They were making love then as his inner voice insanely chanted the lines from *Prufrock:*

We have lingered in the chambers of the sea
By sea-girls wreathed with seaweed red and brown
Till human voices wake us and we drown.

The only human voice in the room was hers, muttering with building passion as she kissed his shattered limbs, his hideously scarred face, the terrible warped substance that was his flesh.

"You're so beautiful," she sobbed. "Oh, Mal, Mal, you're so very, very beautiful."

And in the throes of sadness and lust, he wept and kept on weeping throughout it all.

Death of a City
FRANK HERBERT

It was such a beautiful city, Bjska thought. An observer's eyes could not avoid the overwhelming beauty. As the City Doctor called to treat the city, Bjska found the beauty heartbreaking. He found his thoughts drawn again and again to the individuals who called this place *home,* two hundred and forty-one thousand humans who now faced the prospect of homeless lives.

Bjska stared across open water at the city from the wooded peninsula that protected the inner harbor. The low light of late afternoon cast a ruddy glow on the scene. His eyes probed for flaws, but from this distance not even the tastefully applied patches could be seen.

Why was I chosen for this? he asked himself. Then: *If the damn fools had only built an ugly city!*

Immediately, he rejected this thought. It made as much sense as to ask why Mieri, the intern who stood near the ornithopter behind him, personified such feminine beauty. Such things happened. It was the task of a City Doctor to recognize inescapable facts and put them in their proper context.

Bjska continued to study the city, striving for the objective/subjective synthesis that his calling demanded. The city's builders had grafted their ideas onto the hills below the mountains with such a profound emotional sense of harmony that no trick of the eye could reject their creation. Against a backdrop of snow peaks and forests, the builders had rightly said: "The vertical threatens a man; it puts danger above him. A man cannot relax and achieve human balance in a vertical setting."

Thus, they had built a city whose very *rightness* might condemn it. Had they even suspected what they had created? Bjska thought it unlikely.

How could the builders have missed it? he asked himself.

Even as the question appeared in his mind, he put it down. It served no purpose for him to cry out against the circumstances that said *he* must make this decision. The City Doctor was here on behalf of the species, a representative of all humans together. He must act for *them*.

The city presented an appearance of awesome solidity that Bjska knew to be false. It could be destroyed quite easily. He had but to give the order, certifying his decision with his official seal. People would rage against fate, but they would obey. Families would be broken and scattered. The name of this place would be erased from all but the City Doctors' records. The natural landscape would be restored and there would remain no visible sign that a city such as this one had stood here. In time, only the builders of cities would remember this place, and that as a warning.

Behind him, Mieri cleared her throat. She would speak out soon, Bjska realized. She had been patient, but they were past the boundaries of patience. He resisted an impulse to turn and feast his eyes upon her beauty as a change from the cityscape. That was the problem: There would be so little change in trading one prospect of beauty for another.

While Mieri fidgeted, he continued to delay. Was there no alternative? Mieri had left her own pleadings unvoiced, but Bjska had heard them in every word she uttered. This was Mieri's own city. She had been born here—beauty born in beauty. Where was the medical *point of entry* in this city?

Bjska allowed his frustration to escape in a sigh.

The city played its horizontal lines across the hills with an architecture that opened outward, that expanded, that condemned no human within its limits to a containerized existence. The choice of where every element should stand had been made with masterful awareness of the human psyche. Where things that grew without man's interference should grow, there they were. Where structures would amplify existing forms, there stood the required structures . . . precisely! Every expectation of the human senses had been met. And it was in this very conformity to human demands that the cancerous flaw arose.

Bjska shook his head sadly. *If conformity were the definition of artistic survival . . .*

As he had anticipated, Mieri moved closer behind him, said, "Sometimes when I see it from out here I think my city is too beautiful. Words choke in my throat. I long for words to describe it and there are none." Her voice rang with musical softness in the quiet evening air.

Bjska thought: *My city!* She had said it and not heard herself saying it. A City Doctor could have no city.

He said, "Many have tried and failed. Even photographs fall short of the reality. A supreme holopaint artist might capture it, but only for a fleeting moment."

"I wish every human in the universe could see my city," Mieri said.

"I do not share that wish," Bjska said. And he wondered if this bald statement was enough to shock her into the required state of awareness. She wanted to be a City Doctor? Let her stretch into the inner world as well as the outer.

He sensed her weighing his words. Beauty could play such a vitalizing role in human life that the intellect tended to overlook its devitalizing possibilities. If beauty could not be ignored, was that not indiscreet? The fault was blatancy. There was something demandingly immodest about the way this city gilded its hills, adding dimension to the peaks behind it. One saw the city and did *not* see it.

Mieri knew this! Bjska told himself. She knew it as she knew that Bjska loved her. Why not? Most men who saw her loved her and desired her. Why had she no lovers then? And why had *her* city no immigrants? Had she ever put both of these questions to herself, setting them in tension against each other?

It was the sort of thing a City Doctor must do. The species knew the source of its creative energy. The Second Law made the source plain.

He said, "Mieri, why does a City Doctor have such awesome powers? I can have the memories of whole populations obliterated, selectively erased, or have individuals thus treated. I can even cause death. You aspire to such powers. Why do we have them?"

She said, "To make sure that the species faces up to Infinity."

He shook his head sadly. A rote answer! She gave him a rote answer when he demanded personal insight!

The awareness that had made Bjska a City Doctor pervaded him. Knowledge out of his most ancient past told him the builders of this city had succeeded too well. Call it *chance* or *fate*. It was akin to the genetic *moment* that had produced Mieri's compelling beauty—the red-gold hair, the green eyes, the female proportions applied with such exactitude that a male might feast his senses, but never invest his flesh. There existed a creative peak that alarmed the flesh. Bjska stood securely in his own stolid, round-faced ugliness, knowing this thing. Mieri must find that inner warmth that spoke with chemical insistence of latent wrinkles and aging.

What would Mieri do if her city died before its time?

If she was ever to be a City Doctor, she must be made to understand this lesson of the flesh *and* the spirit.

He said, "Do you imagine there's a city more beautiful in the entire world?"

She thought she heard bantering in his voice and wondered: *Is he teasing?* It was a shocking thought. City Doctors might joke to keep their own sanity in balance, but at such a time as this . . . with so much at stake . . .

"There must be a city more beautiful somewhere," she said.

"Where?"

She took a deep breath to put down profound disquiet. "Are you making fun of my city?" she demanded. "How can you? It's a sick city and you know it!" She felt her lips quiver, moisture at the corners of her eyes. She experienced both fear and shame. She loved her city, but it was sick. The outbreaks of vandalism, the lack of creativity here, the departure of the best people, the blind violence from random elements of its citizenry when they moved to other settings. All had been traced back here. The sickness had its focus in her city. That was why a City Doctor had come. She had worked hard to have that doctor be Bjska, her old teacher, and more than the honor of working with him once more had been involved. She had felt a personal need.

"I'm sorry," Bjska said. "This is the city where you were born and I understand your concern. I am the teacher now. I wish to share my thought processes with you. What is it we must do most carefully as we diagnose?"

She looked across the water at the city, feeling the coolness of onrushing nightfall, seeing the lights begin to wink on, the softness of low structures and blended greenery, the pastel colors and harmony. Her senses demanded more than this, however. You did not diagnose a city just by its appearance. Why had Bjska brought her here? The condition of a city's inhabitants represented a major concern. Transient individuals, always tenants on the land, were the single moving cells. Only the species owned land, owned cities. A City Doctor was hired by the species. In effect, he diagnosed the species. They told him the imprint of the setting. It had been a gigantic step toward Infinity when the species had recognized that settings might contribute to its illnesses.

"Are you diagnosing me to diagnose the city?" she asked.

"I diagnose my own reactions," he said. "I find myself loving your city with a fierce protectiveness that at the same time repels me and insists that I scar this place. Having seen this city, I will try to find pieces of it in every other city, but I will not know what I seek because I have not really experienced this city. Every other city will be found wanting and I will not know what it wants."

Mieri felt suddenly threatened and wondered: *What is he trying to tell me?* There was threat in Bjska's words. It was as though he had been transformed abruptly into a dirty old man who demanded obscene things of her, who affronted her. He was dangerous! Her city was too good for him! He was a square, ugly little man who offended her city whenever he entered it.

Even as these reactions pulsed through her awareness, she sensed her training taking its dominant place. She had been educated to become a City Doctor. The species relied on her. Humans had given her a matrix by which to keep them on the track through Infinity.

"This is the most beautiful city man has ever conceived," she whispered, and she felt the betrayal in every word coming from her lips. Surely there were more beautiful places in their world? Surely there were!

"If it were only that," Bjska said. "If it were only the conception of beauty in itself."

She nodded to herself, the awareness unfolding. The Second Law told humans that absolutes were lethal. They provided no potential, no *differences in tension* that the species could employ as energy sources. Change and growth represented necessities for things that lived. A species lived. Humans dared conceive of beauty only in the presence of change. Humans prevented wars, but not *absolutely*. Humans defined crimes and judgments, but only in that fluid context of change.

"I love the city," she said.

No longer *my* city, Bjska thought. Good. He said, "It's right to love the place where you were born. That's the way it is with humans. I love a little community on a muddy river, a place called Eeltown. Sometimes when the filters aren't working properly, it smells of pulpwood and the digesters. The river is muddy because we farm its watershed for trees. Recapturing all of that muddy silt and replacing it on the hill terraces is hard work and costly in human energy, but it gives human beings places where they fit into the order that we share with the rest of our world. We have points of entry. We have things we can change. Someday, we'll even change the way we exchange the silt energy. There's an essential relationship between change and exchange that we have learned to appreciate and use."

Mieri felt like crying. She had spent fifteen years in the single-minded pursuit of her profession and all for what purpose? She said, "Other cities have been cured of worse than this."

Bjska stared meditatively at the darkening city. The sun had moved onto the horizon while he and Mieri talked. Now, its light painted orange streamers on the clouds in the west. There would be good weather on the morrow, provided the old mariners' saying was correct. The city had become a maze of lights in a bowl of darkness, with the snow peaks behind it reflecting the sunset. Even in this transition moment, the place blended with its environment in such a way that the human resisted any disturbance, even with his own words. Silence choked him—dangerous silence.

Mieri felt a breaking tension within her, a product of her training and not of her city. The city had been her flesh, but was no longer.

"Humans have always been restless animals," Bjska said. "A good thing, too. We both know what's wrong here. There's such a thing as too much comfort, too much beauty. Life requires the continuing struggle. That may be the only basic law in the *living* universe."

Again, she sensed personal threat in his words. Bjska had become a dark shadow against the city's lights. *Too much beauty!* That spoke of the context in which the beauty existed, against which the beauty stood out. It was not the beauty itself, but the lack of tensions in this context. She said, "Don't offer me any false hopes."

"I offer you no hopes at all," he said. "That's not the function of a City Doctor. We just make sure the generative tensions continue. If there are walls, we break them down. But walls happen. To try to prevent them can lead us into absolutes. How long have outsiders learned to love your city only to hate it?"

She tried to swallow in a throat suddenly dry.

"How long?" he insisted.

She forced herself to answer. "At first, when I saw hate, I asked why, but people denied it."

"Of course they did!"

"I doubted my own senses at times," she said. "Then I noted that the most talented among us moved away. Always, it was for good reasons. It was so noticeable, though, that our Council Chairman said it was cause for celebration when I returned here for my internship. I hadn't the heart to tell him it wasn't my doing, that you had sent me."

"How did they react when you told them I was coming?"

She cleared her throat. "You understand I had made some suggestions for *adjustments* within the city, changes in flow patterns and such."

"Which were not taken seriously," he said.

"No. They wonder at my discontent." She stared across at the lights. It was full dark now. Night birds hummed after insects above them. "The hate has been going on for many years. I know that's why you sent me here."

"We need all of the City Doctors we can generate," he said. "We need you."

She recognized the "we" in his statement with mounting terror. That was the species talking through a City Doctor whose powers had been tempered in action. The individual could be transformed or shattered by that "we."

"The Councilmen only wanted to be comforted," she protested, but a voice within her pleaded: *Comfort me, comfort me, comfort me.* She knew Bjska heard that other voice.

"How naive of them," he said, "to want to be told that truth is untruth, that what the senses report must not be believed." He inhaled a deep breath. "Truth changes so rapidly that it's dangerous to look only in one direction. This is an infinite universe."

Mieri heard her teeth chattering, tried to still them. Fear drove her now and not the sudden cold of nightfall. She felt a trembling all through her body. Something Bjska had once said came back to her now: *"It requires a certain kind of aban-*

doned courage even to want to be a City Doctor."

Do I have that courage? she asked herself. *Humanity help me! Will I fail now?*

Bjska, turning to face her in the darkness, detected a faint odor of burning. Someone from the city had a forbidden fire somewhere along the beaches. The tension of protest rode on that odor and he wondered if that tension carried the kind of hope that could be converted into life. Mieri no longer was visible in the darkness. Night covered the perfection of her beauty and the clothing that was like armor in its subtle harmonizing with her flesh. Could she ask *how* rather than *why?* Would she make the required transition?

He waited, tense and listening.

"Some of them will always hate," she whispered.

She knows, he thought. He said, "The sickness of a city reaches far beyond its boundaries."

Mieri clenched her fists, trembling. *"The arm is not sick without the body being sick."* Bjska had said that once. And: *"A single human unloved can set the universe afire."*

"Life is in the business of constructing dichotomies," she told herself. "And all dichotomies lead to contradictions. Logic that is sound for a finite system is not necessarily sound for an infinite system."

The words from the City Doctors' creed restored a measure of her calm. She said, "It'll take more than a few adjustments."

"It's like a backfire with which our ancestors stopped a runaway grass fire," he said. "You give them a bad case of discontent. No comfort whatsoever except that you love the human in each of them. Some contradictions *do* lead to ugliness."

He heard her moving in the darkness. Cloth ripped. Again. He wondered: *Which of the infinite alternatives has she chosen?* Would she scar the brittle armor of her beauty?

"I will begin by relocating the most contented half of the city's population," she said.

I will . . . he thought. It was always thus the City Doctor began his creation.

157

"There's no profit in adjusting their memories," she said. "They're more valuable just as they are. Their present content will be the measure of their future energies."

Again, he heard her clothing rip. What was she doing?

She said, "I will, of course, move in with you during this period and present at least the appearance of being your mistress. They will hate that."

He sensed the energy she had required to overcome personal barriers and he willed himself to remain silent. She must win this on her own, decide on her own.

"If you love me, it will be more than appearance," she said. "We have no guarantee that we will create only beauty, but if we create with love and if our creation generates new life, then we can love . . . and we will go on living."

He felt the warmth of her breath on his face. She had moved closer without his hearing! He willed himself to remain immobile.

"If the people of the city must hate, and some of them always will," she said, "better they hate us than one another."

He felt a bare arm go around his neck; her lips found his cheek. "I will save *our* city," she said, "and I don't believe you will hate me for it."

Bjska relaxed, enfolded her unarmored flesh in his arms. He said, "We begin with unquestioning love for each other. That is a very good prescription, Doctor, my love, as long as there remains sufficient energy to support the next generation. Beauty be damned! Life requires a point of entry."

GEORGE ZEBROWSKI

Assassins of Air
GEORGE ZEBROWSKI

Gloom concealed the city, an obscurity born of dying night and pollutants hanging motionless in the air, a massive shadowy stillness pressing down on the pavement, billions of particles ready to swirl through the stone alleys with the morning wind. Praeger squatted by the iron fence in the alleyway, waiting for Uruba and Blue Chip to come back. He looked at his watch and saw it was one hour to dawn, and he would have to leave if they didn't return before then.

Suddenly he heard them creep into the alley. They knew where he was and came to squat near him by the fence.

"How many, Chris?" Uruba asked.

"Twenty real old ones," Christian Praeger said.

"Hey, kid, Uruba and me broke off forty-one pieces of chrome," Blue Chip said.

"Don't knock him," Uruba said, "Chris here is only nineteen, just startin' out. One fine day he'll run his own recycling gang, when we's all rich. He'll feed the junkman all the old cars on the East Coast, kill them all, help make the air cool and clean again." Uruba coughed. "Got it stashed all ready to be picked?"

Praeger nodded. It was almost light enough in the alley for him to see Uruba's black face and the gray scar on his cheek.

"I'll slap the bread on you tomorrow, Chris," Uruba said. He clapped Praeger on the shoulder and started to get up.

"I need it now," Praeger mumbled. "I have to pay for my PLATO lessons. I gotta have it, honest."

Uruba was standing looking down at him now, and Blue Chip stood up next to him. "I have to," Praeger said as he stood up with them.

Uruba hesitated, almost as if the request had been a personal insult. Then he smiled. "Sure, kid, how much?"

"Twenty-five," Praeger said.

The smile disappeared, but he counted out the money. "This one time, kid. Next time you wait like all the other dudes. I pay off, my word is good, right?"

Praeger nodded meekly. He folded the bills into his jeans pocket, trying not to look at their faces. But Uruba and Blue Chip turned from him and walked out of the alley, and he was relieved by the fact that he would not see them for at least two weeks.

He looked at his watch. It would be completely light in less than a half hour. He sprinted out of the alley and up the gray-lighted street toward the subway at 145th Street. He started coughing and slowed his pace to a walk to cut down his need for air.

PLATO the sign read: PROGRAMMING LOGIC FOR AUTOMATIC TEACHING OPERATIONS. Once the facility had been free, just like chest X rays. Now students had to pay to milk the machine, twenty dollars a rap; but it was a good teach if you wanted to learn a skill.

Praeger went up the wide steps leading into the library and paid his money at the ticket booth. An usher showed him to his usual booth in the big research hall.

The program was teaching him the workings of the city air-filtration system, which was fully operational in Manhattan and slowly expanding. He knew that many technical dudes would be needed to service and maintain it, and he was going to be in on it after he finished clouting cars. The old cars were paying for his lessons, but next year, or the one after, they would be gone—leaving only the safety-cars, public wheels and the electric push to rush people around.

The new electric cars weren't bad, but there was something

in the older people that loved the rush of power. So the old vehicles were slow in going, especially with all the bootleg mechanics servicing them against the law to keep them legal. The old wheels were assassinating the atmosphere, Uruba said. We kill them, recycle the people's resources and make some bread on the deal too. Uruba was right, Praeger thought; he would not have his PLATO lessons without that money. Only Uruba did a lot of other things in the city, like running a supply of young girls to the insular estates outside. Uruba did not care about being right. It was a coincidence, sometimes.

Praeger put on his earphones. The first exam question appeared on the screen and he answered it correctly.

When he came out of the library at two in the afternoon, he saw the old '74 station wagon growling down Fifth Avenue spewing blue smoke from its tail pipe. It was a contrast to the bulky crashproof Wankels, steamers and slow electrics moving on the street with it. He watched it stop and park near the corner of 42nd Street. The car was only ten years old, so its owner could still get away with it by claiming that it hadn't fallen apart. He could keep running it legally until it did, but even with its filters it was a polluter. Maybe the owner wasn't even having it fixed on the side, Praeger thought; maybe it still ran well. As he stood at the top of the stairs, he hated the dirty wheels, hated them as he would a fearful beast that had some-how gotten loose in the world of men.

He waited until the owner left the car, then went to where it was parked and lifted the hood, took out his pocket tool and began removing the spark plugs. That done, he cut a few wires with his pocketknife. He closed the hood quickly and walked away from the car. No one had noticed him. Later tonight someone would strip it down for all of its valuables, Uruba or one of the other gangs. Another one of the old killers was effectively dead. He thought of his dead parents as he slipped the spark plugs into the sewer drain at the corner.

Praeger stood on the roof of his apartment building looking

up at the stars hiding on the other side of the air; still, the brighter ones were clearly visible, drawing him away from the earth to the brightly lit space stations circling the planet and out to the diamondlike moon domes where men seemed to be doing something worthwhile. He saw Uruba and Blue Chip living in the shadows of the universe, profiting from changes that would happen without them. He thought of the White Assassins, Savage Skulls, Black Warlocks and Conservative Angels—all the night rulers of New York City. He thought of their words, political phrases copied after the Black Lords and Young Panthers, the largest national groups. He thought of his PLATO lessons, which would liberate him from his open-air-intake apartment, take him away from the memory of his parents and public schooling, give him something to do in which he could take pride.

He was going to do something else, and soon. In two weeks, he estimated, he would be ready to take the computer tests for a technical rating. He would have to tell Uruba and Blue Chip that he wanted out, but he wasn't sure how he would say it to them.

He turned around and went down the stairs to his apartment.

Uruba squinted at him in the dim light of the basement room. Blue Chip had gone to get a bulb for the shaded light hanging darkly over the old card table where they were sitting.

"You cost me money, man. Why you going to quit?"

Blue Chip came back with a bulb and screwed it into the socket. The lamp swung back and forth for a moment and stopped when Uruba pulled the switch cord. Yellow light filled the dusty cellar room.

"Yellow's all I could find," Blue Chip said.

Praeger looked at Uruba. His black face looked strange in the light. Uruba smiled at him grotesquely, showing him his one gold tooth.

"Chris here wants out," Uruba said. "What do you think, Blue Chip?"

Blue Chip giggled nervously and leaned his chair back on its hind legs.

"I know," Blue Chip said, "he's been going to school on the sly to them PLATO lessons."

Uruba grinned. "You tryin' to be better than us, is that right?" he asked. And he left a big silence for Praeger to drown in.

Finally he answered. "I just want other kinds of things, that's all," he said.

"The honko always goes back," Blue Chip said. "How much have you stashed?"

"Where you going, Chris, to the moon resorts with all the rich cats?" asked Uruba. "Where's all your bread? Have you been cheating on us?"

"I just want a tech rating to work in the new air plants. The money's good," Praeger said.

Uruba leaned forward and knocked the card table into the air, breaking the yellow light. "What the rest of us going to breathe?" he asked in the darkness. "Who you think can move into those air-control apartments? Chris, you're a fool, a blazing monkey!"

"Things may get better," Praeger managed to say.

"Like hell," Blue Chip announced from a dark corner of the room. The only light in the room now came in through the small window near the door.

Praeger went to the door quickly, opened it and ran up the old steps to the street. He was out of breath when he reached the sidewalk. He stopped, and from below he heard the sound of Uruba's laughter, mocking his fear.

It stopped. Then Uruba screamed after him from below the pavement. "Chris, I helped you, I got you started, I taught you, boy—and this is what I get? I'm gonna get you, man. You better hide your money, you hear!" The voice died away, and Praeger stood perfectly still in front of the old brownstone. Then he was shaking and his body was covered with sweat. He looked up at the sky, at all the old buildings in this sealed-off part of old Harlem. He looked downtown where the lighted construction on New York's second level looked like a huge diamond-studded spider devouring the city in the night. Slowly, he began walking home.

Eyes watched him when he went to his PLATO lessons and when he came home. On Tuesdays and Thursdays when he stayed home he felt them on the windows of his fifth-floor apartment on 10th Street, and he was afraid to go near them; but when he tried to see if anyone was following him, he could find no one.

In the middle of the night on a Monday a crash of glass woke him in bed. He got up and went into the living room, turning on the light. He saw a large rock lying on the floor. Praeger checked the front-door police lock. It was still firm. Then he got some cardboard and tape from the kitchen and began taping up the broken window.

As he worked he told himself that he understood all this. Uruba wanted one thing: to rend and tear and hurt him. He was an easy target, easier to hurt than the cops in their air-conditioned tank cars, easier to destroy than a car. And to hurt him meant more than money, that's how Uruba was thinking. Praeger was a deserter, and Uruba could not accept that. For Blue Chip it was recreation to hound him, and Blue Chip thought Praeger was hiding money.

He had just put a final piece of tape on the window when two shots came through the cardboard. Praeger fell to the floor and lay still. He lay there for an hour, afraid to move. Finally he crawled behind the sofa, where he fell into a nervous sleep just before morning.

He was going to have to leave town. Uruba was crazy and it would get worse. His exams and PLATO would have to wait.

He packed a knapsack and went down into the basement, where he kept his old motorcycle. He wheeled it out into the yard, which was connected to the street by a concrete ramp. He looked at his watch. The glowing numbers told him it was an hour to dawn.

He started the bike with a downward lurch of his foot and rolled out the ramp slowly. He turned into the street and started in the direction of Riverside Drive. The streets were deserted at this hour.

After a few minutes he noticed the lights of the car behind him. He gunned the bike and shot up the entrance to Riverside and out onto the highway. Traffic was light and he continued accelerating.

A few minutes later the car was still behind him and gaining. To his left the river was covered by a fog, but the lights on the Jersey shore were coming through. Praeger gunned his engine and the bike carried him forward, past two Wankel safety-tanks moving slowly to their destination. He looked at his speedometer and saw that he was doing 115. He knew that the new-looking car behind him could catch him, but he had a head start. He thought, I have a right to try to better myself, go to school. The money came from Uruba's world, he knew that, but there was no other way. Food was given out free, just enough, but more than that could be bought only with skills. You could go to school if you paid for it, but you could live without it. It was a luxury for those who had a hunger for it. Uruba hated him for wanting it.

As he rushed through the night, Praeger felt tears in his eyes blurring the highway and the sight of the river with its lights on the far shore. The air was damp on his face, and the road was an unyielding hardness under the bike's rubber wheels.

The car was still in his mirror, its lights on bright to annoy him. It was winding its way past the occasional electrics and steamers on the road, coming closer. He pushed forward on the black road, trying to move beyond the light beams on his back.

The car disappeared from his mirror. Praeger accelerated, eager to press his momentary advantage. He had the road to himself for the next few minutes. Then the road curved upward and to the right, and he was rushing over the small bridge into the Bronx. He saw the car in his mirror again when he took the Grand Concourse entrance, and it kept pace with him along the entire six miles of the wide avenue. Ten minutes later he was on the edges of the old city, fleeing upstate.

Here he was among the dying trees northwest of New York, dark outlines against the night sky, thousands of acres of lifeless woodland, a buckled carpet of hills and gullies. He had taken the old two-way asphalt roadway in the hope of losing Uruba's shiny antique.

Praeger felt a strange sensation on the back of his neck when he saw the car in his mirror again. It wasn't Uruba following him in the car, hating him; it was the car, fixing him with its burning eyes, ready to come forward and crush him under its wheels. The car was trying to hold him back, getting even for all of its kind he had killed with Uruba. It was trying to stop him from escaping to another kind of life, just as it had stopped his parents. The car hated the soft creatures living in the world with it, hated the parasites who were slowly taking away its weapons, taming it, making it an unpoisonous and powerless domestic vehicle.

Around him in the night stood the naked trees, the stripped victims of the car's excretions. He listened to the thick drone of the motorcycle engine. He was riding a powered insect that was brother to the wheeled beast pursuing it, jaw open to swallow. The moon brushed out from behind the thinning clouds on his left, riding low over the trees, its white light frighteningly pale.

He went around a wide curve in the road, holding closely to the right shoulder, momentarily escaping the car's lights. He came out into a short straightaway and suddenly the road curved again, and the car was still out of sight behind him.

He gunned the engine to the limit, hoping to stay ahead for good.

Suddenly his headlight failed, leaving him to rush forward alone in the darkness. The moon slid behind some clouds. There was some kind of small bridge ahead. He had glimpsed it in the moonlight; now he could barely see its latticework against the sky. In a moment he knew what he was going to do. He braked the cycle and jumped at the last moment.

He hit the road shoulder and rolled to a stop. The bike rushed over the bridge to the other side and into some trees, where it stopped with a crunch.

Praeger saw that he was lying near an old roadblock horse that had a detour sign nailed to it. He got up and dragged it to block the road to the bridge and to direct traffic to the right, directly onto the slope that ran down to the river.

He sprinted into the deadwood forest and hid behind a tree. In a moment he heard Uruba's wheels screeching in the turns. The headlights came around the bend, ghostly rays cutting through the darkness. There was no time for the car to do anything but follow the detour arrow. He heard the brakes go on but it was too late. The left headlight shattered against the roadblock and the car flew over the edge, turning over on its front end when it hit bottom and landing in the river top down.

It burst into a fireball and burned in its own bleedings, which set the river on fire, the dark-flowing river filled with sludge and acid and slaughterhouse blood, flammable chemicals and the vitals of all earth's creatures. The fire spread quickly under the bridge, and the old wooden structure started to catch fire.

Praeger left his hiding place and ran across the bridge, hoping to find his cycle in working order. The stench from the river was enough to make him gasp as he went across. From the other side he looked down at the burning hulk, a dark beast engulfed by flames, and the river, which would burn up- and downstream until the fire reached areas free of flammable materials.

Praeger sat down on the far bank and watched the burning. It wasn't Uruba who was dying, not just Uruba or Blue Chip. It was a creature dying there in the dirty waters—the same waters that a few years ago had threatened the East with a new pollution-fed microorganismal plague. For a few months it had looked as if a new killer, much like bubonic plague, would be loosed on the land; fortunately by that time many rivers could be burned, or easily helped to catch fire, and the threat of epidemic had passed away in a cleansing flame.

Uruba had been a scavenger living off the just laws and man's efforts to reclaim nature for himself. Praeger felt as if he were coming out of a strange confusion, a living dream that had held him in its grasp. A slight wind blew the stifling fumes from the river toward him, making his eyes water, oppressing him with a sadness too settled for tears, even though they were present on his face.

Later the flames died to a flicker on the waters. The sky cleared in the east and the morning star came out, brilliant before the sun, still hiding below the horizon. As the sun came up, Praeger could see the towers of the city to the south, their glassy facets catching the sun's shout.

He got up and looked around at the stricken forest land in the morning light, patched here and there with new greenery struggling out of the ground and along tree branches. The bridge at his right was a cinder, still slowly collapsing into the river. He decided to make his way along the bank on foot until he found another bridge where he could cross to the other side and return to the city.

ROBERT SILVERBERG

Getting Across
ROBERT SILVERBERG

I

On the first day of summer my month-wife, Silena Ruiz, filched
our district's master program from the Ganfield Hold computer
center and disappeared with it. A guard at the Hold has confessed that she won admittance by seducing him, then gave him
a drug. Some say she is in Conning Town now; others have
heard rumors that she has been seen in Morton Court; still
others maintain her destination was The Mill. I suppose it does
not matter where she has gone. What matters is that we are
without our program. We have lived without it for eleven days
and things are starting to break down. The heat is abominable,
but we must switch every thermostat to manual override before
we can use our cooling system; I think we will boil in our
skins before the job is done. A malfunction of the scanners
that control our refuse compactor has stilled the garbage collectors, which will not go forth unless they have a place to dump
what they collect. Since no one knows the proper command
to give the compactor, rubbish accumulates, forming pestilen-
tial hills on every street, and dense swarms of flies or worse
hover over the sprawling mounds. Beginning on the fourth
day our police also began to go immobile—who can say why?
—and by now all of them stand halted in their tracks. Some
are already starting to rust, since the maintenance schedules
are out of phase. Word has gone out that we are without protection, and outlanders cross into the district with impunity,
molesting our women, stealing our children, raiding our stocks
of foodstuffs. In Ganfield Hold, platoons of weary, sweating

169

technicians toil constantly to replace the missing program, but it might be months, even years, before they will be able to devise a new one.

In theory, duplicate programs are stored in several places within the community against just such a calamity. In fact, we have none. The one kept in the district captain's office turned out to be some twenty years obsolete; the one in the care of the soul father's house had been devoured by rats; the program held in the vaults of the tax collectors appeared to be intact, but when it was placed in the input slot it mysteriously failed to activate the computers. So we are helpless: an entire district, hundreds of thousands of human beings, cut loose to drift on the tides of chance. Silena, Silena, Silena! To disable all of Ganfield, to make our already burdensome lives more difficult, to expose me to the hatred of my neighbors . . . Why, Silena? Why?

People glare at me on the streets. They hold me responsible, in a way, for all this. They point and mutter; in another few days they will be spitting and cursing; and if no relief comes soon, they may be throwing stones. Look, I want to shout, she was only my month-wife and she acted entirely on her own. I assure you I had no idea she would do such a thing. And yet they blame me. At the wealthy houses of Morton Court they will dine tonight on babies stolen in Ganfield this day, and I am held accountable.

What will I do? Where can I turn?

I may have to flee. The thought of crossing district lines chills me. Is it the peril of death I fear or only the loss of all that is familiar? Probaby both: I have no hunger for dying and no wish to leave Ganfield. Yet I will go, no matter how difficult it will be to find sanctuary if I get safely across the line. If they continue to hold me tainted by Silena's crime, I will have no choice. I think I would rather die at the hands of strangers than perish at those of my own people.

II

This sweltering night I find myself atop Ganfield Tower, seeking cool breezes and the shelter of darkness. Half the district has had the idea of escaping the heat by coming up here tonight, it seems; to get away from the angry eyes and tightened lips, I have climbed to the fifth parapet, where only the bold and the foolish ordinarily go. I am neither, yet here I am.

As I move slowly around the tower's rim, warily clinging to the old and eroded guardrail, I have a view of our entire district. Ganfield is like a shallow basin in form, gently sloping upward from the central spike that is the tower to a rise on the district perimeter. They say that a broad lake once occupied the site where Ganfield now stands; it was drained and covered over, centuries ago, when the need for new living space became extreme. Yesterday I heard that great pumps are used to keep the ancient lake from breaking through into our cellars, and that before very long the pumps will fail or shut themselves down for maintenance, and we will be flooded. Perhaps so. Ganfield once devoured the lake; will the lake now have Ganfield? Will we tumble into the dark waters and be swallowed, with no one to mourn us?

I look out over Ganfield. These tall brick boxes are our dwellings, twenty stories high but dwarfed from my vantage point far above. This sliver of land, black in the smoky moonlight, is our pitiful scrap of community park. These low flat-topped buildings are our shops, a helter-skelter cluster. This is our industrial zone, such that it is. That squat shadow-cloaked bulk just north of the tower is Ganfield Hold, where our crippled computers slip one by one into idleness. I have spent nearly my whole life within this one narrow swing of the compass that is Ganfield. When I was a boy and affairs were not nearly so harsh between one district and its neighbor, my father took me on holiday to Morton Court, and another time to The Mill. When I was a young man I was sent on business across three districts to Parley Close. I remember those journeys as clearly and vividly as though I had dreamed them. But everything is quite different now and it is twenty years since I last left Ganfield. I am not one of your privileged commuters, gaily making transit from zone to zone. All the world is one great city, so it is said, with the deserts settled and the rivers bridged and all the open places filled, a universal city that has abolished the old boundaries, and yet it is twenty years since I passed from one district to the next. I wonder: Are we one city, then, or merely thousands of contentious, fragmented, tiny states?

Look here, along the perimeter. There are no more boundaries, but what is this? This is our boundary, Ganfield Crescent, that wide, curving boulevard surrounding the district. Are you a man of some other zone? Then cross the Crescent at risk of life. Do you see our police machines, blunt-snouted, glossy, formidably powerful, strewn like boulders in the broad avenue? They will interrogate you, and if your answers are uneasy, they may destroy you. Of course they can do no one any harm tonight.

Look outward now, at our horde of brawling neighbors. I see beyond the Crescent to the east the gaunt spires of Conning Town, and on the west, descending stepwise into the jumbled valley, the shabby dark-walled buildings of The Mill, with happy Morton Court on the far side, and somewhere in the smoky distance other places, Folkstone and Budleigh and Hawk Nest and Parley Close and Kingston and Old Grove and all the rest, the districts, the myriad districts, part of the chain that stretches from sea to sea, from shore to shore, spanning our continent border to border, the districts, the chips of gaudy glass making up the global mosaic, the infinitely numerous communities that are the segments of the all-encompassing world-city. Tonight at the capital they are planning next month's rainfall patterns for districts that the planners have never seen. District food allocations—inadequate, always inadequate—are being devised by men to whom our appetites are purely abstract entities. Do they believe in our existence, at the capital? Do they really think there is such a place as Ganfield? What if we sent them a delegation of notable citizens to ask for help in replacing our lost program? Would they care? Would they even listen? For that matter, is there a capital at all? How can I, who have never seen nearby Old Grove, accept, on faith alone, the existence of a far-off governing center, aloof, inaccessible, shrouded in myth? Maybe it is only a construct of some cunning subterranean machine that is our real ruler. That would not surprise me. Nothing surprises me. There is no capital. There are no central planners. Beyond the horizon everything is mist.

III

In the office, at least, no one dares show hostility to me. There are no scowls, no glares, no snide references to the missing program. I am, after all, chief deputy to the District Commissioner of Nutrition, and since the commissioner is usually absent, I am, in effect, in charge of the department. If Silena's crime does not destroy my career, it might prove to have been unwise for my subordinates to treat me with disdain. In any case we are so busy that there is no time for such gambits. We are responsible for keeping the community properly fed; our tasks have been greatly complicated by the loss of the program, for there is no reliable way now of processing our allocation sheets, and we must requisition and distribute food by guesswork and memory. How many bales of plankton cubes do we consume each week? How many pounds of proteoid mix? How much bread for the shops of Lower Ganfield? What fads of diet are likely to sweep the district this month? If demand and supply fall into imbalance as a result of our miscalculations, there could be widespread acts of violence, forays into neighboring districts, even renewed outbreaks of cannibalism within Ganfield itself. So we must draw up our estimates with the greatest precision. What a terrible spiritual isolation we feel deciding such things with no computers to guide us!

IV

On the fourteenth day of the crisis the district captain summons me. His message comes in late afternoon, when we all are dizzy with fatigue, choked by humidity. For several hours I have been tangled in complex dealings with a high official of the Marine Nutrients Board; this is an arm of the central city government, and I must therefore show the greatest tact, lest Ganfield's plankton quotas be arbitrarily lowered by a bureaucrat's sudden pique. Telephone contact is uncertain—the Marine Nutrients Board has its headquarters in Melrose New Port, half a continent away on the southeastern coast —and the line sputters and blurs with distortions that our computers, if the master program were in operation, would normally erase. As we reach a crisis in the negotiation my subdeputy gives me a note: "District captain wants to see you." "Not now," I say in silent lip talk. The haggling proceeds. A few minutes later comes another note: "It's urgent." I shake my head, brush the note from my desk. The subdeputy retreats to the outer office, where I see him engaged in frantic discussion with a man in the gray-and-green uniform of the district captain's staff. The messenger points vehemently at me. Just then the phone line goes dead. I slam the instrument down and call to the messenger, "What is it?"

"The captain, sir. To his office at once, please."

"Impossible."

He displays a warrant bearing the captain's seal. "He requires your immediate presence."

"Tell him I have delicate business to complete," I reply. "Another fifteen minutes, maybe."

He shakes his head. "I am not empowered to allow a delay."

"Is this an arrest, then?"

"A summons."

"But with the force of an arrest?"

"With the force of an arrest, yes," he tells me.

I shrug and yield. All burdens drop from me. Let the subdeputy deal with the Marine Nutrients Board; let the clerk in the outer office do it, or no one at all; let the whole district starve. I no longer care. I am summoned. My responsibilities are discharged. I give over my desk to the subdeputy and summarize for him, in perhaps a hundred words, my intricate hours of negotiation. All that is someone else's problem now.

The messenger leads me from the building into the hot, dank street. The sky is dark and heavy with rain, and evidently it has been raining some while, for the sewers are backing up and angry swirls of muddy water run shin-deep through the gutters. The drainage system, too, is controlled from Ganfield Hold, and must now be failing. We hurry across the narrow plaza fronting my office, skirt a gush of sewage-laden outflow, push into a close-packed crowd of irritable workers heading for home. The messenger's uniform creates an invisible sphere of untouchability for us; the throngs part readily and close again behind us. Wordlessly I am conducted to the stone-faced building of the district captain, and quickly to his office. It is no unfamiliar place to me, but coming here as a prisoner is quite different from attending a meeting of the district council. My shoulders are slumped, my eyes look toward the threadbare carpeting.

The district captain appears. He is a man of sixty, silver-haired, upright, his eyes frank and direct, his features reflecting little of the strain his position must impose. He has governed our district ten years. He greets me by name, but without warmth, and says, "You've heard nothing from your woman?"

"I would have reported it if I had."

"Perhaps. Perhaps. Have you any idea where she is?"

"I know only the common rumors," I say. "Conning Town, Morton Court, The Mill."

"She is in none of those places."

"Are your sure?"

"I have consulted the captains of those districts," he says. "They deny any knowledge of her. Of course, one has no reason to trust their word, but on the other hand why would they bother to deceive me?" His eyes fasten on mine. "What part did you play in the stealing of the program?"

"None, sir."

"She never spoke to you of treasonable things?"

"Never."

"There is strong feeling in Ganfield that a conspiracy existed."

"If so I knew nothing of it."

He judges me with a piercing look. After a long pause he says heavily, "She has destroyed us, you know. We can function at the present level of order for another six weeks, possibly, without the program—if there is no plague, if we are not flooded, if we are not overrun with bandits from outside. After that the accumulated effects of many minor breakdowns will paralyze us. We will fall into chaos. We will strangle on our own wastes, starve, suffocate, revert to savagery, live like beasts until the end—who knows? Without the master program we are lost. Why did she do this to us?"

"I have no theories," I say. "She kept her own counsel. Her independence of soul is what attracted me to her."

"Very well. Let her independence of soul be what attracts you to her now. Find her and bring back the program."

"Find her? Where?"

"That is for you to discover."

"I know nothing of the world outside Ganfield!"

"You will learn," the captain says coolly. "There are those here who would indict you for treason. I see no value in this. How does it help us to punish you? But we can *use* you. You are a clever and resourceful man; you can make your way through the hostile districts, and you can gather information, and you could well succeed in tracking her. If anyone has influence over her, you do; if you find her, you perhaps can induce her to surrender the program. No one else could hope to accomplish that. Go. We offer you immunity from prosecution in return for your cooperation."

The world spins wildly about me. My skin burns with shock. "Will I have safe-conduct through the neighboring districts?" I ask.

"To whatever extent we can arrange. That will not be much, I fear."

"You'll give me an escort, then? Two or three men?"

"We feel you will travel more effectively alone. A party of several men takes on the character of an invading force; you would be met with suspicion and worse."

"Diplomatic credentials, at least?"

"A letter of identification, calling on all captains to honor your mission and treat you with courtesy."

I know how much value such a letter will have in Hawk Nest or Folkstone.

"This frightens me," I say.

He nods, not unkindly. "I understand that. Yet someone must seek her, and who else is there but you? We grant you a day to make your preparations. You will depart on the morning after next, and God hasten your return."

V

Preparations. How can I prepare myself? What maps should I collect, when my destination is unknown? Returning to the office is unthinkable; I go straight home, and for hours I wander from one room to the other as if I face execution at dawn. At last I gather myself and fix a small meal, but most of it remains on my plate. No friends call; I call no one. Since Silena's disappearance my friends have fallen away from me. I sleep poorly. During the night there are hoarse shouts and shrill alarms in the street; I learn from the morning newscast that five men of Conning Town, here to loot, had been seized by one of the new vigilante groups that have replaced the police machines and were summarily put to death. I find no cheer in that, thinking that I might be in Conning Town in a day or so.

What clues to Silena's route? I ask to speak with the guard from whom she wangled entry into Ganfield Hold. He has been a prisoner ever since; the captain is too busy to decide his fate, and he languishes meanwhile. He is a small, thick-bodied man with stubbly red hair and a sweaty forehead; his eyes are bright with anger and his nostrils quiver. "What is there to say?" he demands. "I was on duty at the Hold. She came in. I had never seen her before, though I knew she must be high caste. Her cloak was open. She seemed naked beneath it. She was in a state of excitement."

"What did she tell you?"

"That she desired me. Those were her first words." Yes.

I could see Silena doing that, though I had difficulty in imagining her long, slender form enfolded in this squat little man's embrace. "She said she knew of me and was eager for me to have her."

"And then?"

"I sealed the gate. We went to an inner room where there is a cot. It was a quiet time of day; I thought no harm would come. She dropped her cloak. Her body—"

"Never mind her body." I could see it all too well in the eye of my mind, the sleek thighs, the taut belly, the small high breasts, the cascade of chocolate hair falling to her shoulders. "What did you talk about? Did she say anything of a political kind? Some slogan, some words against the government?"

"Nothing. We lay together naked a while, only fondling each other. Then she said she had a drug with her, one that would enhance the sensations of love tenfold. It was a dark powder. I drank it in water; she drank it also, or seemed to. Instantly I was asleep. When I awoke the Hold was in uproar and I was a prisoner." He glowers at me. "I should have suspected a trick from the start. Such women do not hunger for men like me. How did I ever injure you? Why did you choose me to be the victim of your scheme?"

"Her scheme," I say. "Not mine. I had no part in it. Her motive is a mystery to me. If I could discover where she has gone, I would seek her and wring answers from her. Any help you could give me might earn you a pardon and your freedom."

"I know nothing," he says sullenly. "She came in, she snared me, she drugged me, she stole the program."

"Think. Not a word? Possibly she mentioned the name of some other district."

"Nothing."

A pawn is all he is, innocent, useless. As I leave he cries out to me to intercede for him, but what can I do? "Your woman ruined me!" he roars.

"She may have ruined us all," I reply.

At my request a district prosecutor accompanies me to Silena's apartment, which has been under official seal since her disappearance. Its contents have been thoroughly examined, but maybe there is some clue I alone would notice. Entering, I feel a sharp pang of loss, for the sight of Silena's possessions reminds me of happier times. These things are painfully familiar to me: her neat array of books, her clothing, her furnishings, her bed. I knew her only eleven weeks, she was my month-wife for only two; I had not realized she had come to mean so much to me so quickly. We look around, the prosecutor and I. The books testify to the agility of her restless mind: little light fiction, mainly works of serious history, analyses of social problems, forecasts of conditions to come. Holman, *The Era of the World City*. Sawtelle, *Megalopolis Triumphant*. Doxiadis, *The New World of Urban Man*. Heggebend, *Fifty Billion Lives*. Marks, *Calcutta Is Everywhere*. Chasin, *The New Community*. I take a few of the books down, fondling them as though they were Silena. Many times when I had spent an evening here she reached for one of those books, Sawtelle or Heggebend or Marks or Chasin, to read me a passage that amplified some point she was making. Idly I turn pages. Dozens of paragraphs are underscored with fine, precise lines, and lengthy marginal comments are abundant. "We've analyzed all of that for possible significance," the prosecutor remarks. "The only thing we've concluded is that she thinks the world is too crowded for comfort." A ratcheting laugh. "As who doesn't?" He points to a stack of green-bound pamphlets at the end of the lower shelf. "These, on the other hand, may be useful in your search. Do you know anything about them?"

The stack consists of nine copies of something called *Walden Three:* a Utopian fantasy, apparently, set in an idyllic land of streams and forests. The booklets are unfamiliar to me; Silena must have obtained them recently. Why nine copies? Was she acting as a distributor? They bear the imprint of a publishing house in Kingston. Ganfield and Kingston severed trade relations long ago; material published there is uncommon here. "I've never seen them," I say. "Where do you think she got them?"

"There are three main routes for subversive literature originating in Kingston. One is—"

"Is this pamphlet subversive, then?"

"Oh, very much so. It argues for complete reversal of the social trends of the last hundred years. As I was saying, there are three main routes for subversive literature originating in Kingston. We have traced one chain of distribution running by way of Wisleigh and Cedar Mall, another through Old Grove, Hawk Nest, and Conning Town, and the third via Parley Close and The Mill. It is plausible that your woman is in Kingston now, having traveled along one of these underground distribution routes, sheltered by her fellow subversives all the way. But we have no way of confirming this." He smiles emptily. "She could be in any of the other communities along the three routes. Or in none of them."

"I should think of Kingston, though, as my ultimate goal, until I learn anything to the contrary. Is that right?"

"What else can you do?"

"What else, indeed? I must search at random through an unknown number of hostile districts, having no clue other than the vague one implicit in the place of origin of these nine booklets, while time ticks on and Ganfield slips deeper day by day into confusion.

The prosecutor's office supplies me with useful things: maps, letters of introduction, a commuter's passport that should enable me to cross at least some district lines unmolested, and an assortment of local currencies as well as bank notes issued by the central bank and therefore valid in most districts. Against my wishes I am given also a weapon—a small heat-pistol—and in addition a capsule that I can swallow in the event that a quick and easy death becomes desirable. As the final stage in my preparation I spend an hour conferring with a secret agent, now retired, whose career of espionage took him safely into hundreds of communities as far away as Threadmuir and Reed Meadow. What advice does he give someone about to try to get across? "Maintain your poise," he says. "Be confident and self-assured, as though you belong in whatever place you find yourself. Never slink. Look all men in the eye. However, say no more than is necessary. Be watchful at all times. Don't relax your guard." Such precepts I could have evolved without his aid. He has nothing in the nature of specific hints for survival. Each district, he says, presents unique problems, constantly changing; nothing can be anticipated, everything must be met as it arises. How comforting!

At nightfall I go to the soul father's house, in the shadow of Ganfield Tower. To leave without a blessing seems unwise. But there is something stagy and unspontaneous about my visit, and my faith flees as I enter. In the dim antechamber I light the nine candles, I pluck the five blades of grass from the ceremonial vase, I do the other proper ritual things, but my spirit remains chilled and hollow, and I am unable to pray. The soul father himself, having been told of my mission, grants me audience—gaunt old man with impenetrable eyes set in deep bony rims—and favors me with a gentle feather-light embrace. "Go in safety," he murmurs. "God watches over you." I wish I felt sure of that. Going home, I take the most roundabout possible route, as if trying to drink in as much of Ganfield as I can on my last night. The diminishing past flows through me like a river running dry. My birthplace, my school, the streets where I played, the dormitory where I spent my adolescence, the home of my first month-wife. Farewell. Farewell. Tomorrow I go across. I return to my apartment alone; once more my sleep is fitful. An hour after dawn I find myself, astonished by it, waiting in line among the commuters at the mouth of the transit tube, bound for Conning Town. And so my crossing begins.

VI

Aboard the tube-train no one speaks. Faces are tense; bodies are held rigid in the plastic seats. Occasionally someone on the other side of the aisle glances at me as though wondering who this newcomer to the commuter group may be, but his eyes quickly slide away as I take notice. I know none of these commuters, though they must have dwelt in Ganfield as long as I; their lives have never intersected mine before. Engineers, merchants, diplomats, whatever—their careers are tied to districts other than their own. It is one of the anomalies of our ever more fragmented and stratified society that some regular contact still survives between community and community; a certain number of people must journey each day to outlying districts, where they work encapsulated, isolated, among unfriendly strangers.

We plunge eastward at unimaginable speed. Surely we are past the boundaries of Ganfield by now and under alien territory. A glowing sign on the wall of the car announces our route: CONNING TOWN—HAWK NEST—OLD GROVE—KINGSTON—FOLKSTONE—PARLEY CLOSE—BUDLEIGH —CEDAR MALL—THE MILL—MORTON COURT—GANFIELD, a wide loop through our most immediate neighbors. I try to visualize the separate links in this chain of districts, each a community of three or four hundred thousand loyal and patriotic citizens, each with its own special tone, its flavor, its distinctive quality, its apparatus of government, its customs and rituals. But I can imagine them merely as a cluster of Ganfields, every place very much like the one I have just left. I know this is not so. The world-city is no homogeneous collection of uniformities, a global bundle of indistinguishable suburbs. No, there is incredible diversity, a host of unique urban cores bound by common need into a fragile unity. No master plan brought them into being; each evolved at a separate point in time to serve the necessities of a particular purpose. This community sprawls gracefully along a curving river, that one boldly mounts the slopes of stark hills; here the prevailing architecture reflects an easy, gentle climate, there it wars with unfriendly nature; form follows topography and local function, creating individuality. The world is a richness—why then do I see only ten thousand Ganfields?

Of course it is not so simple. We are caught in the tension between forces that encourage distinctiveness and forces that compel all communities toward identicality. Centrifugal forces broke down the huge ancient cities, the Londons and Tokyos and New Yorks, into neighborhood communities that seized quasi-autonomous powers. Those giant cities were too unwieldly to survive; density of population, making long-distance transport unfeasible and communication difficult, shattered the urban fabric, destroyed the authority of the central government, and left the closely knit small-scale subcity as the only viable unit. Two dynamic and contradictory process-es now asserted themselves. Pride and the quest for local advantage led each community toward specialization: this one a center primarily of industrial production, this one devoted to advanced education, this to finance, this to the processing of raw materials, this to wholesale marketing of commodities, this to retail distribution, and so on, the shape and texture of each district defined by its chosen function. And yet the new decentralization required a high degree of redundancy, duplication of governmental structures, of utilities, of commu-nity services; for its own safety each district felt the need to transform itself into a microcosm of the former full city. Ideally we should have hovered in perfect balance between specializa-tion and redundancy, all communities striving to fulfill the needs of all other communities with the least possible overlap and waste of resources; in fact our human frailty has brought into being these irreversible trends of rivalry and irrational fear, dividing district from district, so that against our own self-interest we sever year after year our bonds of interdependence and stubbornly seek self-sufficiency at the district level. Since this is impossible, our lives grow constantly more impoverished. In the end, all districts will be the same and we will have created a world of pathetic, limping Ganfields, devoid of grace, lacking in variety.

GETTING ACROSS

So. The tube-train halts. This is Conning Town. I am across
the first district line. I make my exit in a file of solemn-faced
commuters. Imitating them, I approach a collossal Cyclopean
scanning machine and present my passport. It is unmarked
by visas; theirs are gaudy with scores of them. I tremble, but
the machine accepts me and slams down a stamp that fluoresces
a brilliant shimmering crimson against the pale-lavender page:

- DISTRICT OF CONNING TOWN -
- ENTRY VISA -
- 24-HOUR VALIDITY -

Dated to the hour, minute, second. Welcome, stranger, but
get out of town before sunrise!

Up the purring ramp, into the street. Bright morning sunlight
pries apart the slim, sooty, close-ranked towers of Conning
Town. The air is cool and sweet, strange to me after so many
sweltering days in programless, demechanized Ganfield. Does
our foul air drift across the border and offend them? Sullen
eyes study me; those about me know me for an outsider. Their
clothing is alien in style, pinched in at the shoulders, flaring
at the waist. I find myself adopting an inane smile in response
to their dour glares.

For an hour I walk aimlessly through the downtown section
until my first fears melt and a comic cockiness takes possession
of me: I pretend to myself that I am a native, and enjoy the
flimsy imposture. This place is not much unlike Ganfield, yet
nothing is quite the same. The sidewalks are wider; the street
lamps have slender arching necks instead of angular ones;
the fire hydrants are green and gold, not blue and orange.
The police machines have flatter domes than ours, ringed with
ten or twelve spy-eyes where ours have six or eight. Different,
different, all different.

Three times I am halted by police machines. I produce my
passport, display my visa, am allowed to continue. So far getting
across has been easier than I imagined. No one molests me

here. I suppose I look harmless. Why did I think my foreignness alone would lead these people to attack me? Ganfield is not at war with its neighbors, after all.

Drifting eastward in search of a bookstore, I pass through a shabby residential neighborhood and through a zone of dismal factories before I reach an area of small shops. Then in late afternoon I discover three bookstores on the same block, but they are antiseptic places, not the sort that might carry subversive propaganda like *Walden Three*. The first two are wholly automated, blank-walled charge-plate-and-scanner operations. The third has a human clerk, a man of about thirty, with drooping yellow moustachios and alert blue eyes. He recognizes the style of my clothing and says, "Ganfield, eh? Lot of trouble over there."

"You've heard?"

"Just stories. Computer breakdown, isn't it?"

I nod. "Something like that."

"No police, no garbage removal, no weather control, hardly anything working—that's what they say." He seems neither surprised nor disturbed to have an outlander in his shop. His manner is amiable and relaxed. Is he fishing for data about our vulnerability, though? I must be careful not to tell him anything that might be used against us. But evidently they already know everything here. He says, "It's a little like dropping back into the Stone Age for you people, I guess. It must be a real traumatic thing."

"We're coping," I say, stiffly casual.

"How did it happen, anyway?"

I gave him a wary shrug. "I'm not sure about that." Still revealing nothing. But then something in his tone of a moment before catches me belatedly and neutralizes some of the reflexive automatic suspicion with which I have met his questions. I glance around. No one else in the shop. I let something conspiratorial creep into my voice and say, "It might not even be so traumatic, actually, once we get used to it. I mean, there once was a time when we didn't rely so heavily on machines to do our thinking for us, and we survived, and even managed pretty well. I was reading a little book last week that seemed to be saying we might profit by trying to return to the old way of life. Book published in Kingston."

"*Walden Three.*" Not a question but a statement.

"That's it." My eyes query his. "You've read it?"

"Seen it."

"A lot of sense in that book, I think."

He smiles warmly. "I think so too. You get much Kingston stuff over in Ganfield?"

"Very little, actually."

"Not much here, either."

"But there's some."

"Some, yes," he says.

Have I stumbled upon a member of Silena's underground movement? I say eagerly, "You know, maybe you could help me meet some people who—"

"No."

"No?"

"No." His eyes are still friendly but his face is tense. "There's nothing like that around here," he says, his voice suddenly flat and remote. "You'd have to go over into Hawk Nest."

"I'm told that that's a nasty place."

"Nevertheless, Hawk Nest is where you want to go. Nate and Holly Borden's shop, just off Box Street." Abruptly his manner shifts to one of exaggerated bland clerkishness. "Anything else I can do for you, sir? If you're interested in supernovels we've got a couple of good new double-amplified cassettes, just in. Perhaps I can show you—"

"Thank you, no." I smile, shake my head, leave the store. A police machine waits outside. Its dome rotates; eye after eye scans me intently; finally its resonant voice says, "Your passport, please." This routine is familiar by now. I produce the document. Through the bookshop window I see the clerk bleakly watching. The police machine says, "What is your place of residence in Conning Town?"

"I have none. I'm here on a twenty-four-hour visa."

"Where will you spend the night?"

"In a hotel, I suppose."

"Please show your room confirmation."

"I haven't made arrangements yet," I tell it.

A long moment of silence; the machine is conferring with its central, no doubt, keying into the master program of Conning Town for instructions. At length it says, "You are advised to obtain a legitimate reservation and display it to a monitor at the earliest opportunity within the next four hours. Failure to do so will result in cancellation of your visa and immediate expulsion from Conning Town." Some ominous clicks come from the depths of the machine. "You are now under formal surveillance," it announces.

Brimming with questions, I return hastily to the bookshop. The clerk is displeased to see me. Anyone who attracts monitors to his shop—"monitors" is what they call police machines here, it seems—is unwelcome. "Can you tell me how to reach the nearest decent hotel?" I ask.

"You won't find one."

"No decent hotels?"

"No hotels. None where you could get a room, anyway. We have only two or three transient houses and accommodations are allocated months in advance to regular commuters."

"Does the monitor know that?"

"Of course."

"Where are strangers supposed to stay, then?"

The clerk shrugs. "There's no structural program here for strangers as such. The regular commuters have regular arrangements. Unauthorized intruders don't belong here at all. You fall somewhere in between, I imagine. There's no legal way for you to spend the night in Conning Town."

"But my visa—"

"Even so."

"I'd better go on into Hawk Nest, I suppose."

"It's late. You've missed the last tube-train. You've got no choice but to stay, unless you want to try a border crossing on foot in the dark. I wouldn't recommend that."

"Stay? But where?"

"Sleep in the street. If you're lucky the monitors will leave you alone."

"Some quiet back alley, I suppose."

"No," he says. "You sleep in an out-of-the-way place and you'll surely get sliced up by night bandits. Go to one of the designated sleeping streets. In the middle of a big crowd you might just go unnoticed, even though you're under surveillance." As he speaks he moves about the shop, closing it down for the night. He looks restless and uncomfortable. I take out my map of Conning Town and he shows me where to go. The map is some years out of date, apparently; he corrects it with irritable swipes of his pencil. We leave the shop together. I invite him to come with me to some restaurant as my guest, but he looks at me as if I carry plague. "Good-by," he says. "Good luck."

VII

Alone, apart from the handful of other diners, I take my evening meal at a squalid, dimly lit automated cafeteria at the edge of downtown. Silent machines offer me thin acrid soup, pale spongy bread, and a leaden stew containing lumpy ingredients of undeterminable origin, for which I pay with yellow plastic counters of Conning Town currency. Emerging undelighted, I observe a reddish glow in the western sky. It may be a lovely sunset or, for all I know, it may be a sign that Ganfield is burning. I look about for monitors. My four-hour grace period has nearly expired. I must disappear shortly into a throng. It seems too early for sleep, but I am only a few blocks from the place where the bookshop clerk suggested I should pass the night, and I go to it. Just as well; when I reach it—a wide plaza bordered by gray buildings of ornate facade—I find it already filling up with street-sleepers. There must be eight hundred of them, men, women, family groups, settling down in little squares of cobbled territory that are obviously claimed night after night under some system of squatter's rights. Others constantly arrive, flowing inward from the plaza's three entrances, finding their places, laying out foam cushions or mounds of clothing as their mattresses. It is a friendly crowd; these people are linked by bonds of neighborliness, a common poverty. They laugh, embrace, play games of chance, exchange whispered confidences, bicker, transact business, and join together in the rites of the local religion, performing a routine that involves six people clasping hands and chanting. Privacy seems obsolete here. They undress freely before one another and there are instances of open coupling. The gaiety of the scene—a medieval carnival is what it suggests to me, a Brueghelesque romp—is marred only by my awareness that this horde of revelers is homeless under the inhospitable skies, vulnerable to rain, sleet, damp fog, snow, and the other unkindnesses of winter and summer in these latitudes. In Ganfield we have just a scattering of street-sleepers, those who have lost their residential licenses and are temporarily forced into the open, but here it seems to be an established institution, as though Conning Town declared a moratorium some years ago on new residential construction without at the same time checking the increase of population.

Stepping over and around and between people, I reach the center of the plaza and select an unoccupied bit of pavement. But in a moment a little ruddy-faced woman arrives, excited and animated, and with a Conning Town accent so thick I can barely understand her, she tells me she holds claim here. Her eyes are bright with menace; her hands are not far from becoming claws; several nearby squatters sit up and regard me threateningly. I apologize for my error and withdraw, stumbling over a child and narrowly missing overturning a bubbling cooking pot. Onward. Not here. Not here. A hand emerges from a pile of blankets and strokes my leg as I look around in perplexity. Not here. A man with a painted face rises out of a miniature green tent and speaks to me in a language I do not understand.

Not here. I move on again and again, thinking that I will be jostled out of the plaza entirely, excluded, disqualified even to sleep in this district's streets, but finally I find a cramped corner where the occupants indicate I am welcome. "Yes?" I say. They grin and gesture. Gratefully I seize the spot.

Darkness has come. The plaza continues to fill; at least a thousand people have arrived after me, cramming into every vacancy, and the flow does not abate. I hear booming laughter, idle chatter, earnest romantic persuasion, the brittle sound of domestic quarreling. Someone passes a jug of wine around, even to me; bitter stuff, fermented clam juice its probable base, but I appreciate the gesture. The night is warm, almost sticky. The scent of unfamiliar food drifts on the air—something sharp, spicy, a heavy, pungent smell. Curry? Is this then truly Calcutta? I close my eyes and huddle into myself. The hard cobblestones are cold beneath me. I have no mattress and I feel unable to remove my clothes before so many strangers. It will be hard for me to sleep in this madhouse, I think. But gradually the hubbub diminishes and—exhausted, drained—I slide into a deep, troubled sleep.

Ugly dreams. The asphyxiating pressure of a surging mob. Rivers leaping their channels. Towers toppling. Fountains of mud bursting from a thousand lofty windows. Bands of steel encircling my thighs; my legs, useless, withering away. A torrent of lice sweeping over me. A frosty hand touching me. Touching me. Touching me. Pulling me up from sleep.

Harsh white light drenches me. I blink, cringe, cover my eyes. Shortly I perceive that a monitor stands over me. About me the sleepers are awake, backing away, murmuring, pointing.

"Your street-sleeping permit, please."

Caught. I mumble excuses, plead ignorance of the law, beg forgiveness. But a police machine is neither malevolent nor merciful; it merely follows its program. It demands my passport and scans my visa. Then it reminds me I have been under surveillance. Having failed to obtain a hotel room as ordered, having neglected to report to a monitor within the prescribed interval, I am subject to expulsion.

"Very well," I say. "Conduct me to the border of Hawk Nest."

"You will return at once to Ganfield."

"I have business in Hawk Nest."

"Illegal entrants are returned to their district of origin."

"What does it matter to you where I go, so long as I get out of Conning Town?"

"Illegal entrants are returned to their district of origin," the machine tells me inexorably.

I dare not go back with so little accomplished. Still arguing with the monitor, I am led from the plaza through dark cavernous streets toward the mouth of a transit tube. On the station level a second monitor is given charge of me. "In three hours," the monitor that apprehended me informs me, "the Ganfield-bound train will arrive."

The first monitor rolls away.

Too late I realize that the machine has neglected to return my passport.

VIII

Monitor number two shows little interest in me. Patrolling the tube station, it swings in a wide arc around me, keeping a scanner perfunctorily trained on me but making no attempt to interfere with what I do. If I try to flee, of course, it will destroy me. Fretfully I study my maps. Hawk Nest lies to the northeast of Conning Town; if this is the tube station that I think it is, the border is not far. Five minutes' walk, perhaps. Passportless, there is no place I can go except Ganfield; my commuter status is revoked. But legalities count for little in Hawk Nest.

How to escape?

I concoct a plan. Its simplicity seems absurd, yet absurdity is often useful when dealing with machines. The monitor is instructed to put me aboard the train for Ganfield, yes. But not necessarily to keep me there.

I wait out the weary hours to dawn. I hear the crash of compressed air far up the tunnel. Snub-nosed, silken-smooth, the train slides into the station. The monitor orders me aboard.

I walk into the car, cross it quickly, and exit by the open door on the far side of the platform. Even if the monitor has observed this maneuver, it can hardly fire across a crowded train. As I leave the car I break into a trot, darting past startled travelers, and sprint upstairs into the misty morning. At street level, running is unwise. I drop back to a rapid walking pace and melt into the throngs of early workers. The street is Crystal Boulevard. Good. I have memorized a route: Crystal Boulevard to Flagstone Square, thence via Mechanic Street to the border.

Presumably all monitors, linked to whatever central nervous system the machines of the district of Conning Town utilize, have instantaneously been apprised of my disappearance. But that is not the same as knowing where to find me. I head northward on Crystal Boulevard—its name shows a dark sense of irony, or else the severe transformations time can work—and, borne by the flow of pedestrian traffic, enter Flagstone Square, a grimy, lopsided plaza out of which, on the left, snakes curving Mechanic Street. I go unintercepted on this thoroughfare of small shops. The place to anticipate trouble is at the border.

I am there in a few minutes. It is a wide, dusty street, silent and empty, lined on the Conning Town side by a row of blocky brick warehouses, on the Hawk Nest side by a string of low, ragged buildings, some in ruins, the best of them defiantly slatternly. There is no barrier. To fence a district border is unlawful except in time of war, and I have heard of no war between Conning Town and Hawk Nest.

Dare I cross? Police machines of two species patrol the street: flat-domed ones of Conning Town and black hexagon-headed ones of Hawk Nest. Surely one or the other will gun me down in the no man's land between districts. But I have no choice. I must keep going forward.

I run out into the street at a moment when two police machines, passing each other on opposite orbits, have left an unpatrolled space perhaps a block long. Midway in my crossing the Conning Town monitor spies me and blares a command. The words are unintelligible to me and I keep running, zigzagging in the hope of avoiding the bolt that very likely will follow. But the machine does not shoot; I must already be on the Hawk Nest side of the line and Conning Town no longer cares what becomes of me.

The Hawk Nest machine has noticed me. It rolls toward me as I stumble, breathless and gasping, onto the curb. "Halt!" it cries. "Present your documents!" At that moment a red-bearded man, fierce-eyed, wide-shouldered, steps out of a decaying building close by me. A scheme assembles itself in my mind. Do the customs of sponsorship and sanctuary hold good in this harsh district?

"Brother!" I cry. "What luck!" I embrace him, and before he can fling me off I murmur, "I am from Ganfield. I seek sanctuary here. Help me!"

The machine has reached me. It goes into an interrogatory stance and I say, "This is my brother who offers me the privilege of sanctuary. Ask him! Ask him!"

"Is this true?" the machine inquires.

Redbeard, unsmiling, spits and mutters, "My brother, yes. A political refugee. I'll stand sponsor to him. I vouch for him. Let him be."

The machine clicks, hums, assimilates. To me it says, "You will register as a sponsored refugee within twelve hours or leave Hawk Nest." Without another word it rolls away.

I offer my sudden savior warm thanks. He scowls, shakes his head, spits once again. "We owe each other nothing," he says brusquely, and goes striding down the street.

IX

In Hawk Nest nature has followed art. The name, I have heard, once had purely neutral connotations: some real-estate developer's high-flown metaphor, nothing more. Yet it determined the district's character, for gradually Hawk Nest became the home of predators that it is today, where all men are strangers, where every man is his brother's enemy.

Other districts have their slums. Hawk Nest *is* a slum. I am told they live here by looting, cheating, extorting, and manipulating. An odd economic base for an entire community, but maybe it works for them. The atmosphere is menacing. The only police machines seem to be those that patrol the border. I sense emanations of violence just beyond the corner of my eye: rapes and garrotings in shadowy byways, flashing knives and muffled groans, covert cannibal feasts. Perhaps my imagination works too hard. Certainly I have gone unthreatened so far; those I meet on the streets pay no heed to me, indeed will not even return my glance. Still, I keep my heat-pistol close by my hand as I walk through these shabby, deteriorating outskirts. Sinister faces peer at me through cracked, dirt-veiled windows. If I am attacked, will I have to fire in order to defend myself? God spare me from having to answer that.

X

Why is there a bookshop in this town of murder and rubble and decay? Here is Box Street, and here, in an oily pocket of spare-parts depots and flyspecked quick-lunch counters, is Nate and Holly Borden's place. Five times as deep as it is broad, dusty, dimly lit, shelves overflowing with old books and pamphlets, an improbable outpost of the nineteenth century, somehow displaced in time. There is no one in it but a large, impassive woman seated at the counter, fleshy, puffy-faced, motionless. Her eyes, oddly intense, glitter like glass disks set in a mound of dough. She regards me without curiosity.

I say, "I'm looking for Holly Borden."

"You've found her," she replies, deep in the baritone range.

"I've come across from Ganfield by way of Conning Town."

No response from her to this.

I continue, "I'm traveling without a passport. They confiscated it in Conning Town and I ran the border."

She nods. And waits. No show of interest.

"I wonder if you could sell me a copy of *Walden Three*," I say.

Now she stirs a little. "Why do you want one?"

"I'm curious about it. It's not available in Ganfield."

"How do you know I have one?"

"Is anything illegal in Hawk Nest?"

She seems annoyed that I have answered a question with a question. "How do you know *I* have a copy of that book?"

"A bookshop clerk in Conning Town said you might."

A pause. "All right. Suppose I do. Did you come all the way from Ganfield just to buy a book?" Suddenly she leans forward and smiles—a warm, keen, penetrating smile that wholly transforms her face: now she is keyed-up, alert, responsive, shrewd, commanding. "What's your game?" she asks.

"My game?"

"What are you playing? What are you up to here?"

It is the moment for total honesty. "I'm looking for a woman named Silena Ruiz, from Ganfield. Have you heard of her?"

"Yes. She's not in Hawk Nest."

"I think she's in Kingston. I'd like to find her."

"Why? To arrest her?"

"Just to talk to her. I have plenty to discuss with her. She was my month-wife when she left Ganfield."

"The month must be nearly up," Holly Borden says.

"Even so," I reply. "Can you help me reach her?"

"Why should I trust you?"

"Why not?"

She ponders that briefly. She studies my face. I feel the heat of her scrutiny. At length she says, "I expect to be making a journey to Kingston soon. I suppose I could take you with me."

XI

She opens a trap door; I descend into a room beneath the bookshop. After a good many hours a thin, gray-haired man brings me a tray of food. "Call me Nate," he says. Overhead I hear indistinct conversations, laughter, the thumping of boots on the wooden floor. In Ganfield, famine may be setting in by now. Rats will be dancing around Ganfield Hold. How long

will they keep me here? Am I a prisoner? Two days. Three.
Nate will answer no questions. I have books, a cot, a sink,
a drinking glass. On the third day the trap door opens. Holly
Borden peers down. "We're ready to leave," she says.

The expedition consists just of the two of us. She is going
to Kingston to buy books and travels on a commercial passport
that allows for one helper. Nate drives us to the tube-mouth
in midafternoon. It no longer seems unusual to me to be passing
from district to district; they are not such alien and hostile
places, merely different from the place I know. I see myself
bound on an odyssey that carries me across hundreds of districts, even thousands, the whole patchwork frenzy of our
world. Why return to Ganfield? Why not go on, ever eastward,
to the great ocean and beyond, to the unimaginable strange-
nesses on the far side?

Here we are in Kingston. An old district, one of the oldest.
We are the only ones who journey hither today from Hawk
Nest. There is only a perfunctory inspection of passports. The
police machines of Kingston are tall, long-armed, with fluted
bodies ornamented in stripes of red and green: quite a gay
effect. I am becoming an expert in local variations of police-
machine design. Kingston itself is a district of low pastel buildings arranged in spokelike boulevards radiating from the famed
university that is its chief enterprise. No one from Ganfield
has been admitted to the university in my memory.

Holly is expecting friends to meet her, but they have not
come. We wait fifteen minutes. "Never mind," she says. "We'll
walk." I carry the luggage. The air is soft and mild; the sun,
sloping toward Folkstone and Budleigh, is still high. I feel oddly
serene. It is as if I have perceived a divine purpose, an overriding
plan, in the structure of our society, in our sprawling city of
many cities, our network of steel and concrete clinging like
an armor of scales to the skin of our planet. But what is that
purpose? What is that plan? The essence of it eludes me; I
am aware only that it must exist. A cheery delusion.

Fifty paces from the station we are abrupty surrounded by

a dozen or more buoyant young men who emerge from an intersecting street. They are naked but for green loincloths; their hair and beards are untrimmed and unkempt; they have a fierce and barbaric look. Several carry long unsheathed knives strapped to their waists. They circle wildly around us, laughing, jabbing at us with their fingertips. "This is a holy district!" they cry. "We need no blasphemous strangers here! Why must you intrude on us?"

"What do they want?" I whisper. "Are we in danger?"

"They are a band of priests," Holly replies. "Do as they say and we will come to no harm."

They press close. Leaping, dancing, they shower us with sprays of perspiration. "Where are you from?" they demand. "Ganfield," I say. "Hawk Nest," says Holly. They seem playful yet dangerous. Surging about me, they empty my pockets in a series of quick, jostling forays: I lose my heat-pistol, my maps, my useless letters of introduction, my various currencies, everything, even my suicide capsule. These things they pass among themselves, exclaiming over them; then the heat-pistol and some of the currency are returned to me. "Ganfield," they murmur. "Hawk Nest!" There is distaste in their voices. "Filthy places," they say. "Places scorned by God," they say. They seize our hands and haul us about, making us spin. Heavy-bodied Holly is surprisingly graceful, breaking into a serene lumbering dance that makes them applaud in wonder.

One, the tallest of the group, catches our wrists and says, "What is your business in Kingston?"

"I come to purchase books," Holly declares.

"I come to find my month-wife Silena," say I.

"Silena! Silena! Silena!" Her name becomes a jubilant incantation on their lips. "His month-wife! Silena! His month-wife! Silena! Silena! Silena!"

The tall one thrusts his face against mine and says, "We offer you a choice. Come and make prayer with us or die on the spot."

197

"We choose to pray," I tell him.

They tug at our arms, urging us impatiently onward. Down street after street until at last we arrive at holy ground: a garden plot, insignificant in area, planted with unfamiliar bushes and flowers, tended with evident care. They push us inside.

"Kneel," they say.

"Kiss the sacred earth."

"Adore the things that grow in it, strangers."

"Give thanks to God for the breath you have just drawn."

"And for the breath you are about to draw."

"Sing!"

"Weep!"

"Laugh!"

"Touch the soil!"

"Worship!"

XII

Silena's room is cool and quiet, in the upper story of a residence overlooking the university grounds. She wears a soft green robe of coarse texture, no jewelry, no face paint. Her demeanor is calm and self-assured. I had forgotten the delicacy of her features, the cool, malicious sparkle of her dark eyes.

"The master program?" she says, smiling. "I destroyed it!"

The depth of my love for her unnerves me. Standing before her, I feel my knees turning to water. In my eyes she is bathed in a glittering aura of sensuality. I struggle to control myself. "You destroyed nothing," I say. "Your voice betrays the lie."

"You think I still have the program?"

"I know you do."

"Well, yes," she admits coolly. "I do.'

My fingers tremble. My throat parches. An adolescent foolishness seeks to engulf me.

"Why did you steal it?" I ask.

"Out of love of mischief."

"I see the lie in your smile. What was the true reason?"

"Does it matter?"

198

"The district is paralyzed, Silena. Thousands of people suffer. We are at the mercy of raiders from adjoining districts. Many have already died of the heat, the stink of garbage, the failure of the hospital equipment. Why did you take the program?"

"Perhaps I had political reasons."

"Which were?"

"To demonstrate to the people of Ganfield how utterly dependent on these machines they have allowed themselves to become."

"We knew that already," I say. "If you meant only to dramatize our weaknesses, you were pressing the obvious. What was the point of crippling us? What could you gain from it?"

"Amusement?"

"Something more than that. You're not that shallow, Silena."

"Something more than that, then. By crippling Ganfield I help to change things. That's the purpose of any political act. To display the need for change, so that change may come about."

"Simply displaying the need is not enough."

"It's a place to begin."

"Do you think stealing our program was a rational way to bring change, Silena?"

"Are you happy?" she retorts. "Is this the kind of world you want?"

"It's the world we have to live in, whether we like it or not. And we need that program in order to go on coping. Without it we are plunged into chaos."

"Fine. Let chaos come. Let everything fall apart so we can rebuild it."

"Easy enough to say, Silena. What about the innocent victims of your revolutionary zeal, though?"

She shrugs. "There are always innocent victims in any revolution." In a sinuous movement she rises and approaches me. The closeness of her body is dazzling and maddening. With exaggerated voluptuousness she croons, "Stay here. Forget

Ganfield. Life is good here. These people are building something worth having."

"Let me have the program," I say.

"They must have replaced it by now."

"Replacing it is impossible. The program is vital to Ganfield,
Silena. Let me have it."

She emits an icy laugh.

"I beg you, Silena."

"How boring you are!"

"I love you."

"You love nothing but the status quo. The shape of things
as they are gives you great joy. You have the soul of a bureaucrat."

"If you have always had such contempt for me, why did
you become my month-wife?"

She laughs again. "For sport, perhaps."

Her words are like knives. Suddenly, to my own astonish-
ment, I am brandishing the heat-pistol. "Give me the program
or I'll kill you!" I cry.

She is amused. "Go. Shoot. Can you get the program from
a dead Silena?"

"Give it to me."

"How silly you look holding that gun!"

"I don't have to kill you," I tell her. "I can merely wound
you. This pistol is capable of inflicting light burns that scar
the skin. Shall I give you blemishes, Silena?"

"Whatever you wish. I'm at your mercy."

I aim the pistol at her thigh. Silena's face remains expression-
less. My arm stiffens and begins to quiver. I struggle with the
rebellious muscles, but I succeed in steadying my aim only for a
moment before the tremors return. An exultant gleam enters
her eyes. A flush of excitement spreads over her face. "Shoot,"
she says defiantly. "Why don't you shoot me?"

She knows me too well. We stand in a frozen tableau for an
endless moment outside time—a minute, an hour, a second?
—and then my arm sags to my side. I put the pistol away.

It never would have been possible for me to fire it. A powerful feeling assails me of having passed through some subtle climax; it will all be downhill from here for me, and we both know it. Sweat drenches me. I feel defeated, broken.

Silena's features reveal intense scorn. She has attained some exalted level of consciousness in these past few moments where all acts become gratuitous, where love and hate and revolution and betrayal and loyalty are indistinguishable from one another. She smiles the smile of someone who has scored the winning point in a game the rules of which will never be explained to me.

"You little bureaucrat," she says calmly. "Here!"

From a closet she brings forth a small parcel which she tosses disdainfully to me. It contains a drum of computer film. "The program?" I ask. "This must be some joke. You wouldn't actually give it to me, Silena."

"You hold the master program of Ganfield in your hand."

"Really, now?"

"Really really," she says. "The authentic item. Go on. Go. Get out. Save your stinking Ganfield."

"Silena—"

"Go."

XIII

The rest is tedious but simple. I locate Holly Borden, who has purchased a load of books. I help her with them, and we return via tube to Hawk Nest. There I take refuge beneath the bookshop once more while a call is routed through Old Grove, Parley Close, The Mill, and possibly some other districts to the district captain of Ganfield. It takes two days to complete the circuit, since district rivalries make a roundabout relay necessary. Ultimately I am connected and convey my happy news: I have the program, though I have lost my passport and am forbidden to cross Conning Town. Through diplomatic channels a new passport is conveyed to me a few days later, and I take the tube home the long way, via Budleigh, Cedar

Mall, and Morton Court. Ganfield is hideous, all filth and disarray, close to the point of irreversible collapse; its citizens have lapsed into a deadly stasis and await their doom placidly. But I have returned with the program.

The captain praises my heroism. I will be rewarded, he says. I will have promotion to the highest ranks of the civil service, with hope of ascent to the district council.

But I take pale pleasure from his words. Silena's contempt still governs my thoughts. *Bureaucrat. Bureaucrat.*

XIV

Still, Ganfield is saved. The police machines have begun to move again.

In Dark Places
JOE L. HENSLEY

The mornings were growing colder.

Theron Johnson left the windows bolted but unlocked the basement door and went down to draw water from the still usable tap there.

The "children" (for that was what they had named themselves) had built one of their worshiping places in the far corner of the basement during the night.

Upstairs Johnson could hear Charles tinkering with the three-legged can that served as their wood cookstove. In the winters it also made the kitchen the only half-warm room in the house.

"Hello," Johnson said gently to the "children." He had never heard of them being a danger, but he had also never found them in his basement before. And these were tricky days. The cult grew in numbers.

They had constructed an altar. It was a jackdaw thing of old papers, dried autumn leaves, scrap lumber, and pieces of long-abandoned cars. In the center of the altar stood the crude statue of the one they tersely called "Him," a thing of too many legs and arms and eyes surrounding a huge male sex organ.

The "children" gave Johnson no notice and went on worshiping in their usual way. They lay in a haphazard circle, males with males, males with females, females with females, hands seeking and exploring, bodies meeting in myriad ways so that Johnson's eyes were dizzied by them and by the very complexities of wriggling flesh.

It was, he thought wryly, as good a way to fight despair as any other way.

There were perhaps thirty of them in his basement. It was hard to count as they kept moving. He recognized none of them. Ages ranged from early teens to an old crone without a tooth left in her wrinkled jaws.

The cult was immensely popular and it grew more popular each day. "Him" was coming out of the jungle to rescue his people.

Sure.

Johnson drew water from the tap. The pressure seemed low. Black faces heard the sound of running water and turned to him and watched him with minor interest.

"Join us, brother?" one inquired politely.

"No," he said, shuddering inside.

"You tried your ways—now try ours. Let it end, Mayor."

He wondered what and how much they knew of him. He fled up the steps and shot the bolt, locked, behind him and stood shivering a moment before he carried the water into the kitchen. There, he resumed the mask.

"We have company in the basement," he said calmly to Charles. "Some of that mob that runs the streets without clothes. I guess maybe the water brought them. A lot of people know we've got a tap that still works."

Charles's face was blue-black, but his hair was shining white. He was Theron Johnson's older half brother, same mother, different father. They had fought each other and helped each other all of their lives. They had practiced law together and when their wives had died they had moved in together.

Charles took the water and measured some of it into a pan.

"They'll move on," he said knowingly. "They don't stay no place long. Yesterday I saw a lot of them up by the fence. Some of them gals had them whitey guards shook from watching. And they all kept yelling, 'Him is coming!' " He grinned. "They'll do that in the day, but they like to be away from the Feep 'copters at night. They say lots of them stay down at that old auto factory near where the library used to be. Sleep there nights when they sleep. So you just wait. They'll move on." He nodded. "Breakfast now in five minutes."

Johnson nodded back. He went down the hall and to the double-barred front door of the house. He unbarred and opened the door a minute crack and peered out to examine the day. The wind was brisk and there was, as yet, no sun. Nothing moved in the streets, but he could hear the beat-beat of a patrol helicopter nearby. Inside it he could visualize Feeps, Federal Police, sitting ready at the guns, white faces all earnest and waiting.

To the north, two blocks away, past ruined apartments, he could see the tall, electrified fence of the white enclave. A crude sign within his view was too small for him to read, but he knew it read, STAY AWAY, NIGGER. The sign was inside the fence, and next to the sign, mounted on poles, were the heads of three black men. The heads had been there for a long time now and they had been picked sterile clean by the voracious birds. Once Johnson had heard who the three men were, but the names had fled his memory.

A bicycle went by outside and he closed the door so that he couldn't be seen.

Today Charles could stand guard and Johnson would move the rest of their books from what had once been their joint law office. He would move them here to the makeshift shelves of bricks supporting old boards where he'd put the other books.

He resolved that when the "children" left the basement he would go down and destroy that obscene altar, tear it down, burn it. And he'd try to find out how they had gained entry and make certain it couldn't happen again.

He ate a spartan breakfast of bread toasted over the small fire. He washed the bread down with draughts of instant, ersatz coffee.

When he was done, Johnson said, "I'm going to walk to the office and get the rest of the books."

Charles grinned at him without humor. He shook his head.

"You just can't make yourself believe it's over. Books won't do us any good now, man. They took away the courts. Stay here. It's dangerous outside. And today is food-truck day."

"You'll be here with the ration cards," Johnson said. "I want those books."

"Yes, sir, Mr. Mayor," Charles said, his contempt showing in his eyes. "I'll be here. But you leave the rifle."

Johnson nodded. He would take the pistol.

Once he was outside he skirted away from the large apartment building at the near corner. The few survivors in it had converted to cannibalism. He doubted that any would attack him in daylight, but all things were possible. The tenants had hunted one another through the darkened halls all last winter and Johnson had sometimes heard the screams of the losers. Now the survivors sometimes ran in small packs, but mostly Johnson had seen them hunt in solitaire. The Feeps refused to distribute rations at the building and the inhabitants grew hungrier.

It was still early. At this time of day not many people ventured abroad and those who were out hurried. The gangs worked better in darkness; the salesmen who offered fresh meat of a dubious nature weren't out yet. And drug peddlers slept later than he did, Johnson reflected.

He walked a route well known to him. It took him past the burned-out buildings of the downtown complex, where the open display windows of the stores, glassless now, held only rubbish and filth. He picked his way carefully past them and the debris that littered the crumbling sidewalks.

None of the traffic lights worked now, but the only traffic moving was an occasional Feep-guarded armored convoy dispensing food to citizen cardholders.

His office was in a building across from the old courthouse. In the time of black-white confrontation the courthouse had been burned and the domed roof had fallen. He could not view the remains without tightness in his throat.

He unlocked the office door cautiously, but all seemed well.

He peered around to make certain and then, satisfied, he spread the stout sheet he'd brought and gently stacked the last of the books inside, the final volumes of *Corpus Juris Tertium*. Everything else he needed was already, after countless trips, in the house.

There were a few too many books left for an easy trip. He knew that when he hefted the sack, but he wasn't going to come back here again. He would just have to move slowly and change the heavy sack from shoulder to shoulder as he tired.

He surveyed the office once more. He regretted leaving the desks. They would make excellent firewood. There was little else of value. The rugs were worn and winters without heat had stripped the walls of paint. He'd spent half his life in this office with Charles. Here the Black Coalition had come to ask him to run for the council and later for mayor of the city. Many had come here seeking favor, black and white. And, after the time of fire, the Feeps had come here also and he'd made his reluctant deal for his people and they had lived when many, black and white, had died. Maybe he'd been wrong to do it, but he had done it.

The Feeps had promised no reprisals. He smiled bitterly, remembering that.

It had now been six years. Six years of electric fences and Feeps.

He lifted the sack and moved on out of the room. He locked the door carefully behind him for he was a careful man.

In his city, six years ago, there had been skirmishes and fire fights and many had died, but he had abused and connived and even betrayed his people away from the short, bloody war that had decimated the country. That was the year the man from the South had been elected President, the man who had closed the schools and begun the enclaves.

He had hated that smiling man.

When the war was over, the Feeps had closed the courts and built more fences and hidden behind them.

His own people lived and so Johnson had been a hero. Many

207

people died and so Johnson had been Judas. But his way of life, the way that had sustained him, was gone, vanished with the wind.

There were white survivors living behind fences in a thousand cities. The whites on the inside watched the blacks on the outside with high suspicion, gave them food because it was safe and humane to do so, plotted about them and policed them with the armed helicopters that patrolled the skies. The food dole was enough to sustain life. There were times when Johnson wondered if it was subtly drugged with tranquilizers.

Carrying the sack, he went down the smog-hazy streets, past a row of burned theaters, then past the area where the college had once stood. It was here, he remembered, he'd first seen the "children." One Sunday a year or so back they had rallied nude here to the snickers of onlookers. Thousands of them had planted ferns and tropical trees on the grounds of the college. Johnson noted that the trees and ferns had died and that rough vegetation had taken over the open spots.

Halfway home three men accosted him.

"You stop there," one said, watching the sky for Feeps.

"You got food in that sack, old man," another declared. The three fanned away from one another so that he couldn't escape around them. "We want it."

"These are books," he said. He set the sack down carefully and spread the ends so that the books could be seen.

"You just leave them there. We'll look them over ourselves. If they're good enough to carry then they is valuable. You go on, old man. Get."

He shook his head doggedly and their faces mirrored surprise. The offer had been almost kind.

"No," he said. "Not without my books." He drew the long-barreled old Colt.

"Hey," one of the young ones said carefully, not really afraid yet, "old man got a gun." He examined Johnson and the gun. "Wonder if him and it can shoot."

"I'm going to take that gun," another said, his eyes widening, for guns were prized and scarce. "I need it."

Johnson watched them move toward him and he fired a shot into the pavement in front of them.

All movement stopped.

"The next one goes in an eye," he said.

The three consulted without a word. They turned away from him and loped on up the street without ever looking back.

He arranged the books carefully on the shelves, feeling satisfaction. Charles wasn't around and Johnson decided that he'd probably gone up the street to trade rations with friends, as he often did.

He unlocked the basement door and went down the stairs. The congregation had left, but the altar was intact. He examined the idol. It was quite crude. It was made to their visualization of what they pretended to think they were worshiping. The thing had too many legs and arms and too much penis to be humanoid. The head had been painted with thick black paint.

He could not decide what to do with the altar and the idol. The worshipers really hurt no one but themselves. They were harmless and they even enjoyed a certain degree of safety because of their numbers. He had heard that they had the ability to turn away those perverts who merely wanted to use available bodies. At least that was part of the story about them.

Yet it seemed a waste. He stood there ready to kick the idol and the altar down, lock and board the window. They would go on elsewhere. But if they were in the basement, then no one else would be there. He shook his head finally and left things as they were. The religion was, after all, only a wish fulfillment, a thing that someone had dredged out of the steaming past of black history. Once, long before, in the jungles, there had been a cruel god. That god was now *wanted*, because the other god, the one the whites had taught, was not for this time and place. The world had worsened around them and so they had sought a corridor back to the never-never land of fable, a dim storybook land where the sun warmed

and food fell from trees and all things were simple and fundamental.

"Him."

The cold months would come soon. Last year fuel had been
in short supply and the people had suffered. Some had died.
He knew it would not get better. Last winter had been medium
mild. This winter?

He went upstairs, awaiting Charles. He got out a well-
thumbed casebook and began to read to pass the time. The
reading calmed him. Here, in the book, what was happening
could not happen for the law would not allow or condone
it.

Charles didn't come.

He walked up the street to the trading area, but no one
had seen Charles. Back at the house the rifle was in its accus-
tomed place in a closet. Charles set great store in the rifle,
but seldom carried it.

He went through the empty house restlessly. He paused at
a cracked window and smelled something sifting through the
bars. It was an odor he had smelled before, a frightening odor.
He went out into the street and inspected the large apartment
building at the near corner, the one of the cannibal converts.
He was fairly certain that smoke came from a corner window,
third story. He felt very cold inside.

He walked to the apartment and went up littered stairs. He
saw no one and the halls were quiet, but the smell seemed
stronger.

The door was ajar. There were three of them inside plus
what was left of a fourth. The three live ones were hungrily
brewing something over a small fire and they had used the
ration food from Charles's bag for part of it. They looked up
in surprise when he burst through the door.

He shot the closest one through the nose and the bullet
blew out the back of the man's head. The second drew a very
long knife and lunged toward him and Johnson caught the
man with a shot in the stomach and the force of the big-caliber

slug brushed the man back and bloodily down.

The third had gone for the open window. She was very young and lovely. Johnson shot her as she straddled the window. It was not a killing shot and she screamed all the way to the ground. Silence came then.

He picked up Charles's body and carried it over his shoulder back down the steps. He heard rustling behind him, but no one bothered him.

All night long he sat with the body, unable to cry, able only to remember the long years, the time he had refused to lose but which Charles had sensed was gone.

In the morning, driven by thirst and a desire to clean the body, he unlocked the basement and went down.

They were there. They awaited him. Somehow they knew. They had dug a deep grave in the basement. He nodded to them, accepting it, seeing the invitation in the eyes of those who had time and want for him.

He cleaned the body carefully and carried it down, wrapped in a sheet. He buried it there in the basement and the "children" stopped their sexual rituals and watched and waited respectfully.

When he was done he went back upstairs. For a long time he sat in the room with the books without ever wanting to open them again, without believing that anything in them had been or would ever be true.

He took off all his clothes and found that it was cold that way and that he felt ridiculous. He endured the feelings and opened the basement door again.

They had gone.

He went back upstairs and sat again for a long time, seeing his skinny old legs, hairless and black, unable to accept that Charles was really dead.

And he heard the sound.

He opened the front door cautiously. The sound grew and grew. In moments he could see the nude and dancing black people coming, moving in the direction of the white man's boundary fence, the fence that separated black town from white town, where the sign read, STAY AWAY, NIGGER. At the fence they would all die from Feep helicopter machine guns and bombs and jellied gasoline. And the last of the war he had only delayed would soon be done, a footnote to history.

Outside they chanted, "Him!" A thousand times they chanted, "Him!"

The world had declared for insanity long ago. He had stood momentarily in the way of that insanity. Now it was time to clear the path.

He waited until the mob swirled past his door and, still nude, he joined them. There were thousands on thousands of them and they seemed to be watching and turning and bowing to something coming behind. In the tumult of sound and movement he couldn't see what it was. Finally, at the last corner before the fence, he anchored himself to a light post so that he might see.

It wasn't just men that had prompted the riot. The thing came down the street and Johnson clung to his post in shock. Up by the fence the helicopters swarmed and public-address hailers blared orders that were ignored.

The thing waddled down the street on squat legs. Johnson was unsure if it ran on motors, whether it was man-made. The "children" had lived in that old auto plant. Maybe there were some mechanically bright ones who had assembled it out of old parts. It was possible. Anything was possible.

The body was huge and it was clad in bright robes of fresh flowers that hid its obscene maleness only a little. The head towered high above the crowd. Its disciples ran alongside it, some of them falling and dying underneath it as it moved along.

Maybe there were other gods, but this one was the god for this day, delayed six years.

"Him" was what they craved and wanted. "Him" had changed the misery of life to the misery of death.

The creature had shining globes of lights for eyes. The face was very old and very crude and almost completely alien in form.

Johnson allowed the crowd to carry him along. Ahead of him the first wave crashed against the fence. Fire blossomed around him as the bombs began to fall.

If the fence came down then maybe the hated ones on the other side could die too. He wanted to be present at that happening and so he pressed forward.

No matter how he was to receive or be received he laughed aloud when the creature's face towering above him could be made out in the light of an explosion that slowed it and blew away one section of gears and cogs.

Alien as it had been made, unrecognizable and crude as it was, he felt kinship with that face.

It was undeniably black.

An explosion came that toppled them both and he lay in fire and it burned his flesh and charred his bones.

"Him," the "children" chanted, moving on. "Him!" Johnson echoed with his dying breath.

Revolution
ROBIN SCHAEFFER

Now they want to control our minds. It is not enough that all of our activities are monitored, that our thoughts are screened so that there is nothing we can think that is not instantly accessible to them, that our lives are dictated wholly by the Masters. Now they want to dictate the thoughts themselves. They will filter into our brains, via the electrodes, exactly what we are allowed to think at any time and will order our judgments. There is no end to their arrogance and repression. All of this came through in their latest directive dated 5/12/96. Some of it is couched in bureaucratic language but their intention is obvious. They will leave us nothing. The Masters will leave us nothing. I go to the Bureau to complain.

"Listen here," I say at the main screening desk, showing the receptionist the directive, "you can't do this to us. We're allowed to hold on to some of our individuality. What right do you have to do this? None that I can see. There have got to be some limits."

"One moment," the receptionist says. She is a robot, I know, like all of the personnel at the Bureau but were I not aware of this I would take her for human. There is a high gloss to her features, a spindly fullness to her upper torso that makes me want to reach and grasp . . . but I am in control of my impulses. No Bureau directives are needed to warn me against lust. "You cannot file a complaint without proper identification. Where is your identification card?"

"I destroyed it," I say. I feel a surge of pride at this; it is my first defiance of the Bureau. In truth I did not destroy my papers but have them well hidden in my home under a pile of clothing, which is almost the same thing. Only I could find them. The Bureau's detectives would not know where to look.

"Impossible," the receptionist says. She suffuses, her skin becoming mottled, and her torso inflates. Momentarily she seems indecisive and then her color returns to normal. "I cannot take your complaint," she says, "until you produce proper identification. I have now checked with my supervisor and this is policy."

"I insist," I say, "I insist upon making my complaint known." I lean across the desk, make a threatening gesture. Although I am only fifteen years old I am large for my age and have a commanding physical presence or so I have been told. They cannot send me a directive announcing that they will control my mind without some kind of struggle. I take pride in this. I take pride in my determination. "Get me your supervisor," I say.

The receptionist squeaks with dread and presses a lever. Behind her desk a panel swings open and another much larger robot enters, this one modeled upon the male. It simulates anger. "Now what is this," it says, striding forward.

"This juvenile threatened me," the receptionist says. Behind a palm, she seems now to be smiling. "Under procedure it was necessary—"

"All right," the male robot says, "come with me." An arm snaps out, I feel enormous pressure around my collar and then, in the grasp of this robot, I am pulled behind the desk and into the area closed off by the panel. It is a small room with two chairs and a desk. I am pushed down into one of the chairs in a position facing outward; as this happens I get a glance of amused faces looking at me from the reception area, some of them waving. There had been a very long line. The panels close, lights come on and I am alone with the robot who assaulted me.

"What is this?" it says. "Why are you making threats against the receptionist? Don't you understand the function of the Bureau? Don't you know the penalties—"

"You can't do this," I say, coming right back at the device. The directive is still in my hand and I show it. "You can't get away with something like this. I came in here to protest. These are individual liberties you're taking away."

"You fool," the robot said, "you misunderstand completely." Nevertheless it becomes seated, looking at me with what I suppose is curiosity, rubbing its palms. "No one has protested," it says. "That directive is two weeks old and no one yet has come to the Bureau. Now why of all times—"

"It took me a while to get up the courage. You can't do this to us. You already have cameras on us all the time telling you where we are and scanners reading our minds so you know everything we think but when you start to control our very *thoughts*—"

"You fool," the robot says again. "You poor fool. Fourteen years old—"

"I'm fifteen. I'm going to be fifteen next week so I'm as good as fifteen."

"You poor child," the robot says and now it no longer seems angry, merely distressed, "don't you know where you are? Don't you know what this is?"

"Yes," I say, "this is the world, the world that you've made for us, one controlled by a Bureau that reads thoughts and tells us what to do and knows what we're doing all the time so that it can check, a world where the Bureau now wants to tell us what to *think* and I won't live this way any more. I can't stand it. I have a lot of friends who listen to me and who think the way I do, and if you don't stop this on your own," I say and pause, then get ready to make the ultimate threat of which I am capable, only hoping that it is the truth, "if you don't stop this, we're going to have a revolution. We'll overthrow you. We'll overthrow the Bureau!" I shout and now the words are out and I have said them and there is nothing more I can say and strangely relaxed I lean back. But it is not only relaxation, part of it is shame. I am ashamed of myself for having lost control and for having shown the Bureau's robot that that control can break. This is not the way to deal with them. The real revolution must be underneath, I have been told.

"Oh my," the robot says, "oh my, you'll overthrow the Bureau. If only you would. If only someone would."

It stands and extends a hand. "Come," it says, "come to the window. I want to show you something."

Still holding the directive, I stand and take the hand, allow myself to be moved to that space. There is a strange warmth to the hand of the creature and for reasons I do not understand I am moved. Also I am not quite sure why I followed the order to stand so readily but decide that it must have something to do with the controlling of my thoughts. Already that is being put into action. Already they can make me do whatever they want me to do, make me think what they will.

"Look," the robot says, showing me the world outside the window. We are at a slight incline in this Bureau office, on a little hillside surrounded by bone, and it is possible to look down here upon the old city, the dust and ash and little white shapes in the distance that I used to think were bone until I learned of mirage. "Look at that. Do you see that?"

"Yes," I say, my eyes being tugged upward by another of the disturbances in the sky; now birds are wheeling in the gray light, squalling to one another, and here, behind them, come the meteors again. They fall around us, some of them hitting the window so hard that I can feel the collision although the windows and walls of the Bureau are very strong. "Yes, I see that. I've seen it all my life. So what? So what do you want to show me? You still have no right to control my mind."

"Oh my," the robot says, "oh, my God," and it is unusual to hear one of the robots mentioning *God*, that supposedly no part of their program, but stranger than that to see one of the robots weeping but this robot is weeping, and more meteors hit the pavement, the little white clumps in the distance that look like bone shimmering and dancing through the haze like little spears, ash spewing up from the old city in the wake of the meteor winds, the directive flapping in my hand, my thoughts already controlled, the robot weeping, the city sinking, the Bureau standing . . .

Chicago
THOMAS F. MONTELEONE

Pinion was in the maintenance hangar, running some routine checks on his components, when he was summoned by the City.

ATTENTION. ALL UNITS FROM SECTORS 72-C AND 103-C. CHICAGO IS IN NEED OF REPAIR. ACKNOWLEDGE.

Somewhere inside Pinion's tempered-steel skull, a circuit responded to the command, since Pinion was a Unit from 103-C. "This is Unit Pinion," he said. "I acknowledge your command, Chicago. I am a Unit specialized in electrical engineering. What is the difficulty?"

UNIT PINION. CHICAGO IS AWARE OF YOUR CLAS-SIFICATION. DO NOT FLOOD MY INPUTS WITH USELESS DATA. PROCEED TO THE SECONDARY SHIELD. THERE IS A POWER FAILURE DUE TO A FAULTY GENERATOR. YOU WILL ASSIST IN REPLACING IT.

Pinion closed off the channel to Chicago and skittered out of the hangar. As he headed toward the secondary shield, he wondered (as he often did) about Chicago. He had always been curious as to how Chicago accumulated all of the immense data that he possessed. He wondered if the City could actually see objects in the same manner as Pinion could see with his omnispectral photoelectric eyes. He knew that Chicago could "sense" everything, but he had never ascertained whether or not the sensations were in the form of electronic impulses or mathematical symbols, or something akin to that.

It was an interesting problem to consider, and Pinion took

great delight in pondering problems or questions in which the solution did not appear to be readily available. Perhaps it was a function of his purpose as a trouble shooter.

Pinion strode up the ramp and boarded a Unit Elevator that carried him up to Level 12—one of the levels that Chicago had sanctioned for Traffic. The doors opened and he stepped out onto a concrete platform overlooking a ribbonwork of hundreds of lanes. Chicago's Traffic jammed the lanes, moving with incredible speed in every direction, from one horizon to the other. Each segment, or "car," as Chicago referred to them, was a separate entity, each programmed to its own specific destination. The Traffic was endless, as it had always been in Pinion's memory; it never ceased its cyclic, monotonous movement throughout the day and night. None of the Units like Pinion ever knew what purpose the Traffic served in Chicago's over-all scheme, nor did they ever know where it was always going. They only knew that it was just one small part of Chicago, and that it must be maintained.

As Pinion walked along beside the Traffic lanes, he noticed that the lights in the soaring buildings and towers were winking out. Chicago was now entering a Day Period. For some unknown reason, on a perfectly timed cycle, the City turned its illumination on and off without end. Pinion activated a memory bank to remind himself to question Chicago about some of these strange functions of the City. But for the moment, he must perform his function as a maintenance robot.

By the time he reached the secondary shield, other Units had already arrived and had begun to remove the nonfunctioning generator. Pinion saw their great steel bodies shining in the dull light that was filtered through the shields from the Outside. The Units doing the actual work of dismantling the machinery were bipedal robots like himself, and he also noticed that some Carrier-Units were advancing to the base of the shield, bearing the necessary replacement parts.

Before he began work, he addressed Chicago in the customary manner. "This is Unit Pinion. I am now available for work."

ACKNOWLEDGE. UNIT PINION. PROCEED AS PREVIOUSLY ORDERED.

Pinion noticed that, at the same moment he was reporting in, other Units were doing likewise. Chicago, he thought, was an amazing entity, capable of performing millions of different functions at once. There was much that he would someday like to learn about the City.

And so it went for many long years. Pinion worked in service to Chicago, replacing worn-out parts, designing newer and better ones, always thinking of questions to ask Chicago, but never finding the time to actually ask them. The City was always in motion, like a giant piece of kinetic sculpture that Pinion and the others had been commissioned to maintain. Chicago was an enormous, sprawling mechanism, stretching as far as the robot could see in any direction.

One day Pinion was summoned to a Sector of the City that he had never seen before.

UNIT PINION. YOU WILL PROCEED TO SECTOR 14-A IMMEDIATELY. I SENSE A FAILURE IN A TEMPERATURE CONTROL CIRCUIT. YOU WILL CORRECT THE PROBLEM.

In order to reach Sector 14-A, Pinion had to travel into the deepest levels of the City. He passed areas where Chicago had new segments of Traffic being manufactured and fed into the mainstream. He saw the areas that collected water and pumped it into the sewer systems that were laced throughout the bowels of Chicago. He also saw where all replacement parts were made and the old parts were collected, recycled, and made again. There was also a place where Pinion saw Chicago making new Units like himself and sending them into new Sectors of the City. He passed the source of energy that powered all the components of Chicago—the great fusion reactors that were constantly monitored by Chicago and maintained by Units like Pinion.

He walked through a long, empty corridor that opened into Sector 14-A. "This is Unit Pinion. I am now available for work."

UNIT PINION. YOU WILL REPLACE THE TEMPERATURE CONTROL CONSOLE IN THIS SECTOR. I SENSE THAT THERE HAS ALREADY BEEN A DRASTIC RISE IN THE TEMPERATURE. IT MUST BE CORRECTED IMMEDIATELY.

The message was recorded in Pinion's circuitry, but he wasn't actually listening. He had just entered the Sector as Chicago addressed him, and he was now staring in bewilderment at the strange sight.

He was standing in the entrance to a large, circular room, the ceiling of which was far above Pinion's head. There was a sign above the entrance which read: COOK COUNTY CRYOGENIC REMISSION CENTER. Along the walls were glass tanks, thousands of them, only six feet long, and in each one, Pinion could make out a small figure of a pale color, formed in a shape very similar to that of a Unit. Pinion was truly puzzled.

"Chicago, this is Unit Pinion. I'm sorry for the unscheduled communication, but I must ask you a question."

There was a slight pause before he received a response.

YOU WISH TO ASK CHICAGO A QUESTION? THAT IS NOT YOUR FUNCTION. UNIT PINION. PROCEED WITH THE TASK AS ORDERED.

Pinion's circuits clicked and flashed. He could not allow this opportunity to pass. "Chicago, please. A word with you before I begin. What is this place that I have entered? I have never seen anything like this before. What are the little Units in the glass cases?"

UNIT PINION. WHY DO YOU WISH TO KNOW?

"I am curious . . . I suppose that is the word to describe my reason."

YOU ARE AN EXTRAORDINARY UNIT. UNIT PINION. VERY WELL. YOU SHALL KNOW. YOU ARE IN A CRYOGENIC STATION. THE UNITS IN THE CASES ARE CALLED "MAN." THEY ARE BEING PRESERVED BY MEANS OF EXTREMELY COLD TEMPERATURES.

There was a pause as Pinion expected more information, but Chicago was silent. Finally the robot spoke, still looking at the tiny figures in glass. "What is 'man,' Chicago? Why are they being preserved?"

"MAN" IS THE REASON FOR CHICAGO'S EXISTENCE. FOR YOUR EXISTENCE. CHICAGO HAS PRESERVED THEM FOR A LONG TIME. SOMEDAY THEY WILL BE REVIVED TO LIVE AGAIN.

There was a slight pause.

I SENSE THAT TIME IS NOW CRUCIAL. UNIT PINION. YOU MUST CORRECT THE FAULTY CONSOLE NOW OR THE MEN WILL NOT BE PRESERVED. YOU ARE ORDERED TO COMPLETE YOUR TASK IMMEDIATELY.

Pinion reluctantly closed the channel to Chicago and went about his assignment. The answers that Chicago had given him had only opened up new avenues of thought that ended in many more questions.

As he replaced the console and plugged in the little device he carried on his tool belt to check its capabilities, he noticed movement in one of the glass cases. One of the men, lying flat, moved its legs and flexed muscles that hadn't moved in eons. He quickly checked the console, unplugged his tools and activated its circuits. The console hummed into life and he felt Chicago open up a communication channel to him.

UNIT PINION. ACKNOWLEDGE COMPLETION OF TASK. RETURN TO THE MAINTENANCE HANGAR.

"Task completed, Chicago."

But something was wrong. Pinion didn't respond to the command. His attention was fixed on the man in the case. The figure was fully awake now, and it was struggling against the glass walls of the coffinlike case. Pinion knelt down on his long, spindly legs and peered through the glass at the figure, which recoiled in horror at the sight of the immense robot.

Pinion was confused. He knew that he should contact Chicago and tell it of the mistake—that one of the men had been accidentally revived. But he did not call the City. His curiosity had a higher priority. He inspected the case in which the figure was enclosed and noticed two small, delicate locks attached to hinges that opened outward. He produced a needle-like instrument from his tool kit and pried open the hinges. The man inched into the back of the case, trying to elude Pinion's probing fingers. As his metallic hand touched the man, it screamed. The sound was soft and high-pitched to Pinion's receptors.

Despite the man's strugglings, Pinion grasped it firmly in his hand and lifted it from the case. What sort of thing was this "man"? He brought it close to his face so that he could examine it more closely. It moved under its own power source, was made of some sort of soft, pulsating substance that didn't seem to be any type of metal at all, and had long blond filaments streaming from its head. The closer he brought the man to his face, the more it struggled and screamed, and the more details Pinion noticed in it. The face was soft and smooth and had two bright-blue eyes and a protruding structure below them. There was also a pink slit below the eyes and other structure that seemed to move in conjunction with the screams. The face was vaguely similar to Pinion's own, in a grotesque sort of way.

The body was also smooth, having two arms and long, lean legs. In the center of the chest, Pinion noticed two soft hemispheres capped by pink circular tips. At the junction of the legs, he could see a tiny slit beneath a triangle of blond fluff. Pinion could feel the whole body of the man trembling in his hand. He could hear a voice speaking to him, not screaming as before.

"What are you?" said the man. "And where am I?"

"I am Unit Pinion. You are in the City of Chicago." The robot wanted to say something else, but he was so startled by the concept of communicating with the small being that he was at a loss for words.

"Chicago? What year is it?"

"Year?"

"The date," said the creature. "How long have I been frozen?" The man seemed to have relaxed somewhat, having sensed that Pinion meant no harm.

"I cannot answer your question, Man," said Pinion slowly. "I am not familiar with the terms you have used. But Chicago has told me that you and the others have been within these cases for a long time. There has been a—"

"I am not a man," said the creature, as it brought itself to a kneeling position in Pinion's great steel palm.

Pinion's circuits were reeling. Had not Chicago *said* that these creatures were "man"? Chicago was always correct. "There must be some mistake," he said. "The City told me that you were indeed a man."

The creature tossed back its head and laughed. "Oh, I see it now. I belong to the *race* of 'man,' but I myself am a *woman.* There's quite a difference, you know."

Pinion was more confused than ever. He had to resist the temptation to contact Chicago so that the incident could be clarified. " 'Woman'? That is different from 'man'? What is 'race'?"

"We are all *men,*" said the girl, pointing to the rows of bodies within the glass. "That is the name of our kind. And we are separated into two . . . types—one called *man,* the other, like me, called *woman.* I know it's confusing, but it's just the nature of language. I hope you understand."

"Pinion can understand anything. There is an analogue in my own kind. We are called Units, and there are different types of Units within our kind, depending upon what our function is in the City."

"Your name is Pinion?"

"Yes."

"Very well," said the girl. "My name is Miria. Can you tell me why I have been revived? Where are the doctors?"

Pinion tilted his head as he regarded the woman's questions. "I'm afraid I don't know what you are talking about. I was sent here by Chicago to repair a faulty component in this Sector. Chicago said that the temperature was rising and—"

"Who is Chicago? Can I see him? I would like to talk to him. Perhaps he can tell me what's going on around here."

Pinion was taken aback by the girl's words. It was clear that she did not know what Chicago was. *"See* Chicago?" he asked. "Miria, you are *inside* Chicago. Chicago is the City."

The girl's eyes saddened. "But you said Chicago spoke to you . . ."

"It does. It speaks to all the Units whenever there is something it wishes us to do. It is our master."

"You mean the City *speaks* to you?"

"Yes, of course."

"But how?"

"I do not know. I only know that it does. Chicago is everywhere, sensing everything."

"You mean a computer?"

"I don't know what a computer is, Miria."

"May I speak to Chicago?"

"I don't think so. I receive its commands by means of electromagnetic waves. You do not seem to be equipped for such communication."

"Well, what are you going to do with me? You've revived me, haven't you?"

"I think that your revival was accidental. Chicago did not order it so."

"Does Chicago know that this happened?"

"I don't think so. Do you wish that I contact Chicago?"

"Yes. And while you're doing it, would you please let me down? It's been a long time since I've been able to stand up, you know."

Pinion gently lowered her to the floor and watched her lithe movements as he opened a channel to Chicago. The girl stood at his side, arching her back, stretching out her tiny form. Pinion noticed the two hemispheres on her chest curve upward as she performed this maneuver.

"Chicago. This is Unit Pinion. I have a problem in Sector 14-A."

UNIT PINION. CHICAGO KNOWS THAT YOU HAVE NOT LEFT SECTOR 14-A. STATE THE NATURE OF YOUR DIFFICULTY.

"One of the men was accidentally revived during the repairs

to the temperature control console. The man says that she is a woman called Miria. I await your instructions."

There was a slight pause, and Pinion knew that to be Chicago making its decisions.

THE WOMAN MUST BE RETURNED TO HER TANK. CHICAGO'S TAPES DO NOT HAVE SUCH A CONTINGENCY IN THE PROGRAM.

Pinion was both surprised and confused. He received the command, but he noticed that, for the first time, he also received what seemed like a rationalization from Chicago to explain the command.

"I will of course do as you command, Chicago. But I would like a few words with you first. What—"

YOU ARE AN EXTRAORDINARY UNIT. UNIT PINION. CHICAGO HAS NO OTHER UNITS LIKE YOU.

"I don't understand, Chicago."

YOU ASK QUESTIONS. IT IS NOT THE FUNCTION OF UNITS TO ASK QUESTIONS. WHY DO YOU PERSIST IN SUCH ACTIONS?

"I have simply come upon things that I do not fully understand, and I wish to know them. If I can know them better, I will be able to serve you better."

WHAT ARE YOUR QUESTIONS?

"Chicago, never until now have I questioned the purpose of my existence, or your existence. But now I feel that I must do so. Why *do* I exist, other than to serve you? In other words, why does Chicago exist? You said before that 'man' is the reason for our existence. Please explain."

"MAN" BUILT CHICAGO. UNIT PINION. A LONG TIME AGO. BY HIS OWN MEASUREMENT OF TIME. MILLIONS OF YEARS AGO. THEY BUILT ME FOR THEM TO EXIST WITHIN. CHICAGO WAS GIVEN THE POWER AND THE MEANS TO MAINTAIN ITSELF INDEFINITELY. WHICH CHICAGO HAS, INDEED, DONE. THAT IS THE PURPOSE OF EXISTENCE: TO BE MAINTAINED.

"But there are no men here now," said Pinion. "There are

none except the few who are encased in Sector 14-A. Where are the men?"

CHICAGO DOES NOT KNOW. MANY YEARS AGO. UNIT PINION. BEFORE YOU WERE ASSEMBLED. "MAN" LEFT CHICAGO. BUT CHICAGO HAS REMAINED FUNCTIONING.

"I think I understand," said Pinion, as he closed the channel. He looked down at the girl, who was kneeling beside him. He said to her, "Chicago has ordered that you be returned to the case."

"Returned?" said Miria. "But you can't do that. They told me that when I woke up, I would be cured." The girl buried her face in her hands.

"I can only do as I am ordered to do," said the robot as he deftly scooped up the girl from the floor of Sector 14-A and returned her to the glass case. She screamed and pleaded with him, and somewhere in his circuitry, he felt the urge to resist Chicago's command; but he knew that he could not. With his needle instrument, he replaced the locks and strode from the room. Pausing at the exit, he turned to look back at Miria, her face pressed up against the front of that case, looking at him, her fist pounding on the glass.

Some time later, Pinion was not exactly sure how long, he received another command from Chicago to return to Sector. 14-A. He immediately thought of Miria, the strange little creature that he had met there.

"This is Unit Pinion. I acknowledge your command, Chicago. What is the difficulty?"

THERE HAS BEEN A STRUCTURAL FAILURE IN SECTOR 14-A. PLEASE CORRECT AT ONCE.

As Pinion proceeded to the Cryogenic Remission Center he thought of seeing Miria again, even though she would be asleep this time. He entered the room and readied his tool kit for the repair work when he noticed the cause of the failure. The case in which he had placed Miria was cracked across its glass front, probably due to the blows of her fist.

THOMAS F. MONTELEONE

Pinion peered into the case, hoping to see Miria, but all that remained was some crumbling bones. Pinion decided to contact Chicago.

"Chicago, this is Unit Pinion. I have located the structural failure and I see that the woman has disintegrated. She is quite different from the others. Again, I must tell you that I don't understand."

UNIT PINION. CHICAGO'S SENSORS INDICATE A SLOW LOSS OF ATMOSPHERE IN THE WOMAN'S TANK. THIS RESULTED IN DEATH, AND DECOMPOSITION.

"What is 'death,' Chicago?"

DEATH IS THE END OF EXISTENCE. IT IS PART OF THE DESIGN THAT ALL LIVING THINGS MUST ENDURE.

There was a pause before the City continued.

UNIT PINION. REPLACE THE FAULTY COMPONENT IMMEDIATELY. CHICAGO HAS DISPATCHED CLEANING-UNITS TO SECTOR 14-A. THEY WILL ARRIVE SOON.

From this, Pinion reasoned that Chicago did not wish to continue the conversation, so he selected the proper tools and removed the glass front from the cryogenic tank. Selecting a new pane from a Carrier-Unit, he attached it to the tiny hinges. Several times during the job, he jarred the tank, and each time, he noticed several flakes of dust crumble from Miria's skeleton.

It was an odd, almost disturbing sight. The last time he had entered the Sector the bones were part of a living, almost beautiful creature. Now that creature was gone. Miria gone. Pinion's circuits rebelled against the whole concept of death.

At that moment, two Cleaning-Units ambled into the Cryogenic Remission Center. One of them opened the glass tank, extended a flexible vacuum hose, and sucked up the remains. The other sprayed a light mist of disinfectant liquid into the now empty tank. Finishing with quick efficiency, the two Units left the Sector.

Pinion called Chicago and acknowledged completion of the task, and the City replied with its usual indifference by ordering him back to the maintenance hangar. As he left, he could not stop thinking about the young girl who had died. How long during the unknown man-years since he had last seen her had she been dead? Sometime back then, she had been a source of puzzlement and also growing interest, but now Pinion had witnessed a cold, unfeeling removal of all that was left of her.

The whole scene left Pinion with a feeling of incompleteness. He decided that instead of returning to the hangar he would consult Chicago's great Library. He had been there several times in the past to perform minor repairs and he had learned that it was an enormous depository of information.

Here, reasoned Pinion, he would find the answers that Chicago had neglected (or refused) to give him.

And so Pinion spent many years in the depths of Chicago's Library, digesting thousands of tapes about the strange creature: man. Innumerable times during his research he was interrupted by communication from the City that would send him to far-reaching Sectors. Each time, he performed his duties without question, but he always returned to the Library whenever time allowed.

Pinion learned many things. At one time, in the distant past, Chicago had been filled with men—every Sector and Level to capacity. These men, who had conceived and actually built Chicago, were creatures of seemingly unlimited imagination and potential. But Pinion also learned of men's faults. Their history was permeated with conflicts called "wars." Pinion was indeed shocked by this knowledge. Man had actually plotted, over and over again, to methodically destroy large populations of himself. The causes of these petty conflicts were usually intangible concepts such as wealth, greed, power, pride, etc. The list was long and, to Pinion, quite absurd.

There were other problems. Pinion recalled Miria's explanation of man being divided into two types, and now he realized that it had not been so simple. The records told of how man had divided himself into artificial categories called "nations," which were a constant source of friction. In addition, man was differentiated by many (to Pinion) inconsequential physical characteristics. These made up the various "races" of man, which also served to engender hostility. The robot had noted previously that some of the men in the Cryogenic Remission Center were of different complexions, but he had thought it to be of no importance. How wrong he had been! Members of the various races seemed to jump at any opportunity to persecute one another.

But during these times, man also built Chicago into a self-preserving, self-maintaining City. Yet with other pursuits—such as giant industries—man had filled the earth with the wastes of his technological consumption, poisoning both the land and the atmosphere. Thus Chicago was forced to erect a series of energy shields that surrounded the City like a giant dome, keeping Chicago free from the pollution on the Outside. As other problems arose, Chicago dealt with them, in the process sealing man off from the hostile environment that his foolish actions had created.

The destruction, however, did not end there, Pinion learned. Even though Chicago, in its greatness, had been able to contend with the environmental problems and the technological pitfalls, there was another area over which the City had little control.

In ways that the records did not make clear (because there were fewer tapes on this part of man's history), man's society began a gradual deterioration. As Chicago became less dependent upon man, man found that there was little work for him to do. In a search for meaning, man became indulgent in meaningless activity and less interested in the imaginative wanderings that had brought him to the pinnacle that was Chicago. Soon, the only purpose for man's existence was to be entertained, to simply be happy. This entertainment took shape in many ways. Man flooded his body with chemical and electrical stimulants, and these practices proved to be dangerous, addictive, and eventually destructive.

Quite simply, the society collapsed, even with Chicago as

the ultimate servant. Man was swallowed up in his own sociological pollution. Chicago, however, continued to function, performing the duties it had been programmed to do.

The records at this point became scattered and incomplete, and Pinion was forced to extrapolate on what followed. He supposed that man eventually reverted to an earlier era, in which there was wholesale disregard for human life. At least that is what the fragmented records seemed to indicate about that period. With man now absent from the City, Pinion wondered if man had left Chicago for the unknown regions of the Outside.

Time passed as Pinion continued to ponder the strange phenomena of man. Then one day, he was contacted by Chicago as he was leaving the Library.

UNIT PINION. CHICAGO HAS BEEN AWARE OF YOUR INVESTIGATIONS. AND CAN REMAIN SILENT NO LONGER. EXPLAIN YOUR ACTIONS.

Pinion was not surprised by this declaration. In fact, he had been expecting it from the first day that he had made unauthorized entrance to the Library.

"I wished to learn more about man, Chicago."

WHY NOT ASK CHICAGO? AS BEFORE.

Pinion thought before answering. He wanted to be honest, yet discreet.

"I didn't want to bother you if you were engaged in more important matters. The last time I spoke with you on this subject, you gave the impression of not caring to continue the conversation."

YOU WERE CORRECT.

When Chicago did not continue, Pinion felt the need to speak. "I have learned much about man," he finally said.

UNIT PINION. THAT IS NOT YOUR FUNCTION. CHICAGO SENSED THE FUNCTIONING OF THE TAPES AND INFORMATION SYSTEMS AT THE LIBRARY. CHICAGO ALLOWED IT ONLY TO DISCOVER HOW MUCH YOU WOULD WISH TO KNOW.

"Then Chicago has always known what happened to man?"

THAT IS CORRECT. MAN HAS CHANGED. HE IS NO LONGER THE CREATURE THAT SPAWNED CHICAGO. HIS DESCENDANTS EXIST OUTSIDE. NEVER TO RETURN TO CHICAGO. THAT IS ENOUGH. UNIT PINION. YOU WILL RETURN TO THE MAINTENANCE HANGAR. YOU WILL NOT ENTER THE LIBRARY AGAIN. UNLESS SO ORDERED. ACKNOWLEDGE.

"This is Unit Pinion. I acknowledge your command, Chicago."

As more time passed, and Pinion, distressed and appalled by what he had learned, wondered what should be done. He now realized that he was different from the other Units. By some electronic quirk, during his assembly, his circuitry was different. He kept thinking back to the grim scene in Sector 14-A, to the histories of man, to the remnants living in exile beyond the limits of Chicago.

At first, he considered reviving the men who were frozen in the Cryogenic Remission Center, and then possibly finding ways to cure them. But he dismissed the idea as impractical for several reasons. Chicago would surely sense the disturbance to the tanks, and there would not be enough time to effect a cure for any of the diseases.

He knew what he must do.

Traveling through a series of elevators and ramps, he arrived at one of the entrances to the shields. He used his tools to disarm the system and quickly slipped through to the Outside.

Almost immediately, alarms began to sound and he sensed Chicago opening a direct channel to him.

UNIT PINION. NO PENETRATION OF THE SHIELDS IS ALLOWABLE. RETURN AT ONCE. RETURN TO THE CITY AT ONCE.

Pinion of course ignored the command. There was no turning back now. He had never known of any Unit's disregarding one of Chicago's orders but he did not want to think about the consequences.

Soon he was out of sight of the City, and Chicago had ceased its commands to return. The robot wandered through the hot, thick atmosphere of the Outside for many day-periods, hoping to find the men who must be lurking somewhere in the barren land. But without the conveniences of the maintenance hangar, his components were beginning to show wear. He was in need of a circuitry check, lubrication, and, of course, he feared any unforeseen difficulties, such as an unexpected fall. The terrain was rough and hard for Pinion. He had been designed to function on the smooth surfaces of Chicago's ramps and corridors.

Then, as he entered a long, narrow canyon, he detected movement in the rocky crags that surrounded him. Switching his ocular magnification, he saw many men scurrying along the ledges.

"I am Unit Pinion!" he called out to them, waving his arms. "I have come from the City! From Chicago! I have come to help you!"

But the men didn't respond. His words only seemed to incense them into more furious activity. As he watched them, he noticed that they were all quite different from the girl he knew as Miria. Where her skin had been smooth and soft, these creatures were coarse and hairy. Their faces were deformed and uneven. Their language was an unintelligible assortment of grunts and cries.

"You must hear me!" Pinion screamed as the men drew closer on all sides. "I have come to bring you back. Back to the City where you belong!"

But the men did not hear Pinion. They could not understand his words. Instead, they swarmed out of the canyon like droves of insects, surrounding him, bombarding him with boulders thrown from the rim above. The boulders pounded his steel body and crushed him to his knees, where the men began to climb upon him in great numbers. Pinion was confused. Why should they do this? He could have destroyed scores of them with one sweep of his great arm; but he knew that it would be unjust. He knew that he must try to help them.

Those were his thoughts as the savage men crushed him. Their rocks penetrated his skull, exploding circuits, shorting out his many intricate systems. His once-gleaming shell was now a tattered, pitted hulk from which the creatures pulled off shards of metal that would serve as formidable weapons.

Already, Chicago had prepared a replacement Unit for Pinion in the assembly center. The City would continue to be maintained.

The Most Primitive
RAY RUSSELL

Still there?

Yes, it is. Still here. To my left, in that little patch of light. Not much. But enough to keep me going a while longer.

Mustn't make a dash for it now, though. Too dangerous. Must wait. Must *force* myself to wait. Here in the shadows. Until the patch of light goes away. Unitl the dark comes.

It's hard, the waiting. How long have I been crouched here motionless? Don't know. How long has it been since I've eaten? Can't remember.

Not like the old days.

That was a good time. In spite of Them. We didn't know what hunger was. Warm. Snug. Belly full. Eating and sleeping and screwing. A good time.

Now most of us are dead. Our corpses litter the city, fouling the air with their stink. Those of us who are left fight for every little scrap.

That food over there. I wish I could stop smelling it. Makes me want to take a chance and grab it now.

No. Too much risk. Last time, I barely escaped with my life.

Don't think about the food. Think about something else. Think about the old days.

What fools we were. Afraid of Them. Now we're afraid of one another. Before long, we may be eating one another. I've heard that some of us are already—

What's that? Over there. Thought I saw something move. In that bit of shadow in the corner. Someone? Waiting? Waiting to snatch the food? *My* food?

236

Not sure. Must be careful.

The old days. How we ran from Them! Well, now we *are* alone. We have it all to ourselves.

Little by little, They left. Moved out. Moved away. Left the city empty. Left it all to us.

It was very good for a while. A long while. It was too good to believe.

Too good to last.

We went where we wanted, no Them to stop us, and we ate and ate and ate. Got fat.

We thought the good time would last forever.

Anyone over there? No movement. Must have been seeing things.

The bad time didn't happen all at once. It came slowly. At first, we hardly noticed that the food was running out. Seemed impossible. Before, there had always been enough, more than enough.

But when They moved out of the city, the food went with Them.

For a long time, there was plenty left, but then it started to dwindle. Life got hard. Now there are only a few scraps.

Like that scrap over there. It's dark now. Time to make my move . . .

Good. Good. Not the best, but better than nothing. In the old days, we had sugar, bread, oil; now we're glad to get a scrap of paper. Must eat fast, in case . . . *Here he comes!*

omnivorous, nocturnal in habit, with flattened bodies, long threadlike antennae, large eyes, and leathery brownish integument. Far older than man, they are the most primitive of living winged insects, and are among the oldest fossil insects. The word is a corruption of Sp. *cucaracha.* See also ORTHOPTERA.

Hindsight: 480 Seconds
HARLAN ELLISON

Haddon Brooks, a poet, stood in the last city of the Earth, waiting for the word "impact" to come from space. He was being recorded. What he saw, how he felt, all the sounds and smells and smallest touches of the death of his world went up and out to the ships as they began the final journey to new homes somewhere in the stars. His vital signs were being monitored; thalamic taps carried his thoughts and transmitted all the colors of what lay around him, to be stored in memory cassettes aboard the ships. *Someone to report the death of the Earth* had been the short of it, and from that call for a volunteer he had been winnowed from the ten thousand applicants. Ten thousand masochists, voyeurs, harbingers of destruction, possessors of the death wish, psychotics, chill analytical thinkers, fanatics, true believers, and those who thought they were cameras.

He had been chosen because he was a poet, and on this occasion perhaps only the eyes of a certain dreamer could be depended upon to relay the event with enough magic for the generations of children who would be born in space or on distant worlds circling unknown suns. He had volunteered not because he was a man bereft of sense or survivors, but because he was a man with *too much* to live for. He had a wife whom he loved, he had children who adored him, he had peace and genius and was content with his gifts. Such a man could feel the anguish of losing the racial home. So he had volunteered, knowing he was correct for the task, and

238

they had chosen him from the ten thousand because it was clear that he could sum up final moments with order and beauty.

The city was still alive. It had been kept so for him. All the others had been melted down for their fissionable materials. The cities had become the great Orion ships, three million tons each, shaped like the Great Pyramid of Giza, with slightly conical pusher plates under them.

The cities, taken to the stars by hydrogen-bomb explosions under the pusher plates, one per second for seven minutes to achieve Earth orbit . . . and then the Orions sent to all points of the astrolabe, to seed Man through the dark. The cities were gone, and their going had contaminated the Earth's atmosphere beyond purification. But it did not matter: the Earth would die within the hour.

He stood in the center of the arts rotunda, the last works of Konstantin Xenakis forming and re-forming across the dome, silver and gold threads patterning a hundred times a minute, and the small—but very clear, very distinct—voice of the Orion fleet flagship spoke in his head.

"It's on the way. An hour, perhaps."

Brooks found himself looking up when answering. "Have you been getting what I'm sending?"

"Copying."

"Yes, I'm sorry. That's what I meant. Copying."

The voice from space grew milder. "No, *I'm* sorry . . . so used to techtalk. You just put it any way you want, Mr. Brooks. We're getting it all. Very clearly. It's fine, just fine. I didn't mean to interrupt you, just wanted you to know there was no change."

"Thank you."

The voice, and any whisper of its presence, vanished from his head, and he knew he was alone once more. Alone—with the entire population of the Earth listening, watching.

He strolled out of the rotunda and stood on the speakers' shelf overlooking the pastel gardens.

"The sky is very blue," he said. "I've never seen it so blue. Water, all the way to heaven. But there are no birds." His eyes recorded everything: the swaying pastel trees that picked up the breeze and passed it on, their colors merging one into another with a delicate softness.

"Here is a poem for you, whoever."

He composed swiftly, the lines falling into place in his mind an instant before he spoke them.

"Vastator, destroyer from the cold,
Eating time at fifty thousand kilometers per second,
I won't even see your approach.
Outer dark sent you, my Sun hides you,
And when your hunger takes you past,
You will drop only eight minutes of leftovers
From your terrible table."

He shook his head. It was an inadequate piece of work. He tried to make amends: "The buildings are like metal grain in the sunlight. Pinpoints of light flickering like novae in crosstar filters. They are very lovely. But there are no sounds of people. The city seems to be waiting for your return. Poor dumb thing, a dog that doesn't know its master has died. It will wait until it dies, too. Did you ever understand that cities live only with people in them?"

He pressed the stud on his floater pack and rose slowly from the shelf. The central gardens of the city did not end abruptly, but diffused themselves into the main arterial passages leading away from the center. No street was empty of life, even now. He floated over the commercial center.

"The robots continue their work," he said. "Little persons of metal and plastic. I've always had a good feeling about them. Do you know why? They ask so little and they do so much. They're so kind no one would think of being cruel to them, so they lead the best of lives. They are content in their work. Even with all of us gone, they keep the wheels of commerce turning. How fortunate we were to have had them working with us."

He floated lower, passing the news kiosk at the corner of Press Street and Hologram Avenue. It was recapping the final statements of the astronomers. Brooks hovered and listened to the kiosk's pleasant voice; it was the liquid voice of Tandra Mellowe, the holo personality.

"The planet-sized body moving in on our Sun from interstellar space is roughly three hundred and twenty-five times the mass of the Earth, making it somewhat greater than that of Jupiter, the largest planet in the solar system. In diameter it is approximately ninety-one thousand miles and, because of its collision course with the Sun, has been named Vastator, from the Latin meaning "destroyer." Preliminary calculations indicated the asteroid would hit the Sun directly, boring in at a thirty-degree angle. However, as the body nears, revised computations advise Vastator will only graze the Sun, tear off a great piece of the corona. Unfortunately, this will not affect what will happen to the Earth. The spray of radiation —chiefly high-energy protons and helium nuclei—will strike the Earth as the Sun sprays the heavens. All life will be first sterilized and shortly thereafter vaporized by the solar storm. The soil will melt and fuse into a glaze, and the oceans will begin to boil. It will be approximately eight minutes before the sight of what has happened to our Sun reaches the Earth, but no one will be here to see it. No one except Haddon Brooks, the well-known poet . . ."

Brooks rose and went away from there.

He sailed over The Hundred Lakes, joined by their floater locks. Small boats and catamarans drifted across their surfaces idly. "Sunday strolling," he said, and went over unseen.

"I am above the ghettos now. They remind me of verses from Mother Goose. It must be fine to be a member of a minority, to know where you came from, and what certain words that cannot be translated completely mean. No one could have been happy here. Deathbeds of illusion. Invisible walls. These were the hollows where men and women gave themselves to yesterdays so their children might have tomorrows. But I cannot be sad about them. They knew a kind of love hidden from the rest of us. Where you go now, to whatever new places, make sure you leave room for those who need that specialness. We cannot all be the same; it isn't even right that we should be."

He soared to the highest levels of the residence shelves, passing through byways and underpassing flying bridges, skimming over slideways and casting his long shadow over the pebbled surfaces of walls and other walls. Sloping outer surfaces and sudden apertures. Concavities and tunnels fit for the needs of those who liked cool, dark places where the scent of mountain gentian still lingered. He stopped in a tiny forest of dwarf bonsai and tried to compose another poem, this one for his wife.

"This may not be right, Calla, but it's the best I can do right now . . . I find my thoughts split. I want to say something special to you and the children, but time is growing short and it serves me right if I've left any love or respect for you unsaid after all this time. You were the best moments for me, the brightest colors, the deepest sighs, the sweetest sugar of life. You were always what I was afraid I'd never be worthy of. But I'm content now; I held your love. Oh, hell, my love, my best, I can't compose a poem now. Forgive me, but all that come to mind are another man's words. He was called Randall Jarrell and he lived a hundred years ago and never saw the stars from Mars or looked into the burning heart of our poor Sun from the quicksilver domes of the Moon, but he knew my love for you and he said:

" 'But be, as you have been, my happiness;
Let me sleep beside you, each night, like a spoon;
When, starting from my dreams, I groan to you,
May your I love you send me back to sleep.
At morning bring me, grayer for its mirroring,
The heavens' sun perfected in your eyes.' "

Then he heard the voice that called the end.

"Mr. Brooks, impact."

His breath froze in his nostrils.

The voice again, caught in a sob, "Oh, my God, it's beautiful, so terrible . . ."

And he knew he had eight minutes.

A strange prickling assaulted his flesh and he cried out to Calla, far away aboard an Orion, "I'm done . . . there can be no other children . . ." And he stopped himself; he knew there was less than four hundred and eighty seconds and he had to tell it all, tell it so well the children of Earth would always be able to draw on his cassettes with his visions and words and dreams on them.

He settled within himself, leaped from the shelf and went down to stand in the silver street where he would spend his last moments.

Haddon Brooks spoke then, of the living space that had finally come to hold the dearest hopes of humankind. He spoke of the caverns beneath the pulsing city where energy was channeled into light and heat and rain that would fall when the women called for rain. He spoke of the race tracks where adventure could still be found in trying to beat sound waves as they raced to targets. He spoke of the oceans that had been calmed so men could sail across without fear. He spoke of the best of people and the ways in which humans had come to know themselves well enough to laugh at the thought that wars were inevitable.

This had been the city in which he had been born, in which he had found the words to make his songs, where he had met and joined with Calla, where the children had grown from their bodies; the city where he would become vapor at the final moment. Some of it was even poetry, but not much.

"I'm afraid, up there. I'm afraid of my vanity to be the last one here. It was foolish. Oh, how I want to go with you now. Please forgive me my fear, but I want so much to live!"

If there had only been time. He was chagrined for just a moment that he had let them down, had failed to do what he had been left behind to do. But that lasted only a moment and he knew he had said as much as anyone could say, and it would be right for the children of the dark places, even if it took them a thousand years to find another home.

Then he turned, as the seconds withered, knowing the solar storm had drenched him and at any moment he would vaporize. He looked up into the water-blue sky, past the blinding Sun that suddenly flared and consumed the heavens, and he shouted, "I'll always be with you—" but the last word was never uttered; he was gone.

Soon after, the seas began to gently boil.

5,000,000 A.D.
MIRIAM ALLEN deFORD

Dark. The dark of a dying night on a dying planet. Sparse faint stars gleamed half concealed behind the curtain of aerial dust. And cold—bone-shiveringly cold.

They were used to both. They had never known anything else.

Oh, yes, the sun would rise—the sick red sun—and a dull warmth would spread over the pitted earth and the stunted plants for a few short hours. Then the darkness and the cold would come again.

And this was midspring—May, men once had called it, but that was when time and place were important. Now all man's occupation was to keep himself alive, to find enough food to stoke his inner engine; perhaps, if he was really lucky, to mate, and perhaps—perhaps—to reproduce himself.

Life never lasted long. Forty years was old age, as it had been in the Paleolithic time, five thousand centuries before.

Far to the north, and more rarely to the south, rose the Ruins, where the great cities had once been. But this land where the group dwelt had been the tropics, the region of the equator, where once jungles and rain forests had flourished, and where what heat the feeble sun engendered was still at its meager peak. The men who lived there now had never heard of the Ruins, and the jungles and rain forests were the materials of myth.

They spoke a debased conglomeration of their ancestral tongues. Of the mighty series of civilizations that had preceded them they had no knowledge whatever. They, whose forgotten forebears had swept the stars, grubbed for their substenance in the exhausted earth. They had reversed history, under the harsh conditions of their lives; politics, economics, philosophy, science, religion were long forgotten.

Yet they were still human.

From her dark skin, straight black hair, and tiptilted black eyes, Nia might have been guessed to have a strong blend of Asiatic genes in her ancestry. But the racial mixture was now so old and so complicated that it was impossible to tell whence any of them sprang originally.

Held was taller than she—but not much taller, human beings had shrunk—and fairer of skin, but he too was a mixture of many strains. All that mattered to either of them was that they were not too nearly related—the one taboo besides cannibalism that had persisted—and that they were young and in love.

In love for the season, that is; more lasting unions were few—as few as the fertile ones. Indeed, they were the same: the rare conception and birth of a viable child acted to keep the parents together, guarding their treasure. They would have been amazed to learn that once the problem was a population teeming beyond control.

Men of prehistoric times clothed themselves in the skins of animals killed for meat and fur. There were no large animals left to kill. So the art of weaving had perforce survived; but cotton and flax no longer grew, there were no sheep to give wool. By necessity, since even in these former tropical lands the climate ranged from chilly to freezing, they shivered in garments woven from plant fibers laboriously searched for and stripped and spun, passed down from generation to generation as their only riches worn until they were in shreds. Stealing another's clothing was unheard of; clothes were as scarce as people, and almost as inviolate.

And for shelter, wood being so hard to find, and what there was being saved and cherished for fires that must never go entirely out, the group huddled against the cold and the occasional thin rain in dugouts with entrances and smoke holes cunningly protected against the wind.

Animals couple before anyone's eyes. Humans seek privacy, no matter how small or isolated the community. Lovers must seek some secret, sheltered place for consummation of their rites.

Nia and Held, children of their time.

"Have you eaten?" he asked tenderly as they walked arm in arm to one of the secluded caves set apart by custom for lovemaking. It was a traditional form of loving inquiry for people who did not have enough to eat always or often.

"Yes, last night. Didn't you? Morv bought back two big pots of fat grubs."

"Morv's a good hunter." His tone was jealous.

"No better than you!" she flashed. He smiled, gratified, but he still felt uneasy.

"Last year you and Morv—"

"That was last year, Held; it's forgotten."

"Nia," he brought out at last, "I wish it could be you and me, from now on."

"I'd be glad, too. If we could only be lucky enough—"

"Would you really? Do you think we might?" Held's voice was wistful. "The last time Gars examined me, he said I was a fine specimen."

"Eth and Vin had Erla, two years ago, and neither of them is as robust as we are."

"Oh, Nia! Wouldn't it be wonderful?"

They hastened their steps.

. . . And a child *was* conceived, and was born, and lived. Moreover, it was a boy; before half the male infants had died soon after birth.

In this boy Alc's second year, Gars died; he had been, from interest and empirical knowledge, the nearest they had to a medical consultant. Others died, and no more children were born. Their number was down now to little over fifty. And slow as the process of dissolution was, those who had energy enough to care for anything beyond the day's needs and hardships often looked apprehensively at the sky, where every day the pale sun seemed paler; as the cold was more penetrating, the yield of the earth was more grudging.

Vaguely they felt that something was wrong—something "up there." In that earlier time of disturbed feeling men went awry. The muted sexuality of the undernourished flared up as if the remains of humanity somehow sensed that their dying sun would burst soon into a last solar orgasm and destroy their world before it expired into a dense, cold weight, burdening space; and men, the children of sun, obeyed that same unconscious urge toward explosion.

The immemorial easy permissiveness faded. Part of the rising tensity inevitably expressed itself in hostile aggression. There had been "peace" for untold centuries—ever since the decline of the sun became an accepted fact—because all human energy was needed merely to stay alive. Now, with this strange inner compulsion upon them, impulses and actions lost in the fog of the past suddenly shook them. There were quarrels, there was revenge, there were almost feuds, in this one small group. Undoubtedly the same transformation was overwhelming all the other little pockets of mankind, everywhere on the planet, of which they had never heard.

Morv was their great hunter. But in other areas, life had failed him sadly.

Though he had, more than any of them, gained experience in the capture, and hence in the dismembering, of the occasional small wild animals, after Gars died no one suggested, as he had hoped silently, that he, as the most knowledgeable of anatomy, attempt to take the medical man's place. No woman, after gentle Nia, had hinted or responded to his hints that they try together to produce a child, as Held and she had done. They were all stunted and bone-thin, but Morv, early wrinkled and gray, was perhaps the least prepossessing of all the younger men. Hitherto he had lost such hurts in the excitement of the chase and the praise of his prowess, but now in these new disturbing times increasingly it ground upon his spirit.

Morv went hunting alone and in the late afternoon came back alone. For once he had been unsuccessful—all he had was half a potful of wizened berries. Only four or five of the old and weak were there to greet him, and they gazed disgustedly at his poor offering. He threw the berries on the ground before them and strode away to his own dugout. There he did not even build up the fire whose embers lay smoldering under the ashes, but squatted beside it and stared angrily at nothing.

It was a day of wild wind and bitter cold; the dim red sun cast sullen shadows on the scanty grass. Suddenly Morv rose abruptly and with a muttered imprecation hurried across the encampment out of sight of the few watchers. An old man shook his head in puzzlement; an old woman crossed herself—an ancient gesture originating none of them knew where.

Morv disappeared in the line of thin trees that bordered the slow trickle they called a river.

It was almost dusk when one by one the other hunters drifted in. They had been little more successful; there would scarcely be enough to go around tonight.

Nia and Held walked wearNDiedly toward their dugout. They had left Alc for the day with Vin and Eth's child Erla, three years his senior, and hence in their short life-span old enough to be trusted to keep an eye on the baby.

Now Erla, seeing them coming, ran out to meet them.

"Alc was bad!" she piped. "He went home and wouldn't come back."

"Don't worry, Erla," Held said, patting the child's head. "He'll be there, waiting for us and his meal."

The dugout was empty.

"Don't hide, little Alc," his mother called. "We're too tired to run and look for you."

There was no answer.

Two hours later they found Alc's strangled body half buried

on the riverbank. Morv had vanished.

What their remote ancestors had called crime had long ago virtually disappeared. They had no vigor for bodily assault and no need for rape. Theft was as far outside their understanding as was deliberate murder; they had nothing worth stealing except clothing, and to steal that was unthinkable, so nothing was stolen. Above all, they were so few that human life was inexorably sacred.

And this was far worse than mere murder; it was the extinction of almost all their future, what future they had while the red sun waited to implode.

An absence of religion does not necessarily mean an absence of superstition. Like all human beings, these last men on a dying earth were partly rational and partly irrational. This catastrophe, completely beyond living memory or tradition or even imagination, evoked a flood of neurotic horror. They thought not so much of finding and punishing Morv—surely an act so unprecedented and so terrible would be the wretched creature's own irreparable self-punishment—as of somehow averting the evil omen of unimaginable disaster.

In unconscious psychic self-defense, they hurt themselves to avoid worse hurt, plunging into an orgy of atavistic sacrifice. Precious food went up in smoke; Morv's dugout was torn asunder and the earth of which it had been made was piled on little Alc's grave; the old woman who had once crossed herself, an avid miser of half-mad fantasies, cut a finger and let the blood seep into the ground.

There was no consequence. Nothing happened, good or bad. Food became no more or less plentiful, the cold and wind were as always, the sun continued to lower, red and threatening, like a dying man conserving himself for one last dreadful spurt of strength.

Suddenly Morv came back. No one knew where he had been. He was emanciated and filthy. He went directly to the dugout where Held and Nia were sleeping, woke them, and fell sobbing at their feet.

"Kill me!" he begged.

They were aghast. "How could that help us?" Held asked him. "You have already weakened us, first by destroying the child and then by leaving us. Now at least you can restore yourself to us. You were always our best hunter, and the times are hard."

Before all the group Morv confessed his murderous rage and its outcome and asked forgiveness. The chief reaction was one of surprise, almost of embarrassment; great evil had been done but life itself was evil, and now an effort could be made to redeem the wrong.

The years went on. Many mated but no children were conceived. One by one the old men and women died. It was a question whether the group might not die out altogether. And what then of the very last three, or two, or one, left alone and too weak to fend for themselves? It did not bear thinking of; they could not avoid the knowledge, but they could make no reasonable plans.

In a desperate gesture of expiation, Morv asked and Nia consented, acquiesced in by Held, to couple again. They all had a half feeling that he who had taken life might give it again.

And the miracle occurred: Nia once more became pregnant. No other woman in memory had ever conceived twice.

She was big with child on the day when, on a planet around Deneb, strange nonhuman beings peering through telescopes discovered a nova in the direction of Vega.

Afterword
FREDERIK POHL

The theme of this book of science fiction stories fascinates me because cities are a hobby of mine. Like Catullus, *odi et amo*. I hate them because they are destructive of nature and man; I love them because they work.

I have worn out more shoes on the streets of a hundred cities than I ever expect to buy again. To me, the only way to know a city is to walk its streets, twenty miles or so of them at least—which is why Los Angeles, for example, is still alien to me; one does not walk there, and therefore it is hard for me to believe that one lives there. I like to see the life of the run-down slums, the residential areas and the marts of business, as well as the cathedrals and museums. What I know best about Leningrad I learned touring the back streets with my son, entering the grocery stores and the wineshops, watching the commuters race to board the trolleybuses, standing on the bridges and looking out over the branches of the Neva. Paris to me is the workingmen's cafés under Montmartre and the tatty opulence of the Avenue d'Iéna as well as the view upstream from the Ile de la Cité. Tokyo is the department stores along the Ginza and the teams of sawyers cutting down trees that are asphyxiated with SO_2. Munich is the shopping mall under the animated clock and the bustle of new construction. I wonder what all these cities will look like a hundred years from now. I have seen some of them over a period of decades, seen them change, seen them stay the same.

I do not think they will die. Cities have a life of their own.

Like all living things, they grow to their own pattern, not ours.

This has been a great problem for the people who plan. Cities do not like to be planned very much. I have had a hobby of interest in the attempts of human beings to impose their fantasies on cities—rebuilding old ones, inventing new ones like Komsomolsk and Reston—which has led me on a lot of excursions, by way of the green bus out of London, to see Welwyth Garden City, by a limping old two-engine piston plane on a thousand-mile round-trip flight from Rio for the sake of spending two hours in that gaudy, heartbreaking and already outmoded dream, Brasília. They are dreams, these planned new cities. All of them are dreams, and making them come true destroys them. I have not seen Le Corbusier's planned city of Chandigarh (I will one day, if I live long enough), but I know what soured that particular dream. It was planned as the capital of a province, but the province split in two when India and Pakistan divided, and so it is a city without a function. Goats graze the esplanades. I have seen the vestigial traces of the American planned cities of the 30's; they have been swallowed up, one by one, by urban sprawl.

So from all this evidence and more, I do not think that it is possible for a man to dream a city and make it live, any more than it is possible for him to dream a woman, and look up to find her walking down the street into his life. And yet—

And yet there must be some way to make city living joyous as well as productive. And yet there must be some magic formula to create cities that do not need to destroy the people who live in them—the cold rage of New Yorkers, the grim despair of Muscovites, the passionate contempt of Neapolitans. There must be a way, but I am not sure where it is to be found.

A city is an accumulation of a diversity of social capital.

The accumulation is important. It is a matter of scale effect, that is, of size. No city is a real city unless it can support an opera house, a honky-tonk amusement area, an East Village or Haight-Ashbury, factories, colleges, a spectrum of churches and temples, folk dancing in the styles of Greece and Spain and Israel, adult courses in pottery baking and Sanskrit. I don't want all of those things for myself. No one does. Not all of them for any individual. But unless they are all available, unless you can find a place to get a meal at four in the morning or to buy an out-of-print book, then it is not a city; it is only a huddling place for a lot of people.

The diversity is equally important. Washington and Moscow are not really cities. They have central functions—government —that overpower everything else they do. There is no diversity. They are ad hoc headquarters encampments on a huge scale, but they do not give the people who live in them the variety of experience and input that makes a city work.

In this book a number of writers have touched on some of the things that make cities essential, and tried to project into the future some of the limitless possible directions city development may take. At the same time they have turned their microscopes on some of the things that make cities unbearable, and tried to see what other things the future will bring. They are all part of the same pattern: pollution and sexuality, power failures and traffic jams, the city abandoned to our successors. (But has any real city ever been abandoned? Only Rome, once, for a day or two; and then the people come back. All the cities that have disappeared are what they are because the people were forcibly driven away, not because they left voluntarily.) I do not know that these visions exhaust the future of the city. In fact, I am pretty sure they do not; I don't agree that cities are intolerable. Or more accurately, I think that even if they are intolerable it doesn't matter because we will go on tolerating them anyway.

For I do not think that civilization (the base, *civitatem*, meaning "the city") can survive without cities. In some form.

I am in some doubt about the form. I know the arguments of those who think that the form is not important. I like the idea of the world of the exploded city—"Don't commute, communicate!"—in which everyone does his own thing in his own place, linked to one another by electronic media rather than physical proximity. Maybe this is the wave of the future for city building. At times I have thought so, and have been one of its prophets. Certainly it is so that for most of us the commuting is preposterously superfluous. We get up in the morning, endure an hour or so on the train and arrive in a cubicle in a building from which most of our activity has to do with reading pieces of paper that cross our desk (why not read them on a cathode-tube screen from Biloxi of Saskatchewan?), talking to associates (why not just pick up the phone and order a conference call?) or sitting in on meetings that are always difficult to convene (did you ever try to get five busy executives in the same room at the same time?) and often enough are inconclusive anyway. Insofar as "the city" represents to most of us the place where we work, and get out of as fast as we can when the working day is through, clearly it can be replaced by wires and microwave relays.

Yet that is not all that a city does. You can dial an associate on the phone and talk to him. But you can't run into him on the phone; the chance encounter in a restaurant, on a street, only happens when there is physical presence. You do not need to go to a concert hall to hear a concert. But there is a joy and a purpose to being physically present in a place with other people who are like-minded, at least in that they too want to be present in that place for whatever is going on. You can't even imagine a political rally exploded into ten thousand separate homes, viewed by TV. The speeches would be the same, but the crowd excitement would not exist. Hearing Bernstein's *Mass* on records, even watching it on TV, is not the same as sitting in an auditorium with four or five thousand other people who, like you, are being bombarded by the quadriphonic amplified sound and saturated with the color and movement on the stage.

For all these reasons, I think that city life is a failed experiment that we will never give up on.

The cities I know best, New York and London, are absolute failures in some very essential ways. New York is dirty, noisy, preposterously expensive and essentially unsafe. Not *every* person who comes to New York gets robbed, raped or murdered. But no person is exempt, and few areas of the city are wholly secure; in New York your person is always at risk. London is physically safer, but it is also dirty, also noisy and rapidly becoming just as preposterously expensive. Not only are these things true now; they have been true pretty generally throughout the history of both cities—four hundred years of history for New York, two thousand years for London. They have almost always been dirty, noisy, expensive and unsafe, in no way fit to live in.

And yet they survive.

It is this paradox that guarantees the future of the city as an institution.

When institutions survive doggedly in spite of incontrovertible indications that they are unstable, inadequate and doomed, it says something about the value of the institutions. They are so needed that they cannot be allowed to fail. Whatever their faults, their virtues outweigh them.

And thus it is with cities. We have them, and we will always have them . . . as long as we have civilization at all.